# TABOR
# The First Christian

## Dixie Distler

# ACKNOWLEDGMENTS

I am grateful for the editorial assistance of
Willy Mathes and LaRinda Chapin

Cover design by Robin Ludwig Design Inc.
www.gobookcoverdesign.com

I also thank my husband, family, and friends
who encouraged me to keep writing so
Tabor's story could finally be told.

*"And He will raise you up on eagle's wings,*

*Bear you on the breath of dawn,*

*Make you to shine like the sun,*

*And hold you in the palm of His Hand."*

*Michael Joncas*

# CHAPTER 1



*Spring, 6 B.C.*

A chill rushed over the parched, arid sands, as the sun eased behind the hills of Judea, creating a tapestry of deep crimson and gold among the high thin clouds. Although spring brought daytime warmth to the valleys around Bethlehem, the nights could be bitterly cold. Jonas started the evening fire with sticks and dried sheep dung, while his older brother Jacob counted their herd of thirty-seven sheep for the fifth and final tally of the day. On a distant hill, two more campfires appeared where other shepherds followed a similar ritual.

When Jacob returned, the two men watched in silence, as the fire consumed the dry sticks. Throwing a few small branches onto the burning pile, Jonas said, "I met the new rabbi this morning."

"Ah, your son's circumcision. How is he?"

"Tabor is well. I was nervous because this was Rabbi Asher's first circumcision."

With a grin, Jacob encouraged him to tell more. "And?"

"And—the young rabbi cut in the right place."

Jacob laughed, "Well, what do you think of Rabbi Asher?"

"He bids us to forgive those murderous slayers of the innocent, and be tolerant of their foreign ways."

Jacob shifted on his mat to back away from the fire that now burned hotter. "Our new rabbi tells us to forgive the Romans who fill their crosses with innocent Jews?"

"Alas, o' Lord God, have I done wrong?" Jonas wryly asked, looking up at the first star in the night sky. "Is it a sin for me to not find it in my heart to forgive these—animals? These Romans?"

Jacob shook his head and continued staring into the fire. "You should go home to be with your wife and new son. I can watch the flock tonight."

"No, brother, they're fine. Miriam has fully recovered from giving birth, and besides, Tabor is nearly two weeks old already. He'll be ready to watch the sheep with us before long."

Both men chuckled, acknowledging how fast children grow. Jonas squatted across the fire from Jacob, and reflected on the small two-room home he shared with Miriam and now their son, situated on the second floor of an earthen building that housed five other families living in relative squalor. Looking out at the darkened land and evening sky, he thought, *I prefer these open meadows and hills over the confinement of the village of Bethlehem.*

As his brother pulled from a cloth bag a half loaf of unleavened bread, Jonas stood cautiously, studying a bright light beyond their herd. "I think we have company," he declared, presuming the light to be a torch carried by a nearby shepherd.

"Probably Armon coming to share a meal."

As they continued staring, the intensity of the light changed from the yellow glow of a torch to a light as white as a full moon. And though the light grew brighter, it did not seem to move. For several minutes, the two brothers waited patiently for the mysterious visitor to arrive.

"Jacob, this light is not from fire," Jonas said, taking a few steps ahead.

Rising quickly and walking to where his brother stood, Jacob narrowed his eyes to better focus. "You're right," he replied, rubbing his coarse beard with his hand. "A light that is not made from fire? What phantom of the night could create such a thing?"

The two men walked through their herd, the sheep parting for their shepherds. On the far side of the herd, they stopped and stood still, observing the round orb of light that glowed brightly, yet burned nothing. Jonas saw three other shepherds coming up the hill, illuminated by nothing but the strange glow. "It's as if the moon has come to earth and rested on our hill," Jonas whispered.

As the shepherds approached, Jacob called out to them, "Peace be with you!"

"And with you and your families," came their reply.

Within moments, all five men stood alongside one another in curious wonder. Silently, the mesmerizing glow compelled them to come closer, and moving together as one they did so, even though every step weighed heavily with fear and apprehension. Jonas leaned steadfast against his staff in his right hand, as he clung to the sleeve of his brother's mantle with his left.

The shepherds continued walking forward until they were close enough to see in the center of a perfect sphere the figure of a man whose robe was as white as the light that engulfed him. He had no beard, but upon his head he wore a ring of golden ivy. With caution, they circled the heavenly form. The men walked around in opposite directions, yet the face of the man followed each of them in kind.

Sweetly sung melodic sounds filled their ears, as though an ethereal choir of voices were caroling in sublime harmony. Entranced by the beauty of the angelic figure, each man fell into a strange, euphoric peace. They laid their staffs on the ground and dropped to their knees, for they knew they were witnessing a divine presence.

Finally, each man heard a voice emitting from the heavenly figure encircled in light, though his lips did not move. The soothing words began, *Fear not! For, behold, I bring you tidings of great joy, which shall be to all people. For unto you is born this day in the city of David a Savior, which is Christ the Lord. And this shall be a sign unto you: You shall find the babe wrapped in swaddling clothes, lying in a manger.*

Looking to the herds of sheep in the fields, he lifted his hands out from his side and carefully lowered them. As his arms came down, so too did all the sheep lie where they once stood, freeing the shepherds to attend fully to him without fear of losing a single animal.

*Go, good shepherds,* he continued, *behold the miracle that God has delivered unto you.*

The soothing voice allayed his fears such that Jonas suddenly found his voice and spoke directly to him. "Are you a messenger from God?"

*I am.*

"Where will we find the newborn child of which you speak?"

*Follow my light,* he answered, as the orb in which he dwelled began to glow brighter, its brilliance becoming so great the men could no longer see the angelic figure within. The numinous ball of light rose up and away from the shepherds, who watched in awe as it drifted in the sky westward toward Bethlehem. Climbing ever higher, it stopped near the edge of the city. Then, with a silent burst, a ray of light stretched from the orb to the ground directly below it.

The five men stared at each other in the moonlight as they knelt in a circle, surrounding the void that moments earlier had held the most beautiful being any had ever beheld. For a few moments, no one spoke or stood, each wishing with all their heart to see him once again.

"Men," Jacob finally said, breaking the heart wrenching silence. "He wants us to go into Bethlehem to see the miracle he described to us. We should go, yes?"

Jonas was the first to agree. "Yes, we *must* go."

The astrologer moved swiftly through the dimly lit corridor toward King Herod the Great's chambers. Being summoned by the king in the darkest of night was never a good way to begin a day.

Herod the Great had been known to execute people for nothing more than disturbing his sleep. Stepping just inside the royal chambers of Herod's Jerusalem palace, he dropped to both knees with his head bowed. Crimson stains in the ornately woven rug beneath his knees momentarily distracted his attention.

Within moments, the obese King of Judea, wearing the familiar colored bows at the end of each braid of his beard, entered the chambers from his southern balcony. "Abner! What do you make of it?"

"My lord?" Abner inquired as he took the king's question as permission to rise to his feet.

"Haven't you seen it?" Herod pressed. "Haven't you been watching it? It hasn't moved in hours!"

The king's astrologer walked through the chambers and followed the grossly disfigured man, who smelled of rancid cheese, onto the southern balcony. Even before stepping outside, Abner could see the light in the southern sky. "It hasn't moved?"

"Why do I have to tell my astrologer about the stars?" Herod asked angrily. "Isn't this why you are here, Abner? Aren't you supposed to be the one who studies the stars in the middle of the night?"

"I'm sorry, my King. The small window in my chambers faces north, so I did not see this star before now," Abner explained as he walked to the edge of the balcony, never taking his eyes from the star that was bright enough to cast a shadow from objects below.

"Tell me what this means, Astrologer!" King Herod demanded. "I was awoken by the light from this star hours ago. It has not moved across the night sky with the others. What is this sign?"

Abner hesitated to interpret the meaning of the heavenly light out of fear of Herod's retribution.

"Well?" Herod pressed.

"It's—it's, the prophecy, my lord."

"What prophecy, Astrologer," Herod persisted. "Tell me, while you still have a tongue to speak!"

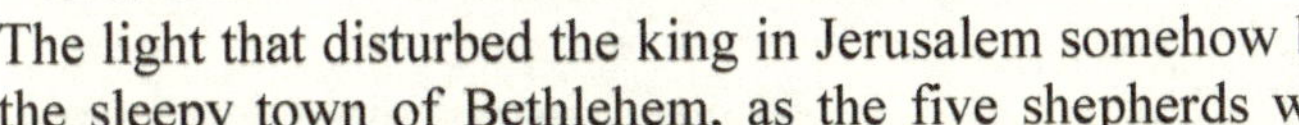

The light that disturbed the king in Jerusalem somehow brought peace to the sleepy town of Bethlehem, as the five shepherds walked along the main road toward the vertical ray of light that shone down from the brightest star in the sky. Dust from packed earth rushed over their sandals with each step, their long wooden staffs deftly moving across the hard ground before them. When the men arrived at their destination, they meekly approached the stable, floored with straw and animal waste. Illumined by the star's light they easily found the humble couple inside, occupying a stall which was best suited for a donkey. With silent reverence, the five men gazed at the newborn baby asleep in a manger of hay, wrapped snugly in cloth, which days earlier had served as a donkey's riding blanket.

As they stared in wonder at the scene before them, the man in the stable said, "Why have you come here?"

The men were slow to respond as they stood before the family. Finally, Jonas replied, "We were tending our flocks in the hills when a messenger from God appeared before us. With a wave of his hand, he commanded our sheep to bed down and the predators to leave our flocks in peace. He told us we would find a baby born this night in a manger and he showed us the way."

"Then you are blessed," the man responded, "for surely you have been chosen by God to witness the truth. I am Joseph of Nazareth."

"Then it is true?" Jacob asked. "This child is the promised one? He is the Christ?"

Mary lifted the sleeping baby from the manger and held him in her arms, still wrapped in the blanket. All five shepherds craned their necks, attempting to catch a glimpse of the tiny newborn.

"Believe what you have heard," Joseph answered, "*and* what you witness. For we too," Joseph motioned toward his wife, "have been visited by an Angel of the Lord, who told us the baby Mary carried was conceived when the spirit of the Lord came upon her."

All five men removed their sandals and knelt in homage before the child.

Mary looked to her husband, then back to the men who knelt before her. "Please rise," she said, "and go tell others what you have witnessed on this night, so they too will know the time of deliverance is growing near. All is well, good shepherds."

The shepherds arose and stepped backwards from the stable. Jonas gazed into the night sky to the bright star that stayed directly overhead, higher than a mountain but lower than the heavens, illuminating the sandy roads amid the dark, sleepy town. The men then hastened toward their respective homes, barely able to contain themselves; eager to share what they'd just experienced.

As Jonas entered his home, the room was dark, except for a single blue flame burning in an oil lamp. From it, Jonas lit a candle made from beeswax, which instantly brought light into the tiny room. Miriam, who slept on blankets piled on the cold wooden floor next to their infant son, sat up quickly, blinking a few times, trying to focus in the light.

"Jonas?" she whispered, so as not to wake Tabor. "What is it, my husband? Are you well?"

Jonas knelt next to his wife, and gently pushed a thick strand of her long, black hair from her face. "I'm fine, Miriam. I have news— wonderful news!" Jonas tried to keep his voice low, but his excitement overtook him.

She propped up on her elbow, "News? What news?"

Jonas told his wife every event as he remembered them, while she sat up and listened intently.

When he'd finished, Miriam stroked her husband's cheek. "Oh Jonas, you must have been dreaming," she said, smiling sweetly and looking into his eyes. "You fell asleep by your campfire and the light confused you. Besides, why would God send a messenger to a shepherd? Wouldn't he choose a priest or king?"

Disappointed, yet not surprised by her doubt, he sighed and pulled the hood of his mantle off his head.

"Jonas!" Miriam exclaimed, reaching for the candle and putting it in front of her husband's face. Tabor stirred at the sound of his mother's voice, but her attention was on her husband. "Your hair, Jonas—what happened to your hair?"

Curious himself, he combed his fingers through his shoulder length hair before responding. "What about my hair?"

Miriam moved the candle from one side to the other, rising to her knees to see the top and sides of his head. "Where your hair was exposed from your hood, it is completely white! But under your robe, it is still black."

Jonas smiled, knowing his wife now had reason to believe him, "It was *as I said*, Miriam. My face was immersed in the light from God's messenger. I was terrified when I first saw him and wanted to run away. But when he began to speak to us, I had a feeling of peace I have never before known."

"Then what you say is true?"

"Come outside with me, Miriam, so you can see this miracle yourself."

Jonas led his wife by her hand through the front door, down the stairs, to the dirt road that passed before their home. Above the stable near the edge of town, the brightest star in the night sky persisted, just as Jonas had described. The beam of light that illuminated the lone stable had faded, but the star still glowed brightly.

<hr>

Miriam shared her husband's story with friends and neighbors the following morning, after Jonas returned to the hills to tend his flock. Everyone watched the strange light in the sky, visible even in daylight, as the story passed from mouth to mouth. The light that hung in the sky, never moving—as the sun, moon, and stars did—quickly became known as the 'Star of Bethlehem.'

With the exception of a few who were certain the phenomenon was a bad omen, most villagers found comfort in the star that chose Bethlehem as its blessed city, even feeling a sense of protection by it. It was Miriam, though, who focused her attention on the new parents in the stable—perhaps because she herself had recently given birth, or perhaps simply due to the amazement in her husband's eyes when he woke her to tell of this mysterious birth in a stable of animals. Still, she knew what she must do. *Hachnasas Orchim demands that we open our home to a stranger in need,* she reminded herself.

With Tabor cradled in her arms, Miriam walked through the crowd of curious onlookers into the stable to find the couple and baby exactly as Jonas had described. Stepping before Mary and Joseph, she said, "Blessed are the parents of this child," as a polite greeting.

"And blessed are the parents of the beautiful baby you carry," Mary replied.

"You met my husband last night," Miriam explained. "He was with a group of shepherds who was sent here by God's messenger."

Mary and Joseph both nodded as Miriam continued. "My husband and I are poor, but what we have is yours. Will you share our home and meals while in Bethlehem? Our home is not much, but surely it is better than sleeping with goats and donkeys."

"It is you and your husband who honor us with your gracious offer," Joseph replied. "If your home is open to another baby who will cry for his mother's breast in the middle of the night, then we humbly accept."

Most villagers didn't give a second look at Mary or Joseph as the days passed. The newest Bethlehem residents were noted more for their strange northern accents than the birth that occurred under the Star of Bethlehem. But for Jonas, he remained reverent to the couple who shared his home and provided much needed relief for the poor family of a shepherd. Mary was five years younger than Miriam, yet very mature and continually helpful around their small home. It was Joseph, though, who fascinated Jonas the most, especially when he shared his stories about the dreams and visions both he and Mary had experienced while living in Nazareth.

"Mary had a vision of an angel who told her she was with child," Joseph said to Jonas, soon after the two couples had begun sharing the humble home. At Jonas' request, Joseph retold the entire story in as much detail as he could recall. "She challenged the angel's statement," he said, "as she had never lain with a man. But the angel told her the Lord God had touched her and made it so. This child, Jesus, would one day become a *king*."

"And you kept her as your wife," Jonas said, "even though she carried a baby who was not of your making."

"Yes, let me tell you, I was prepared to cast her aside until I had a dream that was as real as you are to me right now. In my dream, an angel spoke to me and told me to take Mary as my wife and raise her child as my own. 'For in her womb,' the angel said, 'she carries the Son of God.'"

A feeling of peace came over Jonas when he looked at Jesus,

napping on a blanket next to Miriam as she pushed the bread dough into flat, round patties. Then to Mary who was feeding Tabor mashed grain soaked in goat's milk propped on the tip of her finger, as Miriam had done so often for Jesus, before turning back to Joseph. "And our sons will grow to be as brothers."

# CHAPTER 2

*February, 5 B.C.*

King Herod the Great stood on the balcony outside the bedroom of his palace in Jerusalem, staring at what he'd heard the people were calling "the Star of Bethlehem." "Doran, this star torments me," Herod expressed to the captain of the palace guard who stood two steps behind him. "The light haunts me by day, and blinds me by night."

"Some say the star is God, watching over His chosen people," Doran replied.

"The star does not protect my kingdom, it defies its king!" Herod lashed back. "It demands a sacrifice of which I must pay the price." After a moment to contemplate the meaning of his own words, Herod ordered, "In the chamber next to my pool, you will find twins, brother and sister born to one of my servants."

"Yes my king," Doran confirmed, "I have seen the children swimming in the pool."

"Just before sunset," Herod continued, "throw them from the tower." He turned his attention to the tallest tower in Jerusalem, easily seen from his palace balcony.

Following the evening meal, Herod carried a goblet filled with wine to the balcony where he rested against the banister. As the sun drew long shadows from the buildings below, twin brother and sister walked, tethered behind one of Herod's soldiers, followed closely by two more uniformed men.

*They walk so calmly; so quietly*, Herod observed. *Oh, how I would love to see their faces when they realize what is about to happen.* Twenty minutes of anticipation passed before Herod found perverted pleasure in the distant screams as he watched the young bodies fall to their deaths, yet the star shone brightly through the night.

Two weeks passed before Herod made another attempt to appease the star that drove him beyond his sense of sanity. "Doran!" he shouted to the captain as he walked just beyond his outer chamber.

"My King?" Doran replied with a bow, wary that Herod's increasing depravity and hostility would be directed toward him.

"I want you to take one of my wives, Estelle, to the grounds beneath my balcony and have her trampled to death."

Doran lifted his head to look in Herod's eyes, hoping to hear a clarification to his misunderstanding. However, Herod's determination was apparent in the eyes of a madman.

"I will show this God of Israel who watches me from a star that no sacrifice is too great for me to keep my kingdom," Herod declared, more to himself than Doran. "The God of Israel will not care that Estelle is my least favorite, only that I am sincere."

Swiftly he moved to his balcony and watched with enthusiasm as three soldiers mounted their horses and prepared to fulfill their king's order. Silently he smiled and applauded as a feisty young woman strained against the ropes tied about her wrists. Her panic stricken screams only added to Herod's enjoyment as two guards, each holding a rope, stood as far apart as the ropes would allow, pulling tightly against the arms of the barefoot woman wearing a white, ankle length tunic.

Herod hesitated, not for doubts of his order to execute one of his wives, but to prolong the pleasure of her terror. Finally, with the wave of his hand, the horsemen proceeded forward; each horse crushing the woman's flesh and breaking her bones beneath their hooves, until the pretty maiden was reduced to a bloody mound beneath her husband's balcony.

Herod applauded with elation, the only audience member of his private, barbaric show, but his enthusiasm waned as his attention turned to the star that never moved, the star that rejected his gift and sacrifice.

Three times over the next two months, King Herod dispatched his soldiers to bring him news from the small farming village of the prophesized birth of a king, or with *some* explanation as to why a star would remain fixed in the sky and not move like the others. The first two scouting parties yielded nothing to clarify the mystery. However, the king hoped a small team of his most elite soldiers would be more successful.

"Sorry to disturb you, my king," came the voice of his servant from the doorway of his bedchambers.

"Yes, what is it?" Herod responded, without taking his eyes away from the star.

"Three Magi have requested an audience with you, my king. They are from the east and have traveled a great distance."

"I do not wish to have an audience with anyone. Send them away!"

"They come to speak with you about the Star of Bethlehem, my king," the nervous servant persisted.

Hearing these men might have some insight about the strange star, Herod reconsidered. Turning to face his servant, he recanted, "Give me an hour, and then bring them to me."

"Yes, my king," the servant responded, backing out of the king's chambers and bowing with each step.

Looking into a mirror on the bedroom wall, he grimaced as the putrid aroma of his unkempt body engulfed him. He stared at himself, gave a slight, pitiful laugh and crawled up onto his bed. Lounging on his right side to try to bring some relief to the pain in his left hip, the obese king reclined in bed for nearly an hour. Soon, his servant once again entered his chambers, followed by two sword-wielding guards who took their positions inside, flanking the door for his protection. "King Herod the Great!" his servant announced, "may I present Balthasar of Arabia."

While Herod hefted himself up off the bed, a tall man of dark complexion with a heavy beard entered the bed chamber, dressed in fine linens of many colors and wearing a turban embroidered with jewels. When Balthasar bowed, Herod nodded to his visitor in return before moving further away from the bed in preparation for the next introduction.

"King Herod the Great!" his servant proceeded, "may I present Melchior of Persia."

The second man also touted a full black beard, though his was meticulously braided and decorated with colorful beads. Entering the bed chambers on cue, he bowed gracefully and extended the same politeness.

"King Herod the Great!" the servant once more called out, "may I present Gaspar of India."

The third man had darker skin and was clean-shaven. His wardrobe was a dazzling display of brightly colored silks and braided golden ropes. The wide sash around his waist was an intricate tapestry of men and animals conveying a storyline.

When the three Magi stood shoulder-to-shoulder, they bowed once again to their host and, upon Herod's gesturing, sat on large silk pillows laid out next to each other on the floor. Herod moved back to his bed and took a seated position there. The two guards came forward and positioned themselves on either side of the bed, prepared to sacrifice their lives, if necessary, to protect their king. A fourth man, well-dressed and of calm demeanor, entered the bed chambers and took his place on the floor between Herod and the three Magi.

Herod's servant immediately answered the unasked question, "Their interpreter, my king."

"Your highness," the interpreter began, as he addressed King Herod, speaking fluent Aramaic with a thick eastern accent. "These three Magi have traveled a great distance to find the star that never moves. They come to seek your permission to enter your kingdom, so they may learn the secret of this wondrous, celestial event that pays homage to the great King Herod."

Herod responded with a question of his own, "Do the three Magi understand the nature of this star that lingers over my kingdom?"

The interpreter translated Herod's words to the visitors in a language Herod had never before heard. As Balthasar answered, the interpreter spoke to Herod, "We know only that the star first appeared more than a year ago. We have never witnessed such a sight and seek whatever enlightenment can be had."

"The star is called the Star of Bethlehem," Herod explained, trying to appear as though he was in tune with the star's purpose, "because it took position over the town by that name. My astrologers tell me it has come to announce the birth of a new king. I do not know if this birth has happened, or *will* happen in the near future. None of my soldiers have found evidence of such a birth occurring."

The interpreter finished speaking just a few words after Herod finished. As the three men looked at each other, Gaspar spoke to the other two, both of whom nodded, before returning their attention to Herod, who continued, "I give my permission for you to travel through my kingdom on the condition you will return here and report to me everything you learn about the Star of Bethlehem, in particular, anything you learn about the birth of a king, so that I too may welcome this new king to my kingdom."

The interpreter switched back to speaking Aramaic, as Gaspar responded, "We thank the great King Herod for his hospitality and his permission to allow us safe passage. We will gladly return to share that which we learn about the Star of Bethlehem."

The three Magi rose to their feet, as did their interpreter, and bowed to Herod before turning to leave his chambers, escorted by Herod's servant and guards.

# CHAPTER 3



*May, 5 B.C.*

Joseph and Jonas stood outside their home and watched the horsemen riding at breakneck speed into town. Normally on a street filled with people, the horses would be slowed to a walk, but these were being driven at full gallop. Though people scattered to get out of harm's way, some ran away from one horse to be trampled by another. The two men looked on in horror, as bodies of women and children rolled in the dirt, the bloody carnage claiming victims left and right down the entire length of the main avenue.

Miriam and Mary each balanced a heavy jar of well water on top of their heads with one hand, while respectively toting Tabor and Jesus, with their other. Joseph yelled to both women to get off the road, but neither could hear him, given the screams immediately behind them. Both women turned around, only to see the large black eyes of the horses bearing down upon them.

Dropping their water jars and holding tightly to their sons, they both jumped aside, as the horses and riders passed on either side of the women. In the cloud of dust, Joseph could no longer see Mary and Jesus, and their absence from his view pierced his soul.

"Joseph," came a soft voice. Turning, he saw a tall radiant man whose gown was so white, it was as if it was spun from threads of light. The man was without beard, and his hair was the color of the morning sun. "You must take your wife and child this very night and flee to Egypt. There is no time to waste. Wake, Joseph—rise, take heed."

In the pitch black of night, Joseph sat up quickly in bed, breathing heavily, still reeling from the events of his terrifying dream. Beside him, he felt his wife, and next to her, he could feel Jesus sleeping peacefully.

"Mary, Mary," he whispered, shaking her gently. "Wake up, Mary."

"Joseph? What is it? What's wrong?"

"Come, Mary," he insisted, getting up from their bed of blankets. "We must leave, while it is still dark. An Angel of the Lord just spoke to me in a dream and told me we must leave Bethlehem immediately and go to Egypt."

"Then we go," she said without hesitation. With a sense of urgency, she stood and began gathering her things to prepare for travel.

Joseph went to the room where Jonas and Miriam slept with Tabor, and woke them as well, briefly explaining the vision he'd just had moments earlier. "Come with us," he insisted. "It is not safe in Bethlehem."

Jonas got up and lit a candle from the dim blue flame of an oil lamp. "We are going to Egypt," Joseph said. "You must come with us."

"We cannot go to Egypt, Joseph," Jonas declared. "Dream or no dream, this is our home. My flock is here. My family is here. My *life* is here."

The two families assembled on the dirt road in front of their home where Joseph began securing their belongings to his donkey. To the top of the load, he secured three ornately decorated boxes; one with gold, one with frankincense, and the other with myrrh.

Taking a moment to reflect, Joseph looked directly overhead to gaze upon the star that first appeared the night Jesus was born. *It was that star*, he realized, *that led the three Magi to us earlier this very week. And it was those three Magi who humbled themselves before Jesus as they presented their gifts.*

Both Mary and Joseph continued to plead with their friends, who were now more like family after sharing the same home for the past year. "Alright, Joseph," Jonas finally conceded, "I will take Miriam and Tabor to a cave in the hills near the meadow where I graze my flock, until any danger has passed."

"Promise me," Joseph demanded of Jonas, "you will not return to Bethlehem for three days."

"I give you my word. May God be with you and guide you on your journey."

"And may God watch over you and your family, as you watch over your flock," Joseph replied in kind.

Mary and Miriam hugged as sisters, before kissing each other's son. "We will meet again," Mary promised.

"Sweet Mary," Miriam said. "I will always love you, and dream of the day we are together again."

Mary picked up Jesus and carried him in her arms, as she walked beside the donkey that had been hastily packed with their belongings.

In the opposite direction, Miriam walked beside Jonas, carrying Tabor. Her husband carried a wool sack filled with provisions for a three-night stay in the hills outside Bethlehem.

Slamming a fired clay pot against the wall in his bedchamber, King Herod the Great yelled at Doran, the leader of his guardsmen, "You have betrayed me! You and your men cannot find a *single* child, even when I tell you the town to search. Bethlehem is just a hole in the desert floor, yet none of you can bring me what I ask!"

"But your highness," Doran responded. "We have searched the entire town of Bethlehem. No one claims to know anything about a baby being born the night the star first appeared."

"They don't know, or they won't *tell* you?" Herod lashed back. "And these nomad Magi sat right here and promised to return with information, and now they're gone too! Betrayed by liars and incompetents!"

Herod stormed out onto his balcony, glaring toward Bethlehem. Raising his arms with both hands in fists, he screamed, "Hear me, o' Israel! I am your king! I am your only king!"

While Herod ranted as a man losing his sanity, Doran stood by powerless to do any more than he was told. When Herod returned to the inner room, he stared into the man's eyes. "Now, you listen to me," Herod began with ruthless determination. "You will take an entire division of my best soldiers to Bethlehem tonight. By tomorrow morning, I do not want there to be a single male child living in that rancid sheep town."

"You are ordering me to kill every male child in Bethlehem?"

Herod turned his back on the captain and shouted in a voice

twice as loud, "I am ordering you to kill every male child in Bethlehem who is under the age of two! Tonight, I will put an end to this threat to my kingdom!" Turning around and facing the man, he said, "This would have been done a year ago, if I had just one competent soldier in my guard."

Doran stood, frozen in place, hoping Herod would relent, but instead, Herod sealed his order with two commanding words, "DO IT!"

---

Saul was a stout young man whose quiet disposition made him seem older than his twenty-two years. He knew he was born Jewish, but the years of serving King Herod the Great, first as a palace guard, and now as a member of the King's Army, clouded any memory of his youth. However, Saul was proud of the reputation he had earned as an elite soldier who fulfilled his duties faithfully and followed orders without question.

He rose immediately to his feet when Doran, the Captain of the Temple Guard, ordered Saul and twenty-eight other soldiers to mount their horses. Into the night, the soldiers followed their commander, riding hard until the first sign of daybreak. With the town of Bethlehem in sight, the captain halted his horseback squadron, then turned to face the men and issue the most vile order he had ever given.

"Within this village, a child lives who it is said will one day challenge the King of Israel and Roman authority. As the sun rises on Bethlehem, we have orders from King Herod the Great to kill every male child under the age of two both in and around this town. We should take no honor in the death of these children, but we must take pride in knowing what we do today will preserve Israel for years to come!"

Some of the men took hold of their spears and swords, and nodded their heads, showing they were ready to follow their captain's orders. Saul consciously emptied his mind of thought, for fear of questioning the senselessness of what was sure to come. After a moment's hesitation, he raised his sword high above his head, and hearkened to the commander, who then gave the order to move, shouting out, "For King Herod the Great!"

In full battle gear, with each soldier carrying an array of weapons, the king's men stormed into Bethlehem at full gallop, hollering aloud and trampling anyone who got in their way. Their swords drew blood from any male child they saw in the street. They entered every single home, dragging all young male children outside and murdering them in gruesome, heinous fashion, right in front of their parents.

With his swift steed, Saul chased down a woman who had picked up her son and begun running from the town. As he caught up with the young woman, he grabbed the boy from her arms, but lost his grip. When she picked the boy back into her arms to run in the opposite direction, Saul became enraged at the woman for complicating his task. When he turned his horse to chase her once again, he lowered his spear and ran it through the woman's back, piercing the woman's heart and her son's body at the same instant. Saul stopped and turned to face the woman, who dropped to her knees and stared into the eyes of her executioner for a brief moment before collapsing dead on the ground. Sitting on his horse as it breathed heavily from the chase, he studied the lifeless bodies of a woman and her child skewered with the spear he'd thrust through them both.

Dismounting his horse, he looked out at the dust rising from the streets of Bethlehem. Where he could only hear the beating of horse hooves moments before, he now heard only the screams and wailing of women covered in the blood from their dead sons. The killing and pursuit continued throughout the town, but for Saul, the day was done.

Slapping the rump of his horse and sending it away, he pulled his sword from its sheath and held the point of the blade against his chest, readying himself to fall on the sharpened saber to end his life—the life of a child killer. Closing his eyes and acknowledging his remorse for what he'd just done, he let himself fall forward with all of his weight. The heavy blade dropped beneath him too quickly, however, and the handle failed to stick in solid ground. As he collapsed to the ground, Saul found his face in the dirt and his sword lying flat under the weight of his body.

Not since he was taken from his parents to serve the king had Saul wept. Rolling over onto his back, he stared at the morning sun, while tears fell from the corners of his eyes into his sweat-matted hair. He screamed at the sky for the suffering all around him. For the first time since he'd become a mercenary for the king, he spoke angrily to God, yelling, "Is this what your chosen ones have become? We kill women and children to protect ourselves from a child who wants to be king?"

Saul lay in the desert sands next to the bodies of the woman and child, hoping someone from the village would come end his misery by exacting their own vengeance. When the sound of horse hooves faded in the distance, he knew the soldiers were satisfied their battle was over. He also knew he would not be riding home among them.

The heartrending cries from Bethlehem became a constant siren of indistinguishable voices in Saul's ears. He let the grievous sounds clamor in his soul as the morning sun beat down on him. When his exhaustion and shame were beyond his ability to contain any longer, Saul finally stood and began walking toward the hills, away from the slaughter of so many innocents. Every few steps, he pulled off a piece of uniform and armor until the only thing left was a thin white wrap around his waist. Each step brought him ever closer to the distant hills, where he could die a coward's death and feed the waiting vultures.

Jonas had returned to the hill that overlooked Bethlehem after securing Miriam and Tabor in the cave with their supplies. In the first light of dawn, he watched as thirty horses gallop into the town. Soon, even from his distant vantage point, he began hearing the cries of women and children, and knew death was everywhere in Bethlehem.

Powerless to intervene against the band of horseback soldiers, all he could do was watch, and wait. It was mid-afternoon before the soldiers withdrew. All but one horse carried a rider. *All that death, and they only managed to kill one invader*, Jonas thought to himself.

Even in the light of day, he could not make out the uniforms of the marauding riders, but he could tell most of the soldiers had beards, which told him they were not Roman. *Samaritans*, he thought.

Jonas ran as fast as he could along the path to Bethlehem from the hills where he tended his sheep. As he entered the outskirts of town, he slowed his pace to a walk, forced as he was to take in the carnage around him. Blood covered the streets and bodies were strewn everywhere, many lying in contorted positions. Over most of the bodies, Jonas saw women kneeling and weeping profusely. Men walked past Jonas in shock, tearing at their own clothes.

"They came for the children!" one older woman screamed through her tears. "Why would soldiers murder our children?"

"Who did?" Jonas asked of her. "Who did this?"

She paused as she remembered the bare legs of the horsemen, whose chests were covered with plates of armor and whose heads were crowned with bronze helmets—the uniform she had seen so many times in Jerusalem, near the temple. "Herod—it was *Herod's* soldiers! Why would Herod kill his own people? Why our children? Why?"

Only then did Jonas comprehend the horror of what he had witnessed from a distance. The bodies on the street before him were mostly those of children. Some mothers lay dead, as well, still clinging to the bodies of their babies. A few men who must have fought in vain lay in contorted positions—but mostly, the village was littered with the bodies of very young boys.

In the center of this town that would never be the same, Jonas stood in dismay, as he watched Rebecca, wife of Simon, a woman he had known since his own childhood, cling to the body of her son, as she flung herself headfirst into the town's eastern well.

Those in the village who were not visited by death came from their homes to help those who were. Rabbi Asher moved from body to body, bowing deeply as he prayed and recited scripture. David, a shopkeeper Jonas knew well, carried an armload of white linens to a nearby bench, in order to begin wrapping the bodies.

By that evening, every living soul in Bethlehem was involved in the burial of family, friends or neighbors. A constant stream of grief-stricken families followed solemn men who walked silently through the town, carrying mostly small bodies wrapped tightly in bloodstained sheets to a cave at the foothills just outside of Bethlehem. Even the bodies of Rebecca and her son were retrieved from the bottom of the well and buried in the mass grave.

As darkness crept over the town of Bethlehem, heartsick families mourned, still in shock and horrified by the murderous act of their king. Many in the village were afraid the soldiers would return in a second raid, so they moved to small camps away from town.

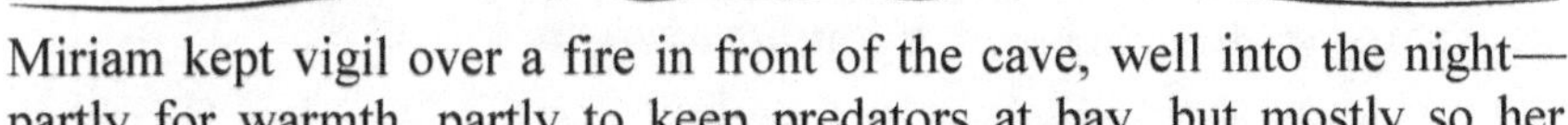

Miriam kept vigil over a fire in front of the cave, well into the night—partly for warmth, partly to keep predators at bay, but mostly so her husband could find her if he returned in the dead of night. She was frightened when she heard the footsteps of a man climbing the rugged hillside toward her fire.

"Jonas? Is that you?" she called out into the darkness. No one replied, but the footsteps grew closer.

Again she called, "Jonas?" but again she received no reply. Miriam backed away from the light of the fire into the mouth of the cave and squatted next to her sleeping son. With each approaching step of a man's sandal, shuffling more than walking, she felt the terror building inside. Her heart pounded and her mouth immediately went dry.

The footsteps stopped, when the figure reached the edge of the fire, and from its light, she recognized her husband. "Jonas! Why didn't you answer me when I called your name? You nearly frightened me to death!"

Jonas stared at the night sky, as if in a trance and unable to respond or even acknowledge his wife. As Miriam approached him, she could see the bloodstains on his clothes and the distant gaze in his eyes.

With both hands, she led him to the fireside and helped him sit. "Jonas, what is it? What happened to you?"

Finally, Jonas turned to face his wife, who knelt in front of him. His mouth was open, as if he wanted to speak, yet was unable to form the words.

Miriam held a bowl with water to his cracked lips and implored, "Jonas, drink. You can speak to me later."

Sipping just a few drops at first, and then more as the moments passed, Jonas's face began to relax. Water washed the desert sand from his tongue as he began to breathe with less anxiety. Eventually, Miriam heard slow and mumbled words that passed through his lips, "Joseph— he tried to warn us."

Miriam began to cry from fear. "Warn us about what, Jonas? You're scaring me! What did Joseph warn us about?"

"They're dead, Miriam. They're all dead."

"Who's dead, Jonas? Is it Joseph and Mary? Are they dead?"

"No, it's the children. Every male child in Bethlehem who is Tabor's age or younger. Herod's soldiers came at sunrise and raided the town, only to kill the youngest boys."

Miriam gasped and screamed in anguish, covering her face, as tears streamed from her eyes. "Why Jonas—why?"

Jonas shook his head and said, "I don't know why. There was nothing I could do but watch, as they rode into town and hunted the children down like dogs. Had we still been there, they would have murdered Tabor, as well."

Miriam shrieked with the realization, jumped up and ran into the cave to touch the blanket that covered her sleeping son. Once she felt her son breathing, she returned to her husband next to the fire. "Jonas? Are they going to come for Tabor? Will they kill our son, too?"

"I don't know, Miriam. I just don't know." Staring back into the cave at their sleeping son, he sighed deeply. "But this much I do know— we can never take Tabor back to Bethlehem. Who knows when the soldiers will return?"

"Then... then we stay here, Jonas. This cave will be our home."

Looking past their campfire into the total darkness covering the hills beyond their cave, toward the town they once called home, Miriam considered the friends who she felt were family. "I pray to God, Joseph and Mary escaped in time to save Jesus."

In the depths of night, King Herod the Great stood alone on his balcony, waiting for word from his returning army to grant him some sense of peace, if not vengeance, from the relentless star that had hung over him for more than a year. As he watched the light which had become his tormentor, a faint glimmer of hope sprung to life when the Star of Bethlehem flickered not once, but seven times. Hope turned to elation as the light faded to nothing, allowing him for the first time since the light first appeared, a view of the millions of stars that filled the night sky. "It is finished," Herod muttered with a sense of victory.

In the darkness, Abner the Astrologer stood alone on the road just beyond the palace walls, watching the Star of Bethlehem fade. "It has begun," he muttered, with a sense of defeat.

# CHAPTER 4

*June, 5 B.C.*

In the ensuing days, many residents of Bethlehem moved to other towns, convinced God had cursed and punished their little farming village. Other's tried to get back to a sense of normalcy and continued on as best as they could.

Jacob left Bethlehem with his wife, Annorah, and their two children to live in Bethany with her family. Wrapped in a white sheet, lying in a tomb next to corpses of other sons of Bethlehem, Jacob's year old son, Adam, stayed behind.

Jonas was among those who moved their families away from the once-peaceful town. As soon as their belongings were safely stored in the cave they'd briefly inhabited, he began turning it into their permanent home. The mouth of the cave was extended by stacking stone with mortar to create a rectangular front, complete with a door, a window on both sides, and a roof. Above the doorway, he mounted a wooden box containing the *Shema*, a Jewish prayer written on a parchment scroll, which he recited every morning when he walked out, and every evening when he walked in.

With the slaughter of so many innocent children still fresh on his mind, Jonas felt the *Shema* held more meaning now than ever before: *Hear, O Israel, the Lord our God, the Lord is One.*

When the home was complete, Jonas continued carrying stones

to build walls elsewhere near their new home, one stone at a time. Crossing the hill below them, he built terraces, never taller than waist. The stone walls served two purposes—to keep the soil from washing down the hill in heavy rains, and as pens for separating and shearing his sheep.

As the cave transformed into a protective dwelling, the small family began returning to a sense of normalcy, feeling safe and secure. The back of the home opened to the cave, which offered some warmth in the winter and plenty of cool air in the sweltering heat of summer. A creek at the bottom of the hill in front of their home provided fresh water most of the year, although the climb from the water to their home seemed to get longer with each passing day.

The cave offered ample storage for their belongings and, as Miriam discovered, provided cool storage for milk, grain and vegetables. When Jonas would go to town to sell wool and buy supplies, Miriam stayed behind with Tabor, fearful that someone would recognize Tabor as a survivor of the slaughter and let word of him escape to Herod's soldiers.

As the first year of living in the hills came to a close, a new life was brought to the shepherd's family. Koda, son of Jonas, brother of Tabor, was born in their cave-home in the hills east of Bethlehem.

---

Walking behind his father with a shepherd's stick as tall as himself, five-year-old Tabor nudged a sheep by tapping the back of its leg, just as he had watched his father do so many times before. "Fire," Tabor said, pointing ahead of the herd. Smoke trailed skyward from a campfire on the side of a neighboring hill.

Jonas turned to see the direction his son was pointing, before spotting the smoke trail himself. "Yes, son. Looks like only one man. I don't know this man, so stay with the sheep."

"Yes, Father."

Jonas left Tabor with the herd and walked toward the stranger sitting by his campfire. Though Tabor stayed with the sheep, the sheep followed their shepherd. Once he got close enough to be heard, Jonas called out, "Peace be with you."

The man stood and held out both hands. "And with you, my friend."

"I am Jonas of Bethlehem." Jonas gripped the stranger's forearm in a peaceful gesture. "This is my herd. My son and I are moving them higher into the hills to graze."

The stranger returned his grip, then stepped back to gaze upon Jonas's flock. "What fine sheep you have, Jonas of Bethlehem. I am Saul of Jerusalem. I have only five sheep, but my flock will grow with each passing year."

Curiosity pulled Tabor away from the sheep as he walked up behind his father where his view of the stranger was partially obstructed. The man appeared frail standing next to his father, as did his sheep when compared to their own.

"If you don't mind my asking, how do you maintain your small herd when you have no ram?" Jonas inquired.

"I get by with what I have," Saul responded. "Occasionally, other shepherds such as you will loan me a ram."

"Saul, the Lord God allowed our paths to cross for a reason," Jonas said, "so I must tell you that your sheep need better food and better breeding. Come, travel with us. I will show you where to find the high meadows."

"God be with you and your household, Jonas of Bethlehem," Saul responded.

Tabor watched as the stranger returned to his campfire, kicking sand and stone onto the smoldering discs of sheep dung. After extinguishing the embers with the bottom of his sandals, he tossed them on his mat, along with a few morsels of dried meat. "Tell me, Saul," Jonas asked as Saul finished rolling his mat and tucking it under his arm for traveling, "how long have you been herding your sheep?"

"These past few years."

Tabor clung to his father's ankle length brown and white mantle as the two men discussed the finer aspects of shepherding. Saul shifted his attention away from Jonas to the small boy who was peering cautiously around his father's leg at the stranger.

"And who is this fine young shepherd?" Saul asked.

Tabor tried to hide himself from the unwanted attention while holding onto the back of his father's mantle. Jonas pulled Tabor's hand and led him to stand in front of him. "This is my son, Tabor."

Kneeling down to address the young shepherd, Saul smiled and said, "Greetings to you, Tabor, son of Jonas."

Instead of responding, Tabor turned his head until his face was buried deeply in the side of Jonas's robe. Other than his family, no one had ever spoken directly to him.

"Tabor!" Jonas's tone was stern to Tabor's ears, but his hand on

Tabor's head was gentle.

Saul stood straight and laughed. "All is well, Jonas. I'm sure my appearance could frighten even the bravest of young shepherds."

Both men talked as they continued walking behind the combined flock of forty sheep. Tabor kept his distance from the men, walking well behind them throwing stones at bushes that, to his imagination, were fierce wolves and cunning jackals.

When they arrived at the grazing plateau, a full moon had begun to rise, so the men decided to make camp. The tall summer grass was lush with green and brown swirls, whipped by the relentless wind that rushed up the hillside. Hunger rumbled within the young shepherd's stomach, yet he held his silence.

Tabor had been thinking about what to say to this man who had talked with his father for hours while they walked, wishing to become part of the conversation. Finally it came to him. "We have thirty-five sheep and three goats."

Saul knelt next to Tabor. "Thirty-five? That is a lot of sheep for such a small shepherd to watch. Do you think you could teach me everything you have learned?"

Tabor searched for the right words to respond, but he could only manage a grin before running to his father, who was bringing life to a campfire.

Saul stood, watching the dimly lit crest of the hill behind Jonas. "We shall soon have company."

Squatting by the fire, Jonas looked over his shoulder before rising to his feet as well.

"Horses!" Tabor pointed to the two riders drawing near. Perhaps they had been attracted by the shepherds' campfire in the last hour of dusk.

"Stay behind me, Tabor," Jonas said as the horses approached. To Tabor, the size of the animals was daunting, and the uniformed men on their backs appeared larger than life. He watched with fascination as the two horses walked through the shepherd's camp.

The Roman on the lead horse shouted at the two grown men, in a language Tabor did not understand, as he led his horse between them. Jonas ducked and moved aside, yet Saul strangely stood his ground. One soldier dismounted while the other turned his steed to face the shepherds. When the soldier on foot walked toward the herd, Tabor backed up a step when he heard his father challenge the intruder.

"You there!" Jonas exclaimed. Saul caught Jonas by the arm at the same time the mounted soldier drew his steel sword, pointing it at the shepherds.

Tabor's mouth felt dry as fear of the foreboding warriors made his heart race. Frozen in place, all he could manage was to watch the Roman on foot pull his dagger. With a quick, practiced stroke, he pulled the blade under the neck of one of the sheep. Before the animal stopped twitching, he had already slaughtered a second sheep.

The soldier heaved one carcass across the neck of his horse, right in front of his saddle, then he placed the other carcass in front of the mounted soldier, who sheathed his sword. After mounting his horse and positioning the dead sheep in front of him, both men turned their horses to ride away with the stolen animals.

Tabor's temper surfaced when the horses passed in front of him. Before the opportunity escaped him, he threw a rock at the second horse, striking it on the rump and causing it to lunge to the side. The soldier spun his horse and drew his sword, raising it high as he prepared to strike.

"Tabor!" Jonas yelled.

Jonas ran to snatch his son, placing his body between Tabor and the Roman steel. At that same moment, Saul distracted the soldier while speaking rapidly in their language.

The heated discussion between Saul and the soldier continued as both men pointed to Tabor, clearly the subject of conversation.

Saul ran toward the herd and grabbed a lamb. Returning quickly to the soldier, he offered the lamb, quite literally in exchange for the lives of Jonas and Tabor.

After a few more words in the same threatening tone, the soldier returned his sword to its sheath once again and took the lamb from Saul.

As the soldiers rode away, Jonas released his grip on Tabor and turned to the man who had clearly saved his life. "You speak Greek?"

---

Without other children his own age, seven-year-old Tabor's companionship was limited to his younger brother, Koda, his father, Jonas, Saul, and occasionally his uncle, Jacob. Saul had become a close confidant to Jonas, providing spirited conversation and pleasant company. To Tabor, though, the family friend was never without an entertaining story or valuable lesson. A visit from Saul was always a welcome surprise.

"Tabor, I brought you a gift," Saul said one day, after greeting Jonas and Miriam, in front of their home.

"A gift, Saul? What is it?" Tabor asked. Saul held out his hand in a fist, hiding the gift he carried, slowly opening his fingers to let the long straps unfurl. "A sling? You're giving me a sling?"

"I am, indeed, Tabor. Now you can fight giants as David once did. He wasn't much older than you when he defeated Goliath, you know."

"Oh, thank you! Will you teach me how to use it?"

"I will be honored, with your father's permission."

"And mine," Miriam added, "but I'd better not see stones flying toward the sheep—or any of us, for that matter, if you wish to keep your sling."

"Oh no, Mother. No, never." Tabor took Saul by the hand and tugged. "Come, Saul, come. Teach me."

Tabor led Saul down the rocky hillside from their home to level ground, where he might receive his first lesson. Saul went to a nearby pile of rocks and stacked eight stones into the shape of a pyramid—to be used as a target—and then counted off ten paces for Tabor. "Now, my young warrior, when you can knock the top stone off without disturbing the stones underneath, you will be ready to take down Goliath."

Saul and Tabor gathered stones small enough to fit in the pouch of the child-sized sling and stacked them neatly together. Saul demonstrated to his young pupil how to wrap one strap around his hand, holding the end of the other strap between his thumb and index finger, and then load a stone. The older man swung the sling twice before sending the stone toward the target, nearly missing it.

"Let me try," Tabor pleaded. When Saul handed him the sling and a few stones, Tabor mimicked Saul's steps, swinging one stone in the sling twice around before letting it fly directly above the two of them. Both Saul and Tabor ducked with their arms over their heads to protect themselves from the falling stone, which landed behind them.

"You must try again and again," Saul said, patting Tabor on the shoulder. "When you are well practiced, you'll be able to feel the stone as it leaves your sling. When you develop this sort of connection with what you're doing, the stones will go where you want, and you'll be using your mind more than your body."

"Really, Saul? I will feel the stone?"

Saul smiled as he lifted the empty sling pouch that dangled from

Tabor's hand, "I'm going to go talk with your father, young warrior. You keep practicing and let me know when you hit your target."

"I will." Tabor wrapped his arms around Saul's waist and hugged his friend. "Thank you for my gift."

Tabor practiced relentlessly with his sling. For months, he refined his technique, initially aiming for his target, then heaving it with all his might and often hitting the base of the pyramid of stones—but never the ultimate prize.

One afternoon, however, he suddenly found himself using his mind to guide the stone directly at the top of the pyramid, and the intended target fell. "Saul! Saul!" Tabor called as he ran through the valley to find his mentor tending his flock. He was so excited he could barely speak. After reaching the shepherd, Tabor tried talking as he caught his breath. "I did it! I hit the target—the stone on top of the stones. Not once, but five times. It was as you said. I can feel it now. I feel the stone, and it goes where I want. Am I a warrior now, Saul?"

"A warrior?" Saul replied. "I say, you are more than a warrior. You are well on your way to becoming a marksman."

"Is a marksman better than a warrior?"

"Most definitely," Saul said. "Anyone can be a warrior. All they have to do is put on the uniform and follow orders. But a marksman is unique in all the world, because he always hits his target. Marksmanship is a gift from God—a gift you must use wisely. You show your father what you can do, and he'll come to depend on your skills to kill the predators that attack his sheep."

Tabor fantasized about going on a hunt for mountain goat with his father as he ran toward Jonas's camp to tell of his accomplishment.

"That's wonderful news, Tabor!" Jonas said to his son. "Remember, though, a live target isn't the same as a rock that waits in place for your stone. A jackal or wolf is always moving and changing direction. You have to anticipate which way it will move and make that spot your target."

Fascinated by his father's expressions and watching as his hands moved from side to side to show a predator's movements, Tabor asked, "How do I do that, Father? How do I know where a wolf will be when I sling a stone?"

"You have to think like the wolf. Remember, it will always sneak up behind its prey to catch it off guard, so think about the way you would be turning to get behind the sheep if you were the wolf."

With so many new things to consider when using his sling, Tabor left his father to go practice against more targets, imagining the movement of animals as they hunted their prey. His techniques evolved with each passing day. Sometimes, he'd go about spinning his sling by his side, but eventually, he settled into perfecting a twirl and release from above his head.

As the weeks passed, his accuracy improved, as did his speed— from the instant he pulled the sling from the rope around his waist to the moment the stone left its pouch to fly toward his target.

It was an instinctive reaction, then, for him to pull out his sling and load a stone the moment he heard the cry of a lamb on the far side of the flock. As he ran past the sheep, he could only see the back end of a large jackal with a newborn lamb in its mouth, heading toward a clump of bushes. Before the wily predator could take two more steps, he felt the sting of Tabor's stone on his hind leg, forcing him to drop his meal and yelp before running away.

Tabor ran for the lamb and checked it over for injuries. The lamb struggled in his arms, clearly distraught after being carried away from her mother. The only damage appeared to be her wet neck from the predator's mouth. On wobbly legs, the lamb walked back to the herd, answering her mother's call. Seeing only the dust trail of the jackal, which he knew wouldn't be feasting on his father's lamb tonight, Tabor smiled, realizing what he had accomplished.

# CHAPTER 5

*Spring, A.D. 6*

"Miriam," Jonas began, as they sat outside by the evening fire, "Passover is coming, and I think we should go together with Tabor and Koda this year."

"Do you think that is wise?"

"Tabor is twelve years old now but has never been to Jerusalem—or anywhere, for that matter. Herod the Great is dead, and his son now sits on the throne. And I don't believe anyone hunts survivors from the slaughter in Bethlehem."

After a moment of contemplation, Miriam responded, "You're right, he should go. We should *all* go. But I promise you this: I will keep a tight rein on both of our sons. Passover is certainly a joyful time in Jerusalem, but it can also be dangerous for the innocent."

Jonas was uneasy about taking his sons to Jerusalem. In their mountain home, he felt protected from the sins of the city, but he knew he was doing a disservice to his sons if he left them unprepared for survival among unscrupulous men.

On the following day, Jonas sat with Tabor to teach him the things he needed to know for Passover. Miriam squatted nearby in front of the stone oven that she used nearly every day to make bread. The scent of the leaven bread provided a fragrant relief to the pungent aroma of burning sheep dung.

"You see, son," Jonas began, "it is important that you know exactly how to behave in the temple. There are places in the temple where only grown men can go, and there are places only for the women. Children usually stay with their mothers, but sometimes you will be with me. You must do exactly as we say, so you won't get lost or hurt."

"I'm not afraid, Father. I have my sling."

"No, son," Miriam interjected. "Passover is not a time for fighting. Passover is a time to remember when our people were set free from bondage in Egypt. It is a celebration, but it is also a time to remember the suffering our ancestors endured in slavery."

"I understand, Mother."

"We will take five of our six male lambs to Passover." Jonas swatted at a fly that had landed on his arm.

"But why do they want our lambs for Passover, Father?"

"This is the temple tax we must pay to be able to live here and raise our herd in peace. Then, like the other Jews who have no sheep, we will buy a lamb for sacrifice. The priests will slaughter the lambs and offer their blood to God, as a sign of respect. You see, in the time of the pharaohs, when our ancestors were slaves in Egypt, God commanded Moses to spread blood from a pure, spotless lamb over the door posts of all the dwelling places of the Children of Israel. That is how God's angel knew which houses to pass over, or leave alone, and which houses to punish with death of the firstborn. So the blood from our lambs will be used to thank God for our ancestors' lives."

"And Tabor," Miriam added, "it is extremely important that you do not speak to anyone in Jerusalem. Not to a man, woman, or child. Do you hear me?"

"Yes, Mother. I hear you."

"There are many good people in a city like Jerusalem," she said, "but there are also a lot of bad people. So you only talk to me or your father."

"Or Saul? Is Saul going to Passover?"

"Yes, you may speak to Saul," his mother said. "And I'm expecting you to help me keep Koda from wandering off."

"Tabor, my son," Jonas said, "Roman soldiers will be there outside the city. Inside the city, you will see Herod's soldiers and even temple guards. Do not look any of these men in the eye. Simply keep your head down and walk quietly with us."

"Will the soldiers try to kill me like they did in Bethlehem?"

Tabor asked, clearly struggling with stories of the past that haunted his thoughts.

"No, those days are behind us," Jonas replied, even though he still suffered with his own nightmares from the slaughter of the innocents. "I will never let anyone harm you or your brother, as God protects us all."

When the day came to leave for Jerusalem, Tabor fidgeted with the ties on a pouch he used to carry food scraps to eat on the journey.

"Calm yourself, Tabor," Miriam said as he paced back and forth near the lambs.

Until his mother spoke, he hadn't realized how excited he was to see the city of which he had heard so much about. "I'm ready to go—can we leave now?"

The lambs were tied in the pen near the front of their home, having been separated from their mothers the day before. Jonas emerged from their home and touched the *mezuzah* that hung above the doorway, before reciting, "Hear, O Israel, the Lord our God, the Lord is One."

"Saul! Saul is here!" Tabor announced, as their friend came walking up the path, carrying two of his lambs, one under each arm.

Jonas eyed his friend before asking, "Are you going to carry your lambs all the way to Jerusalem?"

"I will if I have to," he replied. "You know how picky the priests are. One little blemish and they reject the lamb for being less than perfect."

Miriam led two lambs with ropes around their necks, as did Jonas and Saul, followed by Tabor, who led one of his own. Koda walked next to his brother, poking the lamb with his stick, as a shepherd would to guide his flock. The path into Bethlehem was rocky and slow, but north of the village, the walk was smooth and well-travelled. On the road to Jerusalem, more and more pilgrims joined them in the Procession of the Lambs, until it became so crowded it was difficult to walk. Still hours outside of Jerusalem, Tabor had already seen more people than he had in his entire life.

When they finally reached the city walls, Tabor could do little more than gaze in awe at the number of people and the size of the walls and buildings around him.

"Come, Tabor," Jonas said. "We must bathe ourselves and the lambs before we can enter the city. Nothing about us or our lambs can be unclean, or we won't be allowed to enter the temple."

Miriam held the ropes of all seven lambs and kept Koda with her, while Jonas, Saul, and Tabor went to the pools near Dung Gate to bathe. Afterward, Jonas returned Tabor to Miriam and went with Saul and the lambs to the northern gate to clean them in the Sheep Pool, meant only for sacrificial animals.

A Roman dressed in officer's garb pushed Saul to the side on the crowded road. "Out of my way, Jew," he exclaimed in Greek.

Instinctively, Saul replied in Greek, "My apologies, Centurion."

The soldier appeared to be surprised as he turned and studied the unusual spectacle of a Jewish shepherd who not only spoke Greek, but also recognized his military rank.

Jonas and Saul entered the city through Sheep's Gate from the north, near the Temple, where only men were allowed. Cooking fires dotted the landscape where pilgrims, who had already purchased their Passover lamb, began preparing the meat.

"This is merely another tax," Saul muttered to Jonas, as the two men led their sheep to the table where they would be traded for temple coins.

"It's all part of Passover," Jonas replied.

Saul frowned, knowing the lambs were merely the beginning of the day's taxes. The purchase of temple coins and multiple Roman tables at every exit would leave their pockets empty.

An hour later, while standing in line to purchase a slaughtered lamb from a temple priest, Saul tapped Jonas on the arm and then pointed. "Jonas, look over there, on the temple steps."

"What exactly? What are you looking at?"

"A boy. He can't be any older than Tabor, but he's talking to a group of rabbis and priests sitting on the steps. I've never seen so many rabbis listening to anyone like that before, let alone a child."

Jonas watched the boy who seemed to be teaching the teachers. Then the priest selling lambs called out, "Next!" and Jonas stepped to the front of the line.

After Miriam and Koda bathed in the pool for women, she moved with Tabor and Koda into the crowded line of people who were passing through the gate to enter the great city. Miriam held Koda's arm tightly with one hand and Tabor's hand with the other and led them through a vast area of vendors hawking their wares.

"Feel this, Tabor." Miriam touched a piece of brilliant blue fabric on a vendor's table. "You see how it glistens? This is called silk. They say it is spun by God's angels. It's a good thing we have no money, or I would buy everything here."

Tabor touched it too, but pulled his hand back when the vendor looked his way with creased eyebrows.

Miriam smiled at her eldest as she appeared to be enjoying the day. "Take in the sights, sounds, and smells, my sons," she said. "This city of Jerusalem is alive!"

Tabor marveled at the smells of lamb roasting over fire pits, unleavened bread baking, and toasted figs. He felt as though he had stepped into a different world. In his entire life, he had known fewer than ten people, but here inside the walls of Jerusalem, he was surrounded by thousands. A woman stepped between him and his mother, causing him to lose his grip on his mother's hand and nudging him against a man who stood at his back.

A sudden sense of fear and confinement took hold of his heart, and he tugged on his mother's sleeve. "I want to get out of here, Mother. I want to leave this city."

Miriam continued to admire some cloth, which she held up to see how much light passed through it. "What Tabor?" she asked.

"Mother!" Tabor responded, somewhat more forcibly. "I don't like it here. I want to leave." Tabor's eyes were large and his breathing was rapid.

The fear on his face and panic in his voice shocked Miriam into action. "Yes, Tabor, we will go."

Miriam led her sons by their hands, pushing her way through the crowd until they were outside the city walls. Away from the main gate, she found an isolated bench where they could rest. "We'll sit here, Tabor. Are you feeling better? Do you want some water?"

Tabor shook his head and looked at his mother with tears on his cheeks. "I couldn't breathe. There are too many people."

Miriam sat with her son, holding his head against her shoulder, while Koda sat on her opposite side, clinging to her arm. "I know, son. We'll wait here for your father and Saul. This is where he said to meet them. Then we can go home."

With her reassurance, he nodded his head in agreement against her shoulder.

After resting a few minutes, he lifted his head to study the figures on a hill outside the city walls. Pointing at the activity, he asked, "Mother, what are those men doing?"

Together, they watched as a man in the distance slammed a large hammer toward the ground, followed by the distant sound of a man's agonizing screams. A minute later, two other men pulled ropes to lift a large wooden rail, higher and higher until it nearly reached the top of a vertical pole, against which it came to rest. Attached to the rail were the man's arms, his body dangling below.

Pulling both of her sons closer, she said, "The Romans are crucifying a man. That is how they punish those who break their laws."

"But why? What did he do wrong?"

"I don't know, Tabor. Don't watch."

But watching was all Tabor could do, as the Romans pounded a spike through the man's feet into the vertical pole.

Three weeks after Passover, Jonas sat with Saul at the campfire on a moonless night, the sky ablaze with stars. Jonas watched his friend poke at the embers with a stick. "You seem to be deep in thought."

"Jonas," Saul said, "I would like your permission to teach the language of Greek to Tabor."

Jonas paused for a moment, contemplating Saul's request. "Why would I want Tabor to learn the language of the Romans—the very animals who are bent on our destruction?"

Saul paused, taking time to carefully form his words. "Tabor is a wonderful boy, with whom I know you are well pleased. But when I saw him in Jerusalem during Passover, I sensed only fear. If he learns to speak and understand Greek, I believe it will build his confidence, and he will find the strength that lies within him."

"Where did a Jewish shepherd like you learn to speak Greek?"

Jonas watched Saul stare at the ground, pushing small stones in the sand with his sandals.

Pressing further, Jonas said, "I noticed during Passover that every time we passed one of Herod's guards, you tried to hide your face. If it is none of my business, I'll hold my tongue. But I can't help wonder if you may have crossed paths with the palace guard in the past."

The deafening silence between the two men was broken only by the distant call of a wolf. Saul poked at the fire again with his stick before replying. "Jonas, my friend, I will tell you. And then I won't blame you if you turn and walk away, never to lay eyes on me again. Nor will I blame you if you cut my throat and feed me to that hungry wolf."

"I'll do neither. Go on, my friend."

After another long pause, Saul said, "I was one of them—a member of Herod the Great's palace guard. I swore my loyalty to him with my life. I fought many battles for him and killed many men. I was trained to follow orders without question, no matter how distasteful. I even fought alongside Romans, which is where I learned Greek."

"Bethlehem?" Jonas asked.

Saul nodded. "I was sent to Bethlehem, a member of Herod's elite guardsmen, under direct orders to kill every male child under the age of two, along with anyone who got in my way. I did not stop to question the order or judge the man who gave it. I simply acted as a loyal soldier does. I chased down a woman carrying her child and killed them both with my spear. She was no threat to me. The baby was not part of an army. I killed them because I was a trained soldier who followed orders. When the woman took her last breath, something broke inside of me."

Saul paused as he felt the weight of his words. For years, he had suffered the guilt in silence, but hearing his own admission for the first brought back the anguish anew.

"Go on." Jonas bowed his head, the pain of his friend's confession striking to his very soul.

"Too much a coward to end my own life, I deserted. I pulled off my armor, dropped my sword, and walked into these hills, never to go back. I can't live with myself, but for some reason, God won't let me die. Instead, He punishes me with memories and nightmares that rob me of sleep."

"And Tabor?"

Again Saul nodded. "Yes, I was sent to kill Tabor. Had that woman I chased been Miriam carrying Tabor, they would both be dead now, by order of a madman who called himself *king*. Do you see now why I can never forgive myself? Why God will never forgive me?"

"How do you live with yourself?" Jonas asked.

"I tell you, my friend. If you killed me now, I would consider it a gift. I thought I was a brave soldier once, but in truth, I'm nothing but a deserter. This is why I hide my face from the palace guards. If they knew I was alive, I would be tortured and executed."

. "I was there that day," Jonas began, as Saul lowered his head. "Not in Bethlehem, but close enough to see the soldiers—close enough to hear the screams." Tears filled Jonas's eyes as the memories came flooding back. "Before that day was over, I buried men, women, and children. But mostly children, mostly boys."

"I am an evil man worthy of nothing but death." Saul's voice broke, and Jonas saw tears flooding down his friend's cheeks. "I can never find peace or forgiveness."

Jonas stood and took two steps away before stopping to rest against his walking stick. In the depths of his soul, he weighed the evil acts of Saul the soldier against the gentle heart of Saul the shepherd, who he had come to love as a brother. After filling his lungs and slowly letting the air escape, he turned and faced the broken man. "God kept you alive so you could hear these words from the father of a boy you were sent to kill. From a man who watched the slaughter from a distance and was powerless to stop it—I forgive you, Saul."

Saul looked up to the stars in the moonless night to dry the tears that filled his eyes. Then he looked at the face of the man who had just committed the greatest act of forgiveness imaginable, and he lost control of his emotions and flung himself at the feet of his friend, weeping uncontrollably.

Jonas put his hand on Saul's back, his heart breaking for this man who had truly and completely humbled himself here in the hills of Bethlehem. "Saul," he said, "will you teach my son to speak Greek?"

# CHAPTER 6



*Summer, A.D. 8*

As a fourteen-year-old boy, Tabor was nearly as proficient at herding sheep as his father or Saul—even more so when predators came within range of his sling. On one hot afternoon in midsummer, Tabor left the herd grazing while he climbed a nearby hill to investigate a raucous noise.

In the valley below, he saw two armies in the midst of a battle. Clouds of dust hovered over the soldiers, two or three hundred strong. Cries of battle echoed up the hill, as arrows flew above the orchestrated mayhem.

The men on foot were engaged in hand-to-hand combat, wielding swords and brandishing shields beneath the sweltering sun. Amongst the troops, a few men on horses rode in leisure, each one observing the proceedings around him with almost a studious gaze.

After some commands called out by the tallest horseman, the soldiers broke off their fighting and separated into two lines, facing each other. Another shouted command followed, and the soldiers started their fighting all over again.

*They're only training*, Tabor thought. From his vantage point on the crest of the hill, Jonas's son quickly realized he could, with a simple swivel of his head, see both his herd in the valley behind him and the soldiers in the valley in front of him. And though his sense of responsibility kept him sufficiently attentive to the flock, he nonetheless found the soldiers much more interesting to watch, as they swung their swords, threw their spears, shot their arrows, and skirmished up and down the valley.

When the day was near the end, Tabor watched as the soldiers marched in unison out of the valley, following their commanders on horseback. His youthful curiosity spurred him to run down the hill to the vacant battleground to see if the soldiers had left anything interesting behind.

Searching the ground, he found three broken spears, all with wooden points. He gathered them up and ran back over the hill to find the herd before darkness fell. But Saul was already with the herd and busily starting a campfire when Tabor returned.

"Saul!" Tabor exclaimed. "You won't believe what I found."

Saul spoke Greek as he corrected his young protégé. "Greek, Tabor—remember your Greek. When I get here, I find sheep with no shepherd to protect them. Where have you been? I thought I was going to have to send the sheep out to look for the lost shepherd."

"I was barely over this hill." Tabor pointed, speaking carefully as he struggled to remember the Greek words. "There were soldiers, *real* Roman soldiers, and they were practicing for battle. And look—after they left, I found these spears." Tabor held out the three broken shanks for Saul to see.

In his eyes, Tabor could see Saul's anger flare. With the back of his hand, Saul struck the spears from Tabor's hand, sending them to the ground where the Roman practice points scattered. "You should throw those away and not play with such things. I don't like to see you lured by romantic thoughts of war. Remember, Tabor, you are a shepherd, not a soldier."

Tabor dropped to the ground, cradling his head with his hands. "I know I'm a shepherd, but even a Jewish shepherd can learn to defend himself."

Saul sighed deeply before squatting next to Tabor. "Yes, defend yourself and your family, but promise me—you hunt only for food, not man."

"I promise, Saul."

"Bring Dalia's new lamb to me, Tabor. I need to see if his leg has healed."

Tabor walked through the herd, spinning in circles as he

searched. Finally he returned to the campfire where Saul waited. "I can't find the lamb," he confessed. "I found Dalia, but her lamb isn't with her."

Saul poked the fire with a stick while the realization of the missing lamb worked on Tabor's mind. With resolve, he looked up to stare directly in the young shepherd's eyes. "While you were watching the soldiers, a wolf was watching the herd. He chose the youngest, most fragile for his meal. I found what's left of the lamb behind some bushes over the ridge."

The next morning, after Jonas went to relieve Saul from watching over the herd, Tabor took his broken Roman spears down the hill to the flat ground where he often practiced with his sling. Holding a spear point like a dagger, he pretended to be fighting the same way he had seen the soldiers practicing.

As his imagination grew, the dagger became a sword that he used to fight through hundreds of helpless soldiers who were powerless against his magical weapon. Finally, he took the spear and threw it toward an imaginary rider on a mighty steed. The spear point landed only a short distance from where he threw it.

After running to pick it up, Tabor frowned as he realized it was too short to be thrown any distance. "I wish I could throw my spear as far as I can throw a rock with my sling." He paused and looked at the spear shard, and an idea occurred to him. Holding both straps of his sling, he placed the broken end of the short spear in the pouch of his sling and held the point with the same hand he used to hold the straps. This time, when he threw the spear, the extended length of his sling catapulted the spear nearly three times the distance it had gone before.

Excited with his success, Tabor ran to pick up the spear. He threw it again and again, trying to improve on distance from one throw to the next.

That afternoon, Tabor showed his spear-throwing technique to Saul. "Do it again and let me watch you," Saul said in Greek, after watching Tabor's first demonstration. Following Tabor's second throw, Saul concluded, "I must say, you have some good distance using your sling. I never would have thought of such a thing. But you know, Tabor, you have very little accuracy that way."

"Yes, you're right—and it flips before it lands, so the sharp end won't hit the target. What should I do?"

Saul thought for a moment, as he picked up the broken spear.

"You want it to be sharp as a spear, short as an arrow, and thrown like a stone." After a few more moments of contemplation, he held the spear between both hands and said, "You must make it as long as your forearm, from your elbow to the tip of your fingers. Then you need some weight on the point like an arrow. If you can't do that, then at least burn the sharp point to make it hard. Last, tie a piece of wool or a feather to the back, like an arrow. That will help stabilize it and keep it going straight."

"But won't that reduce how far I can throw it?"

"Some, yes. But you're sacrificing a little distance for stability and accuracy. If you can't control it, you'll never hit your target."

Tabor took the spear from his mentor. "Thank you, Saul. I'll get to work on it right away."

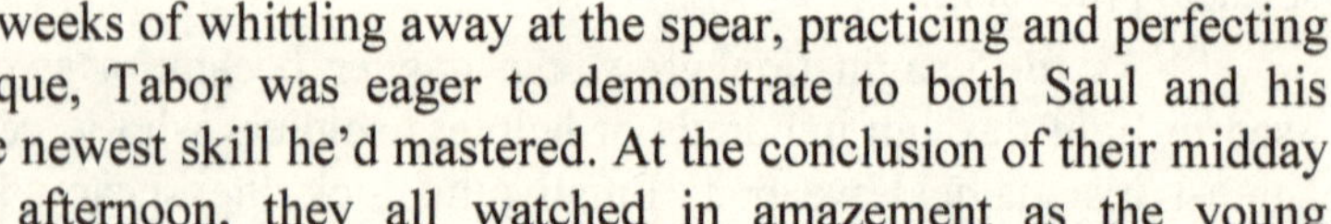

After two weeks of whittling away at the spear, practicing and perfecting his technique, Tabor was eager to demonstrate to both Saul and his parents the newest skill he'd mastered. At the conclusion of their midday meal one afternoon, they all watched in amazement as the young shepherd boy propped a melon on top of the waist-high stone wall of the pen used to hold the sheep for sheering. Then he took his position a stone's throw away, where he loaded the back end of his handcrafted spear in the pouch of his sling. With his left hand pointing toward the melon, he first visualized the spear piercing the stationary target.

"Fly true," he whispered, flinging the short spear at great speed through the air on a direct path into the heart of the melon. The impact was so great, the target exploded into small chunks as the spear passed through it, falling just inside the sheep pen.

When all three adults threw their hands up and yelled, Tabor's eyes widened, and he felt a sense of pride in the accolades being sent his way.

Saul, particularly, admired Tabor's skill and ingenuity. "The Romans forbid Jews from using bow and arrow, but this is neither bow nor arrow! The next time I go hunting for deer or ram, I certainly want you by my side."

The next morning, Tabor gathered his weapons and set out to practice. When he passed his father outside, though, he ignored the promise he had made to Saul and envisioned himself a great warrior. Compulsively fishing for yet another compliment, he stated, "Someday, I'm going to be a soldier, Father. I will kill lots of Romans and free Israel."

Jonas looked at Miriam, who frowned at her son's talk of killing. Turning back to Tabor, he said, "I have a job for you today. Come with me, son."

Jonas picked up a knife and walked down the hill toward the herd, with Tabor following behind him. "What is it you need from me, Father?"

"You are going to learn how to feed our family."

When they reached the herd, Tabor listened as his father explained to Saul, "Today, Tabor is going to learn how difficult it can be to take a life."

Saul patted Jonas on the back. "You are a good father, Jonas. I will stay out of your way."

Tabor was already walking among the herd when Jonas called out, "Tabor, bring Rachel to me!"

As Tabor had done so many times before, he walked through the herd and segregated the sheep his father had asked for. He drove her to Jonas with short taps from his stick on the backs of her legs.

Jonas heaved the animal onto his shoulders, holding her feet in front, and walked with Tabor to the side of a hill, away from the herd before setting her down with his knee pinning her to the rocky terrain. "You think being a soldier would be fun, Tabor?" Jonas held a solemn eye upon his son. "You think killing is something you do with pride?"

"Well, no, Father, I don't think—"

"We take a life because we must, not because we want to. When a man kills for pleasure, he is no longer a man."

"Yes, Father."

"Now we are going to kill Rachel because we *must*. We end her life so that we can live. She will feed and clothe our family. Do you understand, my son?"

"Yes," Tabor answered, trying to interpret his father's instructions. "We kill her because she belongs to us, we raised her, and we—"

"No, son. Not at all. She belongs to God, as does every other creature. God provided her to us so that we may live. Before we kill her, we first give thanks to God for Rachel and the nourishment she brings us. When we take an animal's life for food, we say a blessing of thanks for the *mitzvah*, which requires that we do this in a compassionate manner."

"The *Shechita*, Father?"

"Yes, Tabor, the *Shechita*. Lay your hand on her and say it with me."

Both father and son laid their hands on the animal. She lay quietly, trustful of her shepherds and accustomed to their touch during the shearing season. They both prayed, "Blessed are You, our God, Sovereign of the universe, Who has commanded us regarding *Shechita*."

After the prayer, Jonas offered his knife to Tabor.

"Me, Father? You want *me* to kill her?" Tabor trembled at the idea. Many times, he had used his sling to kill rodents that had invaded their food stocks, and even a jackal once, when the stone hit its head. But those were all from a distance. This was up close, and it was a sheep he had nurtured and protected for five years, from the time she was born. This animal had been more like a pet, and certainly not an enemy.

"Yes, son." Jonas put the knife in Tabor's palm, despite the boy's hesitancy. "I want you to stand over her with your legs on both sides like you do when we shear. Then, pull her chin up with your left hand, reach under her neck with the knife, and pull it across her throat. Cut quick and cut deep, so she doesn't suffer."

Tabor stared from the knife in his hand to his father, hoping for a reprieve. He wanted desperately to postpone this slaughter till another day. Then Jonas laid a hand on his shoulder.

"Remember, Tabor—this is not something we want to do. This is something we *must* do."

Gripping the knife in his sweaty palm, Tabor nodded. He straddled the sheep, his eyes welling with tears. "Like this?"

"Yes, now squeeze her tight with your legs. She will try to kick free when you cut her throat, so hold her as tightly as you can until she stops. That is when you will know she's dead."

Tabor learned later that Jonas's usual technique for slaughtering a sheep was to lay it on the ground and cut its throat before backing away. Today, when Tabor felt this animal's life leave its body, it would serve as an important lesson for a boy so enthused about fighting and killing.

Now, with his legs squeezing either side of the ewe's body, Tabor felt Rachel's muscles tense against his thighs, as if she knew death was near. Her eyes protruded as she strained to look at the young shepherd who hovered over her. Tabor gave serious consideration to releasing his grip and dropping the knife, but his father was watching. He must do this horrible thing.

Struggling to ignore or override all that was drowning him in a dark, anxious flood of emotion, he lifted the ewe's head by pulling up on her chin to expose her throat. Tabor looked at his father once again, hoping he might stop what now seemed a barbaric act. But Jonas instead replied, "It's time, son."

Reaching under her chin, the boy placed the blade against her throat and pulled it across as quickly and firmly as he could. The sheep screamed and kicked as its blood streamed down its neck.

"Hold her, Tabor!" Jonas yelled over the animal's cries. "You didn't cut deep enough. You must cut her again, but this time cut deeper."

Barely able to hold the beast that was struggling against the grasp of his legs, and now suffering from the shallow cut, Tabor reached under to cut her throat a second time, determined to end her torment. Indeed, the second cut severed the ewe's main artery, evidenced by the blood gushing over Tabor's hand and knife. Her struggle ended a moment later. Tabor stared up at his father as the dead silence around them replaced the ewe's death cries. Warm blood dripped from his fingers, and he dropped the carcass to the ground.

"Good, son. Good." Jonas put a firm hand on his son's shoulder. "It's over now."

Tabor looked down at the animal that had been alive mere moments before. Rachel died by *his* hands, the very hands before his eyes, now covered in her blood. He dropped the knife and ran just three steps before dropping to his knees to vomit. After heaving one more time, he sat down on the rocky ground, panting and feeling disgusted with himself. "I'm sorry, Father. I let you down."

Jonas sat next to his son, pulled out a water bag made from a goat's stomach and handed it to Tabor. "Here, son, drink this."

The two sat side-by-side in silence. Jonas handed his son a rag to wipe his hands on. "I am proud of you."

"But how, Father? I failed. I hated killing her. I hated it!" Tabor began to cry, feeling less a man and more a child with each passing second.

"I am proud of you *because* you hated it. Don't you see, son? This is what I've been trying to tell you. There is *no* pleasure in taking a life, *any* life. When you find pleasure in killing, then your life has no meaning. You will no longer be a man. You're not even an animal. You're nothing."

Tabor wiped the tears from his eyes. "Then—you're not disappointed in me?"

Jonas put his arm around Tabor's shoulder and pulled him close, "No, not disappointed. I'm proud of you. And I'll let you in on a little secret. I vomited the first time I killed one of my father's sheep, too—same as you."

Looking up at his father, Tabor saw he was smiling at the son in whom he was well pleased. Jonas slapped Tabor on his knee and said, "Come, the hard part is over. Help me skin it and dress it out."

# CHAPTER 7

*Early Spring, A.D 9*

"This is going to be a killing storm," Jonas proclaimed, as he and Tabor stared beyond the herd at the brown wall of sand to the west.

"Is it coming this way?" Tabor asked, not taking his eyes from the brown wall, even as the mountain on the other side of the valley disappeared, consumed by the encroaching sandstorm.

"It is, and we don't have much time. We need to get all of the animals inside. Let's move!"

With shouts to startle the animals, and swats from the shepherds, Jonas and Tabor herded the flock toward their home. Miriam was swiftly bringing in loose items that might otherwise blow away when the sheep entered the pens that linked to their front walls.

Tabor stood uneasily at the entryway to the cave in which he had been raised, holding a lamb in his arms. His attention was divided between handing this newborn to his mother and wondering how the rest of the sheep would all fit inside. That task fell to Tabor's brother.

Koda kept the sheep pushed to the rear of the cave as more and more joined the flock indoors. "Here are two more," Jonas called out to Miriam, his voice barely to be heard over the howling wind that forced sand through the crevices in the stone walls of their home. Jonas released his grip on the two sheep, and the animals bolted into the safety of their new home to escape the gritty wind that stung their eyes.

Miriam lit two torches and set them in their holders near the animals, while Jonas constructed a temporary pen by laying two poles between crevices in the rock walls to separate the animals from the front of the cave. "I don't think this cave could hold even one more lamb," she concluded while using her sleeve to dab at the grit that coated her face.

The sudden light from the torches startled the already nervous flock, causing a lamb to dart from the herd, under the pole that separated shepherds from sheep, and escape through the door as Tabor was pushing it closed. "I'll get her!" Tabor cried out as he ran into the storm.

"Tabor! No!" Jonas yelled. Miriam and Koda guarded the pen to keep any more animals from following the lost lamb into the blasting sandstorm. To reinforce the pen, they began lashing ropes together, weaving them into a more secure fence.

Outside, blinded by the thick dust, Tabor held his arm across his nose and mouth so that his sleeve would filter the air. Still, he struggled to breathe and to see. Within a few steps, he tripped over a waist high stone wall and fell to the ground. He got to his feet again, listening carefully, faintly hearing the lamb's cries over the howling wind that whipped around hills and trees. Following the sound, he practically stepped on the young animal where it had collapsed and lay still, bleating for its mother. "I found you!" he yelled, barely hearing his own words through the storm. Kneeling beside it, he lifted the lamb and covered it with his garment.

From his crouched position, he looked for a familiar landmark to help him find his way home. In every direction, all he could see was shades of brown, stinging his eyes, filling his nose and mouth. "I can't see," he said to the lamb. "I don't know which way we should go."

"Tabor!" A man's voice came from directly ahead. Looking up, Tabor saw the shadowy figure walking directly toward him. He wore a scarf wrapped around his head, leaving only a small opening for his eyes.

"Father! I found the lamb, but I can't find my way home." He hugged the lamb tight to his body.

"I know. I'm here." He picked up both boy and lamb in his arms and climbed the hill toward the home, hidden behind a wall of blowing sand. "That was very brave of you to save the lamb, but you must be careful. You still have much to do."

"I'm sorry, Father."

When they reached the door to the home, he lowered Tabor to walk inside with the lamb.

"Tabor!" Miriam grabbed her son and quickly checked him over. His eyes were badly swollen, red and puffy from exposure to the blasting sands. He carried the lamb to the back of the cave and set it down next to its mother.

"I have to get your father," Miriam said. "He's still out there."

"He's right behind me," Tabor called back.

Miriam looked down at the rope in her hands that continued to pull through the doorway. "I don't think so!" With three heavy jerks on the rope, she began reeling it in until the door opened just long enough for Jonas to step inside.

"Is he here?" Jonas asked his wife.

"He's safe," she replied.

Though his eyes were burning, Tabor approached his father. "You carried me home!"

Jonas ignored his son's statement and scolded the young shepherd, "You risked your life and put us all in danger by running after that lamb. You must be smarter than that."

When all were safe, Jonas, Miriam, Tabor, and Koda began settling into the notion of sharing their home with thirty-seven sheep, three goats, and a donkey.

Jonas told his eldest son, "Tabor, it's up to us to keep these sheep fed and watered. However long they're here, we need to ensure they're tended to."

For the next two days, while the sandstorm raged, they each took turns bringing water and as much hay as they could gather, always tethered to the end of a rope for safety. Miriam did her part, as well, struggling to both protect their food supply from the massive herd in their home and prepare what she could to nourish her husband and family. Their home, which had seemed so large to the family of four with the combined cave and two rooms constructed beyond the cave entrance, suddenly felt cramped.

Constrained and anxious, the sheep bleated and threatened to break loose from their roped in sheepfold. Compounding all of this, the intensely strong wind made it impossible to build a fire to use for cooking or warmth. Nuts, dried figs, and a few strips of sun-dried mutton sustained the family as they listened to their outdoor sheds and belongings buckle to the will of the wind.

The morning after the second day of storms blossomed with a stillness that was in stark contrast to the violence of the previous days. Jonas was the first to step out to survey the damage. Miriam, Koda, and

Tabor quickly followed. Jonas lifted two wooden poles that had once held a roof over their cooking pots and hand tools, as if standing the poles upright would reconstruct the broken lean-to. Seeing his disappointment, Miriam said, "At least we are safe and well."

Jonas dropped the poles and looked at his wife and sons. "You're right. God brought us through the storm and protected our herd." Wrapping his arms around Miriam, Tabor, and Koda to form a family circle, Jonas looked to the sky and began to pray. "God of Abraham, we give thanks for your mercy and protection that saved us all and our flock from the wrath of this terrible storm."

After his prayer, Jonas said, "Tabor, take the sheep to the meadow to graze. Koda and I will start cleaning up and salvaging what we can."

"Yes, Father," Tabor replied. He walked back into their home and began leading the sheep into the peaceful daylight. Once the last animal emerged, he ushered them toward the path they knew so well, which eventually led to the open meadow. After counting all thirty-seven head, Tabor picked up his walking stick and followed the last straggler.

With the flat edge of a shovel, Miriam began carrying mounds of sheep dung from the back of the cave to the gravel slope in front of their home, where each pile would dry in the afternoon sun. After a few days of drying, the smelly dung would become usable fuel for the cooking fire.

Jonas and Koda began separating broken pots and splintered wood from the intact, reusable supplies. The damage done by the fierce winds would require a trip into Bethlehem and, of course, the expenditure of funds the family did not have. The two were deep into the process of rebuilding, repairing, and cleaning up when a familiar voice rang out from the bottom of the hill.

"Friend, Jonas!"

Turning around, Jonas saw a shepherd approaching, one he had known for years. "Armon! Glad to see you're still among the living!"

Jonas walked down the hill to greet his friend with clasped forearms before embracing him. "How did you fare?" Jonas asked.

"Most of my herd is intact. I found two dead lambs, and three sheep are still missing. Have you seen any strays among your herd?"

"No, but I'll help you search for those still missing. Come, Koda, we have lost sheep to find."

Jonas and Koda promptly left their chores for another day to join

with Armon to search for his lost animals.

While the herd grazed throughout the peaceful afternoon, Tabor enjoyed taking some time to practice with his sling. With his left hand pointing at his target, one swift-flying stone after another hit its mark. By studying the composition of the stone, he found some stones to be better for speed, while others were better for accuracy.

From the corner of his eye among the larger boulders, Tabor caught sight of feathers moving with the wind. Curiously, he approached to find a bird, larger than any he had seen before, lying motionless on the ground. "Poor creature," he said, "you must have been blown out of the sky during the storm."

Tabor secured his sling in the rope around his waist and knelt by the bird to inspect it. As he folded back the wing that had been extended upward, he noticed a slight movement in the bird's eye. Its open beak slowly closed when he brought the wings back against the bird's side. Turning it upright, the bird's neck and head drooped, and it let out a croak.

Tabor stroked the bird's wing, feeling its softness. "Are you alive, feathered one?" Lifting his pouch, Tabor opened the end to let some water spill into the palm of his hand. "Here, drink this," he urged. The bird was so weak and exhausted, it didn't have the strength to move toward the water.

He lifted the bird's head onto his wet palm and let its tongue touch the water. As if by instinct, the thin gray tongue moved in and out of the large, curved beak as the bird pulled the water droplets to the back of its throat. Sitting on the ground next to the bird, Tabor pulled some small pieces of dried meat from his pouch and put them next to the bird's beak. Much to his disappointment, the bird ignored the offering.

"You will not live, feathered one, if you do not eat," he lectured the dying creature. Then he got the idea to do for this bird what he had observed mother birds doing for their young. He took the dried meat and chewed it until it was soft and moist before placing it in the bird's beak. Instinctively, the bird closed its beak around the morsel and appeared to swallow it.

"Good!" Tabor exclaimed, realizing they could work together.

Within a couple of hours, the bird was resting in his lap with its head upright, looking side to side. "It may be a day or two," he said to the bird, "but as quickly as you've recovered, you'll soon resume your journey. I have never seen a bird as large and majestic as you. Your curved beak and large talons are those of a hunter. But I don't know exactly what kind of bird you are."

The bird did not yet have the strength to stand, but it seemed comfortable nestled in Tabor's lap, eating morsels of food that had been chewed by its new friend. Around mid-afternoon, Tabor caught sight of Saul walking behind a dozen or more sheep, moving them to graze in the clearing.

"Saul!" he called out.

Saul stopped and turned around, quickly catching sight of Tabor sitting on the side of the hill. "Peace be with you, Tabor."

"Come and see what I found."

"What do you have there?" he asked, continuing to climb the hill. "Is that a black lamb?"

"I think I made a new friend."

Saul kept enough distance between himself and Tabor so as not to startle the animal. "That's quite a bird you have. Did you catch it, or did it catch you?"

Tabor chuckled. "I found it this afternoon right here, nearly dead. I've been caring for it while I keep an eye on the herd." Tabor fed the bird another morsel of chewed meat.

"I have seen birds like this before," Saul said. "You have a golden eagle there. Many years ago, Caesar gave one to Herod the Great as a gift. I don't wish to give you concern, but that is a young female eagle. I can tell by the shape of her beak. She will grow half again that size by the time she is fully grown. You should know, a full-grown eagle can tear a man apart if she wants."

Tabor looked down at the bird in his lap with a newfound sense of pride, knowing she was completely dependent on him for survival. "Don't worry. As soon as this feathered one is ready, she will be on her way."

Tabor walked home with the young eagle tucked under his arm. At the door, he greeted his parents as he had Saul earlier in the day, "Look what I found! Saul told me she is a golden eagle, like they have in Rome. She was hurt in the storm, and I've been nursing her back to health."

"We can't keep a Roman bird in our home." Miriam planted her hands on her hips, blocking Tabor from coming inside. "I just cleaned up after an entire flock, and now you want to bring another animal inside?"

"Don't worry, Mother." Tabor stroked the bird's head. "As soon as this feathered one can fly, I'll let her go."

Miriam looked at Jonas, who had been silent on the matter. However, he frowned as he shrugged his shoulders, clearly not taking Miriam's side. Miriam threw up her hands and turned away, saying to herself and anyone willing to listen, "We're living like animals when we open our home to animals." She disappeared into the depths of their cave home.

Koda knelt to get a closer look at Tabor's latest acquisition. "It looks large and fierce, brother."

"Can she stand on her own?" Jonas asked.

"Not yet," Tabor replied. "But she's getting stronger. This morning when I found her, she couldn't even lift her head." He set the bird on the ground to see if she was ready to stand. The bird sat with her breast flush against the earth, surveying her surroundings with quick head movements.

"What do you think she eats?" Tabor asked his father.

"Rodents, small game. But she can't hunt if she can't fly." Then, Jonas warned, "But you must realize, a hunter such as this would also carry off a lamb. She can't stay here if she is a threat to our animals."

"I understand, Father. And don't worry, I'll hunt for her! I've even given her a name. Since she blew in on the fierce winds, I'm going to call her Storm."

"Best you keep Storm out of your mother's way," Jonas said with a chuckle. "She didn't seem too happy to have another animal to care for."

The two stood and watched Storm as she stretched her left wing to her side before retracting it. Then, she did the same with her right wing, which all by itself, told the story of a desert wind that blew so strongly, it snapped the bone of this noble bird in flight, sending it hurtling to the ground in an uncontrolled crash among the rocks.

Immediately, Tabor reached for Storm's right wing and gingerly helped her fold it once again to her side.

"Ah, too bad," Jonas said, surmising the damage done. "With a broken wing, she'll never fly."

"No, Father. I can fix her. Please, let me try."

"Tabor, God gives a gift to every creature. To a bird, he gives the gift of flight. A bird that has lost the ability to fly will surely die," Jonas said. "You don't want her to suffer through death, do you?"

"Killing isn't always the answer, Father!" Tabor snapped back, lifting Storm under his arm and carrying her inside their home.

Once he made his way to the main table, Tabor sat on a wooden chair with the bird in his lap, contemplating his options. He did not want the animal to suffer or starve, simply because she was unable to hunt.

Soon, Jonas followed his son into the house and after a moment of studying Storm, suggested, "Perhaps we could wrap her. If you could get the broken ends of the bone lined up, then we could bind the wing to keep her from moving it. That might give the bone time to heal."

Appreciating his father's change in perspective, Tabor replied, "Yes! We should try that. If she wants to fly again, God will help her heal. I know it!"

Tabor held Storm gently, yet firmly, while Jonas took some old wool strips about as wide as his hand and bound the bird's wings to her body to immobilize them. Tabor meticulously sewed the loose end of the strap to the material beneath it, completing a temporary body cast. "There," Jonas concluded. "She's in God's hands now."

By the next morning, Storm was able to stand and hobble about for short distances. With her wings bound, she eventually stopped struggling against the bandages and accepted her fate of having to walk to get around. Determined to provide her with the best nourishment he could find, Tabor sat Storm up on a log near the entrance to their home and then went out to hunt a game animal for his new friend.

Shortly thereafter, he returned, carrying a dead mouse by the tail, and dropped it on the ground in front of Storm. The bird looked at the motionless creature and then out beyond Tabor, across the hill, as if looking for a more appetizing meal.

After watching for a few minutes, Jonas asked Tabor, "She won't eat?"

"I don't understand her. I brought her a fresh kill and now she won't touch it."

"You know, Tabor," Jonas said. "Storm is a hunter, not a scavenger. She is used to killing her own meal, not eating someone else's kill."

"Then I should bring her a live animal?"

"She can't chase her prey, but if you offered her a mouse that was stunned yet still breathing, she may take it."

Within the hour, Tabor returned with a rabbit he had hit on the back with a rock from his sling, breaking the animal's backbone. When

Storm saw the helpless creature on the ground in front of her, breathing and twitching, she reached a talon forward to grab the animal, pinning it to the earth. With a single, snapping bite to its neck, her mighty beak ended the life of her meal.

As the recovering golden eagle regained her strength, she became more alert, more agile when she walked, and louder with her ear-piercing cries for attention. Miriam made a sheepskin vest for Tabor to wear, so Storm could perch on his shoulder without puncturing his flesh with her razor-sharp talons.

Quickly the two became inseparable, as Tabor now went about his daily chores while Storm perched on his shoulder with a vigilant eye. In addition to the young shepherd's responsibilities was the morning and evening hunt for Storm's meals. Stunning a rodent with his sling, yet not killing it, required a level of marksmanship that challenged his resolve and improved his skills.

After three weeks of carrying Storm on his left shoulder so he could use his sling with his right hand, the two developed a bond of trust and camaraderie. Tabor learned to use Storm's superior vision and hearing to find his prey by observing her posture. When her head movements slowed to a focused stare and her claws tightened against her sheepskin perch, he knew she was watching an animal he could not see. Following her lead, he closed the distance until he could spot the target himself.

Storm even became a working member of the shepherds, watching over the flock while perched on Tabor's shoulder. More than once, the maturing fifteen year old thought to himself, *her presence alone among the sheep is enough to keep many predators away.* Occasionally, Storm would spot those who ventured too close long before the shepherds. More often than not, the predator became the prey after receiving one of Tabor's short spears or a stone hurled at tremendous speed.

By the end of the month, even Miriam realized Storm added value to their family. Since Storm had been in her home, she had not found a single mouse or rat with which she had to contend. One morning, she called her son over to the table and motioned for him to sit down. Jonas, who had been coiling a rope nearby, stopped what he was doing and took notice. "Tabor," Miriam began, "it has been four weeks since you wrapped Storm's broken wing. I think it is time to remove the bindings."

Tabor looked over at his father, who silently nodded in

agreement.

For days, Tabor had been concerned that if the time ever came when Storm could fly, she would fly away, never to return. But he also knew he could not keep her bound forever, and whatever happened had to be her decision.

"Yes, Mother, I understand. I'll get my knife and see how well her wing has healed."

Tabor carried Storm to perch on a low branch of a willow tree just beyond the front entrance where the entire family had gathered to watch. There, he cut the threads that held the bindings together, careful not to damage her wing as he unwrapped them. Then he backed away and watched her intently. Storm sat on her perch, turning her head first to one side, and then the other, seeing black feathers where her white bindings once were.

With her beak, she began preening the newly exposed feathers on her breast. Then, in slow motion, both wings spread from her body for the first time in a month. "It looks good!" Tabor exclaimed. "Her wing is straight."

"Look at her!" Koda yelled.

Miriam clapped her hands in relief. Tabor stood behind Storm and lifted her wing out to her side, "I'm not going to hurt you, Storm. I only want to feel the bone."

Jonas watched his son and quietly told Miriam, "If any person other than Tabor were to pull that bird's wing out like that, they would find their missing finger in her beak."

"I can feel a small bump on the bone where the break was," Tabor said, as he moved his fingers along the outer ridge of the wing. "But it is straight and feels strong." Smiling now, pleased with the success, he proclaimed, "I think we did it Mother, Father. I think she will fly again."

Storm stretched her wings frequently, sitting on a perch or walking on the ground. Tabor continued to hunt for her, bringing her small game both morning and night. For a good while, the increasingly mobile bird could flap her wings, but she did not have the strength to take flight. Four weeks of immobility had caused her to lose significant muscle mass in her once mighty wings.

To help Storm exercise her legs and wings, Tabor often set her on the ground, while they watched over the flock. He thought, *This will encourage her to walk and flap her wings, which will ultimately help her when she gains the strength to fly again.*

While filling his water pouch in the stream on a cloudless afternoon, Tabor heard Storm's familiar screech, but somehow her call seemed more a cry for help. He dropped the pouch and ran with all his strength to find her stretching her wings in an effort to chase the three wolves that surrounded her, each searching for a vulnerable opportunity to kill.

Mere seconds later Tabor had loaded a rock into his sling and sent it traveling at tremendous speed, crashing into the wolf's skull and dropping it lifeless. The other two wolves turned to see the young shepherd loading another stone into his sling and watched as he twirled it above his head. When one of the wolves yelped after feeling the impact on his left hip, they both turned to run—stopping to look back only once.

Tabor tucked his sling in his belt and sat next to Storm, who still maintained her defensive posture. After folding her wings to her side, he cradled her in his lap. Her beak stayed open and her body trembled with fear for several minutes. "I'm sorry, Storm—I will never leave you alone again. I'm sorry. Your best defense is your gift of flight, and until you fly again, I will protect you."

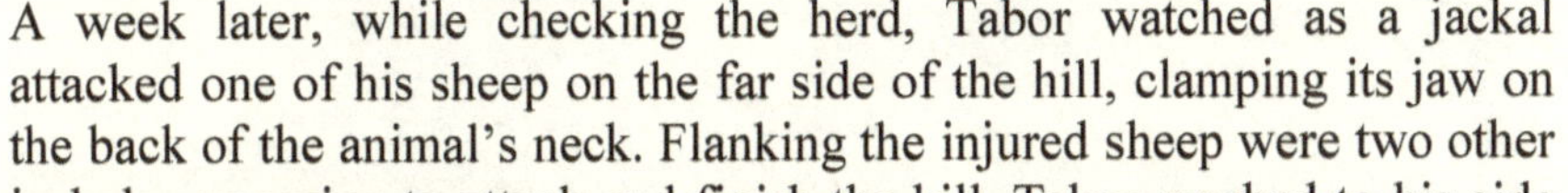

A week later, while checking the herd, Tabor watched as a jackal attacked one of his sheep on the far side of the hill, clamping its jaw on the back of the animal's neck. Flanking the injured sheep were two other jackals, preparing to attack and finish the kill. Tabor reached to his side to pull out his sling, but realized too late he had left it at home after killing a mouse for Storm.

Tabor felt a sudden draft of wind on the back of his neck, as a black shadow swooped closely over his head. Storm's familiar screech announced her intent to attack as she dove directly at the jackal's head, striking it with a painful blow. The jackal released the sheep and scurried off with his two companions. Tabor again felt the power from Storm's wings, as she flapped one last time to settle on his left shoulder.

Looking at the majestic bird that sat proudly next to his face, Tabor felt a sense of quiet awe at what he'd witnessed. Storm, however, continued surveying the sheep herd and the hills around it with short jerks of her head, assuming her role as protector. Tabor smiled and asked, "Have you been waiting until I need you, to show me you can fly?"

# CHAPTER 8

*Fall, A.D. 11*

Tabor taught Storm to respond to his whistle. Even as she flew away to hunt for sometimes hours at a time, she returned instantly when her superior hearing detected Tabor's call. The two learned to hunt together, for both food and predators alike. By watching Storm in flight, Tabor knew when wolves or jackals were stalking his herd, and thus became the predator himself, hunting the stalkers before they were within sight of the sheep.

In nearby Bethlehem, word spread among the villagers about the son of a shepherd who was protected by a mighty eagle. The sight of them garnered a measure of awe and fascination when Tabor carried Storm into the town. Most kept a safe distance from the shepherd who strode about town with the large hunting bird on his shoulder. Those who did approach out of curiosity were usually warned away, when Storm opened her beak and extended her wings.

One day when Tabor was pushing a wooden cart full of wool through town to sell at the market, he heard a girl's voice say, "You are *him*, aren't you?" Turning toward the voice, he saw an olive-skinned girl with wavy black hair walking in the same direction. She trotted a couple of steps to catch up to him.

"Do I know you?" Tabor responded somewhat rudely, given what little contact he'd had with people outside of his small clan.

"No, but I know of you. I have heard stories about the shepherd who lives in the hills. They say he can talk to the animals, and they do what he commands. Are you that shepherd?"

Tabor stopped pushing his cart and faced the girl, intrigued by her interest in him. She looked barely thirteen, although her small frame may have given the illusion of a girl who was younger than her years. She wore a scarf tied around her head to partially cover her hair, which draped below her shoulders in a tangled mass, seeming to blend with the smudges on her face.

He laughed and replied, "I may talk to animals, but that doesn't mean they listen to me."

"I think your bird is beautiful," she said, staring up at the creature on his shoulder. "What's his name?"

"*Her* name is Storm. And my name is Tabor, son of Jonas."

"My name is Ruth," she replied, oddly neglecting to mention her family lineage. "May I touch her?"

"Storm doesn't let other people touch her," Tabor stated, yet before he could finish his sentence, Ruth was already stroking Storm's feathers down her back. The gentleness of her touch and kindness in her voice apparently relaxed Storm's defensive instincts.

"I must go. I hope I see you again sometime, Tabor, son of Jonas. And you, Storm."

As suddenly as she had appeared, Ruth turned and walked away. Amazed at the girl's lack of fear while stroking Storm, Tabor looked at his companion and asked, "You like her, don't you?" Storm opened her beak and Tabor immediately set a strip of dried meat on her tongue before resuming his trek to the market. Tabor returned home with an empty cart and a heart full of feelings he couldn't explain. He had always disliked being in town, even though his parents had taken him there several times to help him grow accustomed to other people. However, after meeting Ruth, he suddenly found a passion for Bethlehem. Week after week, any excuse to buy or trade supplies for his family would entice him to the village streets.

"I knew you were coming when I saw Storm flying below the clouds," Ruth said from behind Tabor.

He recognized her voice, even before turning to see who was speaking behind him. With a smile he couldn't control, Tabor replied, "Good day, Ruth."

Tabor watched Ruth's eyes as they followed Storm's mighty

flaps just before perching on his shoulder. Without fear, she reached up to stroke the feathers on Storm's breast. Her tender affection toward Storm stirred emotions of desire within his heart.

In the early morning hours, before the air was filled with the smell of cooking fires and bread ovens, the raven-haired girl stacked dates in the street display for the shopkeeper.

"Ruth, I must speak with you."

Ruth stopped her chore and nervously turned toward the man whose words often preceded an unprovoked lashing with a stick. She looked no higher than his feet. "Yes, Yasim?"

Sounding more like a father than her self-proclaimed master, Yasim said, "I have seen you with the shepherd boy who carries the eagle."

"Yes, Yasim?"

The man, who was easily three times her age, put his hand under her chin and lifted her face to see her eyes. "Remember, you belong to me. I took you in, fed you, and raised you, when no one else would. Do you remember this?"

Ruth's mind went to the feces-laden hay where she had slept for years, in a stable where she was allowed to pick through the food scraps that were fed to the goats. She was afforded those privileges in exchange for her labor in the stable and at her master's food stands in the street market. "Yes, Yasim, I remember."

Yasim's breath reeked of onions. His face drew nearer hers while his grip on her chin tightened. "Hear me, Ruth. No man can have you without my blessing. My price is high to compensate me for the years I have cared for you."

Ruth stared at the foamy spittle that hung beneath his lower lip, above the beard that was more grey than black. With a final squeeze, he released his grip after flipping her face to the side. She watched as he turned to walk away, spitting at the ground where he had stood.

On a chilly afternoon that reminded everyone of the changing season, before buying grain for his mother, Tabor approached Ruth as she drew water from Bethlehem's eastern well. Her face brightened when she saw him approach.

"Do you have good well water where you live?" Ruth asked.

"We have a stream that runs near our home," Tabor replied as he watched Ruth hoist the heavy jug to rest on the top of her head. He walked with Ruth toward the market, not wanting to draw attention to their friendship, but wishing for all the world to prolong their time together.

"And the water from your stream," Ruth continued, "is it clear and sweet, or does it hold sand and dirt?"

"The water is normally clear, but after a heavy rain, it turns brown with the desert sands. When that happens, we pour it through a basket of wool and it comes out clean." Not wanting the conversation to lag, Tabor boldly continued, "I would like to show you my home someday."

The awkward silence that followed led him to believe he had made a mistake, and he felt his face grow hot with embarrassment. After an uncomfortably long pause, Ruth replied, "I would like that, too."

Tabor released the breath he didn't realize he was holding, and he felt an uncontrollable smile pull on his lips.

Joy turned to fear when Yasim angrily approached the young couple, waving a stick. "Ruth! You have been gone too long simply to get water."

"Yes, Yasim, I'm sorry." She hastily departed toward Yasim's vegetable stand in the market without even acknowledging Tabor's presence.

"And you!" Yasim continued, turning his attention to Tabor. "You are nothing but a shepherd. What gives you the right to come here day after day to keep Ruth from her chores?"

Still uncomfortable around people other than his family, Tabor took a step back in fear of the threatening gesture Yasim made with his stick—the very stick that had been used to whip Ruth.

"Leave this place, you dirty shepherd!" Yasim shouted. "Go back to the hills where you belong."

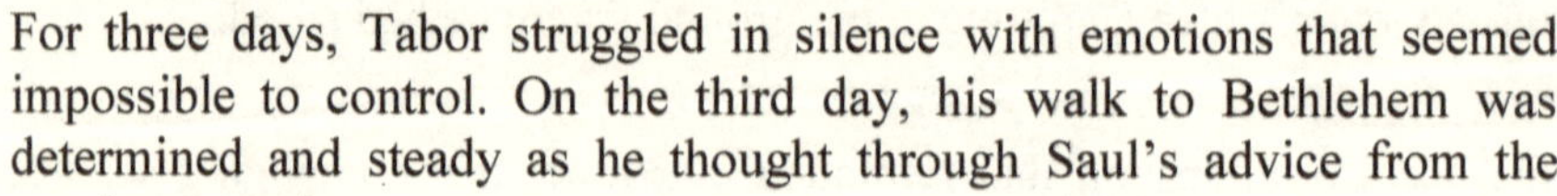

For three days, Tabor struggled in silence with emotions that seemed impossible to control. On the third day, his walk to Bethlehem was determined and steady as he thought through Saul's advice from the previous evening.

"She is all I can think about," he had explained to Saul.

"If you truly love her," Saul had replied, "you will conquer your fears. This man who threatens you is a coward. He cannot harm you."

"Ruth must surely hate me. I let Yasim come between us. I am the one who is a coward."

"Had you confronted Yasim, he would have backed down from you, but taken his anger out on Ruth. No, Tabor, what you did was to protect Ruth, not yourself. Joy in this life seldom lasts, so when it finds you—embrace it."

Now, with renewed confidence, Tabor walked directly into the street markets in the late afternoon where he spied Ruth sweeping straw. "Will you walk with me?"

Ruth paused for a moment, and then turned to see Tabor standing behind her. Her eyes were red and tear swollen, but she still managed a smile when she saw the young shepherd who she feared she would never again see.

As they meandered the streets together, Ruth boldly bumped her shoulder against Tabor's arm, always leery of onlookers, before asking, "Will I see you again?"

Tabor stopped walking and turned to face Ruth as the disappearing sun painted orange and red streaks above the western hills. "I need to tell my parents the truth—why I have come here so often."

"And what is the truth you will tell them?" Ruth asked.

Tabor lifted the girl's chin and gazed into her still puffy eyes, "The truth that I found love, and that love found me."

Ruth managed to smile before responding, "Then go to your family, but carry with you my love for their son."

When Ruth took a step back, she smiled and released a girlish giggle before covering her mouth with both hands. With the speed of a gazelle, she turned and ran with youthful euphoria.

That very evening, Tabor was sitting next to his father by the fire after their evening meal. "I met a girl in Bethlehem," he began.

Miriam was close enough to hear Tabor's statement and jumped into the conversation before Jonas could respond. "Tabor, you do not need to be meeting a girl on your own. When the time is right, your father will choose the girl who is right for you."

"How do you know I haven't already?" Jonas replied somewhat irritably.

Miriam abruptly got up stomped her foot before going inside their home.

"A girl in Bethlehem, you say?" Jonas asked Tabor.

"Yes, Father. I speak to her and we walk on the street every time I go there."

Jonas nodded his head. "I thought you were going to town a little more than necessary these past few weeks."

After a few moments of silence, Tabor asked, "Father, am I old enough to have a wife?"

Before he could answer, Miriam burst out of the house and took the conversation back. "No, you are *not* old enough to have a wife. Hear me, Tabor—I don't want you going anywhere near Bethlehem, ever again!"

"Woman!" Jonas snapped back. "This is a conversation between a father and his son. Since you are neither, I would thank you to stay out of it."

Again, Miriam stomped her foot and went back inside, obviously close enough to hear the conversation that was sure to continue without her.

After taking a moment to calm down, Jonas asked Tabor, "So, who is this girl? What family is she from?"

"Her name is Ruth. She is kind and gentle and quite shy, but she loves Storm and Storm loves her."

"And her family?" Jonas inquired for a second time.

"Well, that's just it," Tabor said. "She was born without a father, and her mother disappeared years ago. She does odd jobs for the vendors in the market in exchange for food. She cleans stables to earn a place to sleep."

"And you think that by marrying her you can rescue her?"

"No, it's not that at all. I really care for her, and I can tell she cares for me."

Jonas looked at the fire and tossed a couple of sticks on it. After pushing the logs together, he studied the sparks that rose in the night sky. With his voice lowered so even Tabor could barely hear him, he said, "Miriam, you can come out now."

As an admission to her eavesdropping, the door to the home opened slowly and Miriam walked to Jonas's side without uttering a word. "I realized something tonight, Miriam," Jonas said. "I realized that our boy has left us, and he has been replaced by a man."

Miriam and Tabor remained silent as Jonas spoke, but Tabor blushed at the compliment and felt pleased with the tone of his father's voice.

"One week from today, Koda will stay with the herd, and the three of us will go into Bethlehem to meet the girl Storm has chosen for our son." Jonas looked directly at Tabor. "This gives you one week to discover if this girl feels for you as you do for her."

High above the small town of Bethlehem, Ruth watched Storm circle. Dropping the rake she had been using to clean stalls, her heart began racing, and moments later her own feet were flying down the road that led east from town.

Away from spying eyes, she continued until Tabor was in sight. Here, she stopped running and waited for the young man to approach. "Good day, Tabor," she said.

Tabor smiled a nervous smile but said nothing. Instead, he looked for Storm in flight and whistled for her to return.

As Storm began her quick descent, Tabor started his rehearsed speech. "When God sent the great floods, yet spared the lives of Noah and his family, all seemed lost as they drifted helplessly at sea."

"Tabor?" Ruth asked, confused by the sudden scripture lesson.

"In his quest for land," Tabor continued, "Noah sent forth a dove that returned to him with a branch from an olive tree. It was the olive branch, you see, that showed him he was saved."

Ruth searched Tabor's eyes for meaning to his speech that had been delivered with a trembling voice. Storm's talons reached for Tabor's shoulder, as the final flap from her wings slowed her descent to land on his body's natural perch. Ruth smiled at the sight of the majestic bird, quickly noticing the twig with green leaves protruding on either side of her beak.

As Storm leaned forward, Ruth lifted her hand, and Storm dropped the branch into it. Ruth studied the small twig from an olive tree, then turned her attention back to Tabor.

"Before I met you, I was lost," Tabor said. "Will you save me, Ruth? Will you take my family as your own?"

Ruth's lips curved into a smile and her eyes widened. "I will."

"Will you protect me from those who would do me harm?" Ruth asked in return as tears began to pool in her eyes.

"I will," he replied. "Will you bear my children and love them as you love no other?"

"I will," she replied. "And will you love me with all your heart, never forsaking me for the warmth of another woman?"

"I will," Tabor said as they clasped hands. "Ruth, will you be my wife?"

"I will."

As they entered the outskirts of Bethlehem under the heat of the midday sun, Jonas and Miriam watched Storm take flight after Tabor pointed skyward following his whistle.

"How will we find this homeless girl?" Miriam asked Tabor, as he entered the village with his parents.

"Her name is Ruth," Tabor corrected his mother, somewhat irritated at her judgmental attitude toward a girl she had never met. "And we do not need to find her. She always finds me."

Tabor led, while his parents walked beside one another a few paces behind. Without warning, a girl ran between Jonas and Miriam from behind, pushing hard enough against Jonas to cause him to lose his balance and fall against a basket of olives, spilling them to the ground.

Tabor turned to see his father on the ground with olives rolling past his feet, and watched as his mother went to her husband's aid. Unfortunately, the loose olives rolled under her sandals, causing her to lose her footing and fall as well. Jonas was barely able to break Miriam's fall when she reached for his hands, and she let out a short scream before landing in his arms.

The vendor, who had every intention of selling the olives before they were spread across the main road through town, lashed out angrily as he watched the scene unfold. "Ruth! You're going to pay for every one of those olives."

Ruth knelt and began hastily picking up the olives from the dusty road, completely unapologetic to the couple who had fallen as a result of her childish enthusiasm. "I'm sorry, Yasim. Look, I'm picking them all up, and the basket is not damaged."

"Ruth?" Miriam sat in the dust with olives all around her. She looked up at her son, who had carefully stepped between the olives to stand in front of his parents. "Please tell me this isn't *your* Ruth."

Completely embarrassed by the awkwardness of the introduction, which he had imagined quite differently only moments earlier, Tabor had no alternative than to press on. "Father, Mother, I would like for you to meet my friend, Ruth."

Ruth froze when she heard this exchange between Tabor and the woman who was sitting amongst the olives she was frantically trying to pick up. With fear and embarrassment, she struggled to look in the eyes of the woman on the ground, who was now glaring at her. Ruth realized, only a few seconds too late, that her clumsy behavior had just destroyed her chance of pleasing the one person she needed to please the most.

With a sudden lunge, she dropped the olives in her hands and cowered behind Tabor, squatting behind his legs and holding the bottom of his mantle in front of her face. She peered around his legs at the two adults who had, in her mind, every right to whip her until she bled.

Tabor stared at his parents on the ground, trying his best not to laugh at the incident, but it was more than Jonas could hold in. With a deep bellowing laugh, Jonas pointed to the young girl who was embarrassed beyond fright, and then at his wife who looked angry enough to eat sand. When Miriam saw Tabor laugh along with his father, it didn't take long before her demeanor began to soften and she too found humor in the sequence of events.

"I like her already, Tabor," Jonas announced, loudly enough that the bystanders found themselves laughing along with the shepherd and his wife, who were still sitting on the ground. Reaching out his hand, Jonas said, "Tabor, give me a hand up, and then help your mother."

Ruth did not rise to her feet until Miriam was standing, but even then, she hid behind Tabor. While Miriam brushed the road dust from her mantle, Tabor pulled Ruth around in front of him and completed the introduction. "And Ruth, I present my parents, Jonas and Miriam."

Ruth stood with her back pressed against Tabor and both hands in front of her mouth, shaking her head back and forth in disbelief at her own indiscretion. "I'm so sorry, so very sorry."

Ruth appeared underdeveloped, due to a lifetime of malnourishment. She wore a tattered mantle without a headdress, covering a tunic meant for a girl much younger. Her large dark eyes sparkled with a gentle spirit that offered a glimpse into her vulnerability.

Yasim reacted harshly when Ruth stopped picking up the spilt olives. Many of the vendors tolerated Ruth's clumsy exuberance in the market in exchange for her light chores, but Yasim was known to whip the girl when her performance was less than appreciated. "I said pick up those olives, you street urchin!" he yelled, raising his stick.

Jonas caught the man's forearm as it swung to strike the girl, even though she had already covered her head with her arms. "You will not be striking this girl today," Jonas said in a threatening tone.

"And who is she to you?" Yasim sneered at him.

While still grasping the man's forearm, Jonas turned to Miriam who had a horrified look on her face, then to his eldest son. Tabor had put his arms around Ruth and pulled her to the side, placing his body between Ruth and the merchant to help protect her. Jonas then looked at the frightened girl in his son's arms and said in a proud, thunderous voice, "This girl is going to be my son's wife, and I would appreciate it if you would not break her before the wedding."

# CHAPTER 9



*December, A.D. 11*

On the morning of his wedding, Tabor felt anxious for the day to end. Knowing the next time he laid eyes on his home, it would be with his wife.

"Tabor, it is time," Miriam said. As he turned to face her while kneeling near the fire, separating coals that would be reignited the next day, she tenderly asked, "Are you ready?"

With his parent's blessing, and a day of celebration still to follow, he stood and released a deep breath, smiled and replied, "I'm ready, Mother."

Jonas led the donkey, laden with the carcass of a sheep and two lambs, through the early morning shadows along the path toward Bethlehem, while Miriam and Tabor followed behind. "Where's Saul?" Tabor asked.

"Saul and Koda started out yesterday," Miriam explained. "By now, they should have the tents up and fires burning."

"And wine!" Jonas said, joining the conversation behind him. "Saul promised lots of his homemade wine, and my brother promised to bring all he could carry as well."

"Jacob and Annorah are coming?" Tabor asked enthusiastically.

"Indeed they are," Jonas said.

Fifteen minutes outside Bethlehem, the groom's family approached the two tents where Koda and Saul greeted them and offloaded the animal carcasses. While the men loaded the lambs on a rack over the low, open flames and prepared the sheep to be buried with a layer of hot coals, Miriam proceeded into Bethlehem.

"It was in this very stable," Miriam began, "where I first met a young girl who was about your age."

Ruth gasped when she first heard the woman's voice behind her. Turning quickly to see Miriam, she blushed while bathing herself with water from the trough meant for donkeys.

Miriam approached the young woman who was destined to become her daughter and took the soapy wool cloth from her hand while proceeding to clean the skin not covered by the tattered tunic. Ruth lifted her hair while Miriam washed the back of her neck. "Soon after Tabor was born, another baby boy was born right over there," Miriam continued, motioning to a bed of hay against a stall. "On that night, a star appeared over Bethlehem and stayed in the sky for more than a year, both day and night."

"I've heard stories of the Star of Bethlehem, but it was gone before I was born," Ruth said.

Silently, as Miriam gently combed the tangles from Ruth's hair, her thoughts drifted back to the time when they had opened their home to the travelers from Nazareth. Memory of Mary's words from the day they first met while she carried her infant son warmed her heart, *And blessed are the parents of the beautiful baby you carry.*

Miriam returned her attention to preparing the bride. Turning Ruth to face her, she kissed both of her cheeks and smiled. "And now, blessed is the woman who is to marry my son."

As the sun followed its familiar trek across the sky, word spread among shepherds and villagers alike of the wedding celebration. Fires burned for warmth and torches burned for light. Food and drink filled mats under a canopy. The more the wine flowed, the louder the singing and celebration grew.

When dusk settled, all eyes were on Jonas, who stepped from the flap of one of the tents and announced, "Friends and family, I present my son, Tabor."

Tabor stepped through the same tent flap and stood under the canopy smiling, yet somewhat embarrassed by the attention, while the crowd of onlookers applauded and cheered.

As the cheering settled, Miriam stepped from the second tent and held the tent flap open for the bride, whose head and face were covered by an ornately laced headdress. An anxious hush fell over the crowd as she moved to the canopy where Tabor waited. Ruth took her place next to her betrothed, and the quiet was interrupted with a celebratory cheer. Two men ushered Tabor to the center of a circle of men who surrounded him with arms interlocked. Women and men clapped in unison to keep time with songs as the men danced around the red-faced groom.

Saul and Koda unearthed the fragrant mutton, steaming with freshness, and began pulling tender portions of meat apart and loading platters. Before anyone tasted the food, Rabbi Asher stepped forward, carrying a cup of Saul's wine. The crowd gathered around the bridal couple, who once again stood together under the wedding canopy.

In the stillness of the darkened torch-lit night, the rabbi approached the young couple and said, "Tabor, Ruth, stand before me."

As Tabor and Ruth stepped to face him, Rabbi Asher extended the goblet. Tabor took the cup from the rabbi and turned to face Ruth. Rabbi Asher began, "God blessed them, saying: *Be fertile and multiply; fill the earth and subdue it. Have dominion over the fish of the sea, the birds of the air, and all the living things that move on the earth.*"

Next, Tabor took a sip from the cup. Then, after accepting the cup from Tabor, Ruth worked the cup under the veil that still covered her face and sipped the sweet nectar, which led to a spontaneous cheer from the crowd for the newest married Bethlehem couple.

Ruth's head and face remained covered, and would remain so until she consummated the marriage with her husband in his father's home, which would not happen until the food and wine were all consumed. But through her veil, she watched the man she had come to love greet every man who wished him well—and offered humorous advice on marriage.

"Jonas! Jonas of Bethlehem," a voice called from the darkness, beyond the torches that surrounded the celebration.

"Who calls me?" Jonas shouted toward the desert beyond.

"You stole something that belongs to me," the voice continued.

Jonas peered into the darkness, trying to identify the man. "Step into the light so that I may see my accuser," he called back.

From cover of darkness, a man approached Jonas and stopped

next to a burning torch. "I am Yasim." He pointed to the crowd gathered behind Jonas. "Everyone here will tell you that I am Ruth's father. She belongs to me, and you have taken her without my permission or my blessing."

Jonas looked at the crowd on either side, waiting to hear a single man validate Yasim's claim, but none stepped forward. Tabor moved to stand next to his father, but Jonas turned and said, "Step back, son."

Miriam grabbed Ruth's hand and pulled her back into the tent.

"Ruth had no parents before today," Jonas told Yasim. "Come, Yasim, and eat, drink—celebrate with us."

Yasim took another step toward Jonas, his fists balled and his face dark. "I will celebrate my daughter's wedding after I receive her dowry."

Jonas raised his hands in a gesture of welcome. "A cup of wine and the sweetest tasting lamb is all I have to offer you."

Again, Yasim stepped toward Jonas. "Perhaps you would care to explain to these villagers of Bethlehem how your son survived the slaughter so many years ago, while all of our sons perished. Perhaps Herod Antipas would like to know of a child who escaped his father's will."

"You go too far with your threats, Yasim," Jonas replied angrily.

Saul walked up to Jonas and grabbed his friend's arm. "I will negotiate with my new friend Yasim. Please, Jonas—this day belongs to Tabor and Ruth."

Before Jonas could protest, Saul approached Yasim, put an arm across his shoulders, and walked him into the darkness.

Tabor moved to stand next to his father who watched as the two men faded into the night. "Should we go help Saul?" Tabor asked.

"Saul can take care of himself." Turning back to the crowd of onlookers, Jonas smiled and called out, "My friends—eat, drink, no one goes home until their bellies are full."

When Saul returned less than an hour later, he smiled at Jonas and said, "Yasim decided he has no claim over Ruth. I don't think he will bother you again."

When Tabor was not watching his sheep, he was carrying flat stones up the hill to stack beside his family's home, specifically, the portion that extended from the mouth of the cave. "It won't be long," he said, loudly enough for Miriam and Ruth to hear as they tended the fire. "Two more stacks of rock like these, and I'll be ready to start building the walls."

Ruth walked over to stand proudly next to her new husband. She looked at the hillside that would soon be the structural backbone of where they would live—a much desired separate third room, somewhat removed from the other two. "Imagine, our very own home," she said with delight.

"Yes, and I can finally stop sleeping so close to my parents," Koda said, joining the conversation while carrying stones to add to Tabor's stacks.

Tabor laughed, hearing his brother's half-serious comment. "So that is why you are working so hard to help me build this addition."

Koda smiled as he stood next to Ruth and patted her ever-growing belly. "Well, yes, that—and the fact that I'm hoping to sleep through the night after my nephew is born."

Tabor laughed at his brother's humor and put his arm around Koda's shoulder. "All right, brother, let's go. We have more stones to gather."

By the next morning, the stones were stacked and ready to be moved into place. Tabor leveled the ground that would be the dirt floor, while Koda cut the wood to specific lengths before framing the doorway and window. Jonas and Saul pitched in as well, gathering clay from the bed of the stream and mixing it with straw. When packed around sticks, the clay would dry into a solid roof. In three days' time, the additional room was complete. At Ruth's request, Tabor's home had its own outside entrance, so that even though it shared a wall with Jonas's home, they chose not to make a doorway between them.

The first night in their new home was marked by a celebration. Miriam seared fresh meat over the fire as the sun set behind the western hills. Saul brought two large jugs of wine—each hanging from either end of a yoke across his shoulders—and set them by the entrance to the new home. Jonas's brother Jacob and his family also joined in the festivities, bringing with them a basket of bread and goat cheese.

The entire group of gathered family and friends ate, drank, and danced in a joyous tribute to the new home built to honor the young couple and soon-to-be parents. Miriam and Annorah, Jacob's wife, caught each other up with rumors from the village, having not seen each other since Tabor's wedding nearly a year earlier, while the men entertained Ruth with stories from Tabor's childhood.

"Ruth," Jacob began, half-drunk from the long night of drinking wine. "Did I ever tell you about the time the sheep herded Tabor?"

"No, Uncle, I don't believe I've ever heard that story," she said, smiling at her husband who knew this was the third time in the evening Jacob would tell his favorite story of Tabor's childhood.

"Ah, yes!" Jacob continued. "Tabor couldn't have been more than five when he followed me and Jonas to the meadow. He watched as we tapped the sheep to pack the herd tighter. Being a fast learner, he decided he would poke the sheep with his stick, too. But when he did, they immediately turned around to face him—and he turned and ran!"

Laughing hysterically at his memories of the comical sight, Jacob could barely continue. "So, this terrified small boy who had already dropped his stick runs past me, followed by three of the angriest sheep you ever saw. They chased him until he jumped into the creek below the willows—and I *do* believe they only stopped chasing him because they were laughing too hard."

Ruth stood and kissed Jacob on his cheek, to thank him not only for the story, but for the joy he had while telling it. "You are a wonderful storyteller, Jacob. Soon you will have new stories to tell—about Tabor's son!"

When Ruth rejoined the women, Saul praised Tabor for bringing new life into the family. "You have a wonderful wife there, Tabor. Treat her well and she will bring you a lifetime of happiness."

"I will, Saul, and thank you for all you have done for us." Tabor carried a small pitcher to Saul and poured more wine into his cup. "Here, drink more—and keep the compliments coming."

All the men laughed at Tabor's encouragement, then passed the pitcher around to top off their own cups.

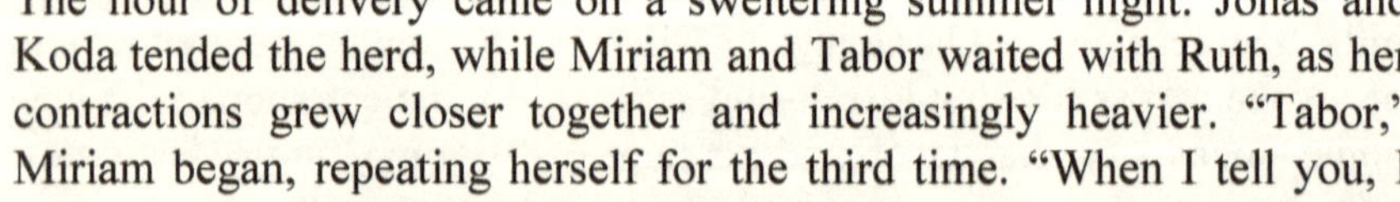

The hour of delivery came on a sweltering summer night. Jonas and Koda tended the herd, while Miriam and Tabor waited with Ruth, as her contractions grew closer together and increasingly heavier. "Tabor," Miriam began, repeating herself for the third time. "When I tell you, I want you to sit behind Ruth and let her lean against you. With each contraction, she will push against you, but it is your job to support her back."

"I will, Mother. Now, is it time to pray for Ruth and the baby?"

Miriam chuckled at Tabor's nervous questions. "My son, there is never a wrong time to pray for your wife and child. Ask God to give Ruth strength and a quick delivery for your baby."

Ruth cried out loudly before Tabor could finish his prayer.

"Tabor!" Miriam yelled, "Get behind your wife! I can see the baby's head showing. It's time."

Tabor rushed to take position behind Ruth and wrapped his arms around hers. "Push, Ruth! Push!" Miriam hollered.

As the young mother-to-be's contractions eased, Miriam let her rest. Storm sat on her perch across the dimly lit room and spread her wings, as though she too sensed the tension in all present. Miriam placed a short willow stick in Ruth's mouth, both ends poking out past her cheeks. "From now on," she said, "when you push, I want you to bite down on this stick as hard as you can."

Once the stick was positioned between her teeth, Ruth nodded. Sweat streamed down her face and dripped continually from the ends of her hair.

When Miriam felt Ruth tightening up at the onset of her next contraction, she said, "Now, Ruth, this time I want you to push with all the strength God has given you." Spreading her knees, Ruth grabbed them with her hands, while Miriam began to call out, "Now, Ruth! Push, push, push!"

Ruth bore down, biting hard on the stick, her loud groan breaking into a painful scream. Moments later, the baby's head left her body. Storm flapped again, this time letting out a call of her own, followed by the faint cough and subsequent cry of the young couple's new baby daughter.

"A girl?" Tabor asked, as though he wanted his mother to check again. "My son is a girl?"

Ruth's head still rested against Tabor's shoulder with their cheeks nearly touching. She reached her hand back to stroke Tabor's beard before responding, "No, my love, our *daughter* is a girl."

Tabor kissed Ruth on the cheek, while Miriam laid their daughter on her belly with the umbilical cord still attached. Abruptly, Jonas threw open the door and rushed in, asking, "Has the baby come? I heard screaming."

"Out!" Miriam yelled. "You cannot come in here yet!"

"Woman!" Jonas protested. "Please tell me, is my grandson here?"

Miriam stood and turned Jonas to face the door. "No, your grandson is not here. Your grand*daughter* saw to that. Now, get outside until I call for you."

Jonas stepped outside and contemplated Miriam's words. Tabor,

Miriam, and Ruth all laughed together, listening to Jonas in front of their home scream at the top of his lungs, "A granddaughter! I have a granddaughter!"

For the next few minutes, Ruth reclined in her husband's arms, while Miriam tied and cut the cord. Then, once she'd delivered the afterbirth, she gazed over at Tabor and asked, "Are you happy, my son?"

"I am in a room with three of the most beautiful women on God's green Earth. What man couldn't be happy with such a blessing?"

Then to Ruth, she asked, "Have you a name for her?"

Ruth smiled and looked to her husband for approval before responding. When he nodded, she said, "We're going to name her Evia. I'm told it was my mother's name."

Miriam smiled at the plucky young woman before her. Picking up a cloth rag and soaking it in warm water, she began working to clean the blood from Ruth's legs. "Evia, what a pretty name for such a pretty girl." Turning to Tabor, she said, "Tabor, I will stay with Ruth and Evia. They both need to rest for now. Will you please go save your father, before he loses his voice by announcing your daughter's birth to the entire world?"

Late one evening, Jonas walked among the sheep that parted to let their shepherd pass. His campfire had burned down to a large pile of orange-hot coals in the valley below, so he began his routine of taking one last head count for the night. "Forty-nine is the total," he whispered to himself, "as it has been for most of the year. The largest it has *ever* been, thank you, God. But so too is the growing family it supports."

It was the quiet times such as this, when he thought most deeply about God's blessings—two strong, caring sons, a "daughter" who they could now claim as their own, a safe and secure home conditioned by the constant temperature of a cave, a good herd of sheep, and now a new life in Evia.

Suddenly, a faintly familiar voice came from behind him, as he stood on the hill overlooking his barely visible campfire below. "Good Shepherd..."

A cool dry wind brushed against his face, sweeping upward from the valley floor. When Jonas stopped and turned, he somehow knew he would be facing the very Messenger of God who had approached him on this same hillside eighteen years earlier.

He did not run in fright or drop to his knees in awe. Nor did he beg for mercy or hide in shame. He merely gazed into the eyes of this loving angel, intuitively grasping why he called him "Good Shepherd." In fact, as he felt the touch of the angel's hand in his, he immediately understood everything.

In the early morning hours, Saul stood at the bottom of the hill and called toward the three-room home that held tightly to the side of the hill, "Miriam! Tabor! Koda! Come quickly! It's Jonas!"

Storm flew ahead and began circling over the rich fertile valley that fed the herd. Miriam ran toward Saul. "What is it? Where's Jonas?"

"Come this way," Saul replied, directing all three with a gesture of his hand. "Jonas is down. It may be his heart. Hurry!"

Storm continued to circle high overhead, watching the three men and one woman approach the robed figure who lay motionless on the hillside next to a shepherd's cane. She watched as Tabor shook the lifeless form. She heard the wailing from Miriam, who threw dirt and sand in the air and eventually collapsed on the one who was her husband. From high above, she flew silently along, following the small procession of those carrying the body of their loved one home.

# CHAPTER 10

*August, A.D. 25*

"Rest for a weary shepherd?" Tabor called out, as he tapped on the door of Koda's home.

"Come in, come in!" Koda said, warmly inviting in his older brother.

Naomi got up from her chair and kissed her husband's brother on both cheeks. "You're *always* welcome here, Tabor," she added. "Please, come in and rest. Can I get you some water?"

"The beauty of my brother's wife is enough to make any man thirst," Tabor replied, mostly to make Naomi blush, but also wishing to accept her offer.

Seeing Miriam on a chair near the corner of the room, he leaned over to kiss her on both cheeks. "How are you, Mother?"

Miriam's eyes sparkled with her son's kisses. Taking his hand in both of hers, she asked, "How are Ruth and Evia?"

"All are well, Mother. Evia is twelve years old now, and helping Saul watch the flock. Like her father, she is at her best when she walks among the sheep."

"And Storm?" she enquired further.

Tabor smiled as he raised his hand and circled it above his head with his finger pointing up, which was his signal to Storm to fly high and circle.

"Uncle Tabor!" a young boy's voice called from across the room. "Did you bring me a gift?"

"Daniel! That is not polite," Naomi chastised her son. "You go give your uncle a hug and greet him properly."

Daniel ran to Tabor, hugging him around the waist. Tabor smiled at his eleven-year-old nephew and said, "*My*, Daniel, you get bigger every time I lay eyes on you. A gift, you say? I certainly may have something for you."

Tabor knelt in front of Daniel, where he stood ready to receive his uncle's gift. Koda and Naomi watched as well, wondering what he'd brought their son. Tabor watched Daniel's eyes, as they were following his hand reach under the rope around his waist. Slowly, he held his hand out and turned it palm down to let a child-size sling drop, suspended by the straps squeezed between his fingers.

Daniel's mouth dropped. "A sling, Uncle Tabor? You're giving me a sling?"

"That I am, young Daniel. This is the very sling Saul gave me when I was not much older than you. But you must promise me you will use it only as your father teaches you. Promise?"

'I *promise*," the delighted boy quickly agreed, twirling it around in front of himself, eyeing it and its presumed limitless range of possibilities in his mind.

"If you practice every day, you will soon be as good as your father."

Naomi frowned and said, "Perhaps when you are a little older, Daniel."

"Mama!" Daniel protested.

Koda stepped between his son and his wife and offered a compromise. "Daniel, as your uncle said, you must do as your parents say." Then, he leaned down to whisper into Daniel's ear, loud enough for Tabor and Naomi to hear as well. "And I say I will teach you how to use it as soon as I return."

Naomi relented. "You heard your father, Daniel. You can begin practicing with it when he comes back in a few days."

"Where is he going?" Daniel asked.

"He and your uncle are going to Jericho."

"We should go, then," Tabor said, encouraging Koda to prepare to leave.

Miriam got up, walked over and stood between her two sons, dwarfed by the two tall shepherds who were easily as tall as their father. Giving each a hug, she said, "I have anticipated and dreaded this day for months. What we do today, we do for the man who once loved us as we loved him."

Once Koda had gathered his sack of goods, the trio left the house and began down the dirt road out of town, the men walking slowly for their mother's sake. As they approached the home of the village rabbi, they heard a voice call out to them, "Shalom, my friends!" Rabbi Asher said, approaching them with open arms.

Both Tabor and Koda greeted the spiritual teacher with a warm smile and embrace, for they had known this man who bequeathed his love and wisdom their entire lives. As all four walked along into the morning sun, Rabbi Asher took advantage of his own captive flock. "Tabor, Koda, I must speak with you about the Sabbath. It is written, *Remember the Sabbath day, to keep it holy. Six days you shall labor, and do all your work, but the seventh day is a Sabbath to the Lord, your God. On it, you shall not do any work, you, or your son, or your daughter, your male servant, or your female servant, or your livestock, or the sojourner who is within your gates.*"

Tabor looked at his brother before responding, "Yes, Rabbi, we do our best."

"No, no, no, Tabor. You continually work your sheep. I hear you even hunt on the Sabbath." The rabbi stopped walking and faced Tabor fiercely. "It is not me, though, Tabor. It's the Pharisees who make and interpret the laws. There is even talk these days that they will arrest and punish those who do not observe the Sabbath by their rules."

"I do not hunt on the Sabbath, Rabbi," Tabor replied as they resumed their slow trek, "but I must confess I have killed predators that are hunting my sheep on the Sabbath. If protecting my herd on the Sabbath upsets the Pharisees, then they can watch over my sheep and I promise I will rest the entire day."

Looking skyward at the great eagle circling the travelers, the rabbi questioned, "And your hunting bird? Do you hunt with your bird on the Sabbath?"

Looking up at the same majestic bird, Tabor laughed a hearty laugh, "Storm? No, Rabbi, she is not my hunting bird. She is my friend and my eyes."

"Your eyes, Tabor?"

"Yes, Rabbi. She leads me and my flock away from danger and

warns me when I'm in harm's way. I can tell, by watching her, when I am being stalked by predators. More often than not, the sight of Storm drives the predators back into the shadows and crevices in the hills."

"We're here," Koda said, interrupting the discussion between Tabor and Rabbi Asher.

Tabor grasped Miriam's arm and prepared to steady her as they approached a stack of rocks. Next to the rocks sat a wooden ossuary that Tabor had made and placed there the day before.

"Are you alright, Mother?" Tabor asked.

"Yes, I'm fine. We should have done this years ago."

Rabbi Asher stood next to Miriam, while Koda and Tabor began removing the stones that had concealed the opening to the small cave for the previous thirteen years. Indeed, the opening was so small that all Tabor could manage was to reach inside and pull the tattered linen from the hole, dragging it to rest next to the bone box.

Koda reached down and lifted the lid from the box, then stepped away, as did Tabor. Rabbi Asher bent over and opened the white bundle to expose the skeletal remains of Jonas. Miriam covered her mouth, but did not divert her eyes from her husband's remains.

One at a time, the rabbi placed the bones in the box in a very specific order, a rite which had been ordained for generations. With each bone, he offered a prayer until the entire skeleton was in place.

Standing between her sons, Miriam reminded them both, "Promise me, my sons. One day, my bones will be in the same box with your father's."

Koda wrapped his arm around his mother's shoulder and squeezed, "We promise, Mother."

"Are you sure the two of you can carry this all the way to Jericho?" Miriam asked Koda.

"His family tomb is in Jericho," Koda responded. "This is what sons do for their parents."

"May the road rise to greet you," Rabbi Asher said, offering his blessing. Then he turned to walk with Miriam back into Bethlehem, while Tabor and Koda began their journey toward Jericho, with a long pole resting on each of their shoulders and the ossuary hanging from the center of the pole by ropes.

Tabor knew, as did Koda, that the ritual entombment of their father's remains was one of the most important means of respecting their Jewish heritage. Still, the trek was slow and difficult as the two men strained to support the pole with the ossuary swinging beneath it. Tabor broke the silence with a question that weighed heavily on his mind, "Have you ever wondered why it is so easy to forget the good things in your life, yet struggle with the memories of your sins?"

"I suppose God wants us to remember our sins so we won't repeat them," Koda replied.

After a long moment to consider his brother's response, Tabor confided his thoughts, "We carry the bones of our father, yet I can't remember what he looked like. He was the most important man in my life, but if I saw him in a crowd today, I don't know that I would recognize him."

"Perhaps it is easier for me," Koda said. "You look so much like our father that I am reminded of him every time I see you."

Tabor smiled at the complement before continuing, "I want to remember him, yet I am haunted both day and night, reliving every sin that I wish to forget. I know I have sinned against God, but it is the sins I have committed against Ruth and my family that torture me the most."

"Don't be so hard on yourself, Tabor. You are a good man. Our father would be proud of you."

Tabor stopped short of naming the sinful acts that weighed heavily on his soul, but the burden of their memories fluttered within his thoughts as they walked in relative silence.

"Did you hear something?" Koda asked, as the two brothers walked along the shore line. "It sounded like a man yelling."

Tabor listened, but other than the sounds of flowing water from the Jordan River, he heard nothing.

"Repent!" came a distant voice, which Tabor could now hear as well. Every few steps, the brothers could hear the same voice calling out, even louder than before, "Repent, before it is too late!"

"Look," Tabor said, pointing to a hillside near the river's bank. "I wonder why that crowd has gathered."

A large group of people were mustered on the hill, primarily men, all seeming to be watching something or someone. A number of bystanders stood along the road that followed the river, and while they too were watching, they were doing so from a distance without engaging. A man sat watching and listening intently from the branches of a tree that stretched out above the water.

Walking into the crowd of people who were mostly seated in the fertile grass growing along and up the hill from the river bank, Tabor and Koda found an area clear enough to set themselves and the ossuary down, so as to listen to the man who was standing waist deep in the river. Behind the man, across the Jordan they could see the ancient city of Bethabara.

"Repent, I tell you!" the man screamed. "The time has come for each and every one of you to lay down your sins and walk with the Lord God Almighty!"

Koda asked an elderly man sitting to his left, "Who is this man and why has this crowd gathered to listen to him?"

"We have been following him for days," the man answered. "He is John. We call him John the Baptist, because he cleanses men with *mikvah* who are truly repentant, to prepare them for a new beginning."

"Behold, I am baptizing you in water! But one is coming after me who will baptize you in the Spirit of holiness and everlasting forgiveness!" John yelled out to the crowd.

A man sitting near the front of the crowd stood and walked into the water in front of John. After a few words between the two, which neither Tabor nor Koda could hear, John put his hands on the man and pulled him backward until he was completely submerged. While he held the man under water, he called out to the crowd, "Repent!"

A moment later, the man who was held under water stood, looking toward the sky with his arms outstretched. John patted the man on the back and said, "Go, brother, and sin no more." As the man walked out of the water, he held his arms stretched to either side. The smile on his face was exaggerated, but his eyes glowed with a profound bliss.

"Come, Tabor. We should go," Koda said, as he prepared to stand and walk away.

"No—wait," Tabor replied, grabbing his brother's arm to keep him from standing. "I want to hear what he has to say. Did you see that man's eyes when he came out of the river?"

Koda didn't respond, but looked at Tabor with bewilderment.

"I have come to prepare you," John cried out at the top of his lungs, "for the one who is greater than me! A new king walks among us who will bring us into the Kingdom of Heaven! Repent of your sins, so you can be saved!"

"Saved from what?" a voice in the crowd asked.

"Saved from the burden of your sins!" John declared. Pointing across the crowd, from one side to the other, he asked, "Who among you has not sinned? Who among you has not broken the laws of Moses? Truly I tell you, if you have broken just one of the laws, then you have broken *all* of the laws in the eyes of God! Repent I say, before it is too late!"

"How can you forgive sin?" another man called out. "Only God has the power to forgive sin."

"True!" John yelled in reply. "I baptize you with water, but through the water, it is God who washes away the sins of the man who is truly repentant!"

Two more men got up and waded into the Jordan, each walking out of the water a few moments later with looks of wonderment and peace.

"Repent and wash your sins away! Prepare your soul for salvation!"

"Can he really do that?" Tabor asked, turning to Koda. "Can he cleanse a man of his sins?"

The brothers stayed, watched and listened for a long time, while the man in the water who appeared to be the poorest, unkempt man they had ever seen, spoke of riches of the heart and purity of the soul—of a kingdom that was yet to come.

One by one, men walked into the river and stood before John, who pulled them underwater and then back up, never stopping or stumbling in his speech. For every question, he had an answer, and those who ridiculed him were eventually baptized by him. Tabor watched as one man after another rose from the Jordan River, beaming with a sense of peace and tranquility. His heart ached for the days he could look in the eyes of his wife and daughter, free of guilt and self-loathing.

A priest standing at the edge of the crowd called out, "Who are you?"

"I am the voice of one, calling out in the desert!"

It was not until John caught sight of a man walking along the bank directly toward him did he become silent, watching as a dove landed on the man's shoulder and stayed. The lone man did not join the crowd, but instead walked directly toward him in the river. "John, will you baptize me?"

The crowd was so silent that every man present could hear their conversation.

"My Lord, it is you who should baptize me," John replied.

Both men stood face-to-face. John carefully planted his feet firmly in the rocky river bed and placed one hand behind the man's back and the other on his forehead, pulling him backward into the water. This time, John said nothing while the man was underwater, nor did he speak when he helped the man stand.

As this freshly baptized, solitary man walked from the river, he lifted his face to the sun, which bathed him in light. Staring up into the sky, he watched the outstretched wings of an eagle circle high overhead. Even though John was speechless, the entire crowd heard a single statement of sanctified words swirling in the air around them, engulfing them with a sense of peace: *This is my Son, whom I love, with Him I am well pleased.*

Many fell to their knees in response to the voice they heard, while others hid their faces in fear. As the crowd watched in silent reverence, the man resumed walking the shoreline of the Jordan River.

It was not until he was out of sight that the silence was broken by John. "Repent!"

"Koda, I need to do this," Tabor said to his brother. "Will you wait for me?"

Koda nodded and said, "I will be here, Tabor."

Tabor stood and walked to the river's edge. Stepping into the water to approach John the Baptist, he realized for the first time how tall the man stood. With each step, tears streamed down Tabor's cheeks. He thought, *Perhaps God's forgiveness of my sins will allow me to one day forgive myself.*

John continued yelling to the crowd, as though he didn't see Tabor standing in front of him. "He who walks with the Lord God will have everlasting peace, but he who walks away from the Almighty will suffer in everlasting agony!"

John suddenly acknowledged the man who stood before him, whose shoulders drooped from the weight of the guilt he carried. In a calm, fatherly voice, he asked, "Do you truly repent of your sins?"

Tabor's tear-filled eyes earnestly looked into John's. "I do," he whispered.

Feeling John's powerful hand on the small of his back and the other on his forehead, Tabor allowed himself to be submerged into the river. He did not struggle as a drowning man might react. Instead, he felt himself completely surrender to something intangible, yet fully present there in that moment. Consciously holding his eyes open beneath the slow moving water, Tabor could see a halo around the bright sun, shining beams through the water all around him. From under the water, he could still hear John yelling, "Repent!" to the crowd—but the words Tabor clearly heard with his own ears were, *"You are forgiven."*

# CHAPTER 11



*Thursday, March 21, A.D. 26*

In the early hours of dawn, Ruth and Naomi packed their travel bags with dates, dried figs, and strips of meat still warm from being smoked overnight as they prepared to accompany both of their families on the trek to Jerusalem. Twelve year old Daniel and thirteen year old Evia each walked two lambs with their ropes, while Tabor and Koda followed their families, having earlier gathered the remainder of the herd into stone corrals for safety.

Halfway into Jerusalem, Saul joined the six of them, leading his three lambs in similar fashion. "You two would make Jonas a proud man," Saul said to the sons of his friend. "Is Miriam already cooking for Passover?"

"Cleaning first," Naomi responded. "Tomorrow she will clean, and the next day, she will clean some more!"

Ruth added, "If it is possible for a floor made of dirt to ever be clean, Miriam will find a way."

"Look, the city." Daniel called out, excited to be the first to spy the tallest pillars of the temple over the horizon.

As they ascended the hill overlooking the Hinnom Valley, the families paused to look upon the heart-stopping sight of Jerusalem in all its glory. The temple gleamed white and gold, and the mighty walls of the Temple Mount astounded them. The sheer magnificence of the temple reminded them they had arrived at the center of Jewish life.

While descending the hill and upon their crossing the Hinnom Valley, the group's excitement grew, especially the children's. The road was crowded with pilgrims, all making their way to enter through the southern gate at the end of the road from Bethlehem.

The men, along with Daniel, left the seven lambs with the women and went to bathe in the temporary pools for men, which had been constructed for the crowds entering the city for the week of Passover.

After bathing, it was the men's turn to watch the lambs, while Ruth, Naomi, and Evia left for the women's pool. "Father?" Daniel asked. "Can I go with you to the temple this year?"

Overhearing Daniel's question, Tabor thought back to his own childhood, following his mother to the Court of Women, wishing he could be with his father instead—but the rules were clear.

"You're too young, Daniel," Koda replied. "Two more years."

Tabor smiled at the innocence of his nephew, listening to the father-son conversation. Across the road, he watched Ruth pouring bowls of water over Evia's hair, while standing knee deep at the edge of the pool, soaking their tunics with the water that had already cleansed hundreds of women before them.

Tabor studied the gate, dwarfed by the towering walls of the great city. "Such walls make this place a cold fortress rather than a warm city to welcome visitors," Tabor said loud enough for Koda and Saul to hear his disdain for Jerusalem. "I can't figure out if the walls were built to keep me out—or them in."

"I'm fine with either," Saul replied as he slapped Tabor on his shoulder.

Once the women returned, Tabor told them, "The four of you go into the city through this gate. Koda, Saul and I will take the lambs around to the Sheep Pool on the northern side and enter the Temple from there. When we're finished, we will look for you in the Lower City."

As their father had done before them, and his father before him, Tabor and Koda took their lambs to the Sheep Pool near the northern wall to clean the animals for ritual slaughter. With Saul following behind the brothers, the three men entered the temple and proceeded directly to the table, behind which stood the priests, where their lambs would be inspected for purity before being accepted as sacrificial animals to be purchased by pilgrims for Passover.

A dozen or more priests in their black robes stood behind the tables. Behind the priests were pens, packed from one side to the other with anxious white lambs, all calling out to mothers too far away to answer.

Each man stood before a temple priest, who recorded their names to credit their donation. "Name?"

"Tabor of Bethlehem."

"Koda of Bethlehem."

"Saul of Bethlehem."

After scribbling in a ledger, the priests each asked the same question of the respective shepherd before him. "How many?"

"Two."

"Two."

"Three."

"Let me see them," each priest demanded, as they had already done a hundred times that morning. One at a time, each man stood a lamb on the table and held it until the priest took the animal. After tugging on the lamb's coat to look for blemishes and checking his eyes and mouth, the priest tossed the innocent beast into the pen with the other animals, all of which were living their last day.

"Let's go get in line," Saul said to the two men who were the closest thing he would ever have to sons of his own. The three walked over to an appointed area and stood in line for the money changer, who would exchange their denarius for faceless shekels, the temple tax coins—at an unfavorable exchange rate. Only the purity of temple coin was permitted when purchasing a sacrificial lamb.

Studying the handful of Roman denarius coins in his hand, which were unacceptable tender in the Temple, Tabor angrily said, "It's bad enough we have to thin our herd, but I truly resent being expected to buy someone *else's* lamb with useless temple coins."

"If we don't buy the lamb that has been blessed by a priest," Koda replied, "then it will not be acceptable to God for sacrifice."

"We do what we must to stay in favor with Rome and Herod. After they finish with us, though, there is so little left," Saul added. "Passover has become more of a political tax day than a holy day of remembrance."

"Passover is *supposed* to be a day of celebration, about faith and piety," Koda responded defensively.

"Passover is about *money*," Tabor replied cynically.

In the outer courtyard of the Lower City, the bazaars were in full vigor with vendors displaying their goods for sale to the countless hordes of pilgrims, many of who entered the city only once a year, often with more money than sense. Ruth and Naomi were no less taken in by the flashy displays of fabrics and food than any other. While their mothers inspected the colorful tapestries and tasted exotic delicacies, Evia and Daniel watched a street performer who demonstrated his acrobatic skills for a crowd of curious onlookers.

Walking amongst the crowd were the ever present palace guards and Roman soldiers, each charged with the duty of controlling the crowds and arresting thieves. Two of these soldiers were interested in more than thieves, their eyes open for any children not under the watchful protection of their mothers.

"You! Come! Me!" a Roman soldier demanded in broken Aramaic, while grasping Daniel's arm. At the same time, his fellow soldier sternly grabbed the back of Evia's neck, pulling her toward him.

"What? What have we done?" Evia yelled, a sudden fear making her legs feel weak.

Neither soldier responded, as neither understood her question. Instead, the children were quickly and forcibly escorted from the Court of Women, through the colonnades of the Eastern Gate, where there would be fewer witnesses. Next to the outside wall, two other soldiers sat on horseback, patiently waiting. Without a word of explanation, Daniel and Evia were each thrown across the back of a horse, chest down, in front of the horse's respective rider. Both riders immediately kicked their horses into a gallop and sped away. Screaming and kicking, Evia and Daniel were forced to look at the ground racing by them, pinned as they were to the horse by the rider's hand on their backs.

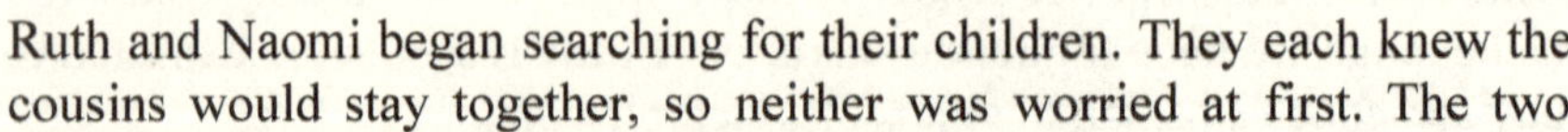

Ruth and Naomi began searching for their children. They each knew the cousins would stay together, so neither was worried at first. The two mothers agreed their children *were* easily distracted by the sights and sounds of Jerusalem during Passover festivities.

"They've probably found their way to a vendor who's captivating them with some odd item, or their fathers have found them and are now looking for us." Naomi concluded, as their search started to take on more urgency.

"I know one little girl who is going to be milking the goats for a month, after wandering off like this," Ruth added.

After hunting all over the marketplace in the Court of Women with no sign of them, the two mothers' worst fears turned to panic.

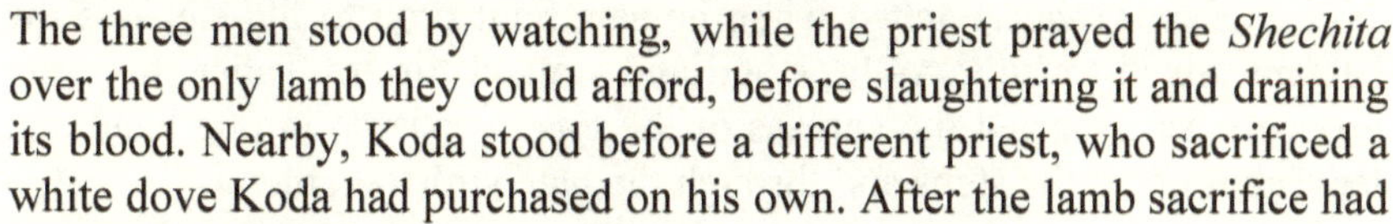

The three men stood by watching, while the priest prayed the *Shechita* over the only lamb they could afford, before slaughtering it and draining its blood. Nearby, Koda stood before a different priest, who sacrificed a white dove Koda had purchased on his own. After the lamb sacrifice had been performed, a commotion caught Tabor's attention.

"Look at that man," he said, directing Koda and Saul's attention toward the tables of the money changers.

Dozens of men were leaving the lines where they stood to run toward coins flying through the air and scattering on the ground. Tabor laughed at the man who was shouting in anger, as he flipped one table after another. Temple guards ran from three different directions toward the disturbance.

"Is he crazy?" Koda asked, watching the man flip another table. "A man can get himself executed for far less around here."

"He's only doing what I wish I had the courage to do," Tabor replied.

"We better leave before the entire temple army comes in here and arrests us, too," Saul cautioned.

As they walked toward the outer courtyard to find their families, Tabor couldn't help but smile, thinking, *Here is a man who is even angrier than I am about the exchange rate for temple coins.*

"Tabor! Koda!" Ruth cried out, running toward her husband. In tears and breathless, she fell against his arm, catching herself on his sleeve. "We've lost the children! We can't find them! I hoped they were with you, but they're not! Oh Tabor! Where could they be?"

Only steps behind Ruth, Naomi ran to Koda, confirming, "We can't find Daniel or Evia! They were right behind us one moment and gone the next. We've looked everywhere."

Tabor handed the lamb carcass to Saul and ran back up the stone steps to look through the crowd from a better vantage point, hoping to see the children. Without concern for what anyone thought, he called out at the top of his lungs, "Evia! Daniel! Evia! Daniel!"

Koda made his way quickly through the crowd, after telling both women, "Try to stay calm and focus on searching inside the Court of Women where you last saw them."

Tabor continued calling out, over and over, while Koda and the two women separated and resumed searching in different directions.

Tabor noticed two temple guards watching him. Turning to his friend, he said, "Saul, ask those guards if they can help us find Evia and Daniel."

Tabor's heart ached when he saw Saul drop to the steps as the captain talked to him. As he stood and walked toward Tabor, his head drooped. Saul carried the carcass of the Passover lamb in one hand and led Tabor down the steps and through the gate with the other.

"Likely, Roman soldiers took them," Saul explained.

Tabor dropped to his knees on the road, while Saul continued scanning the crowd for a sign of Daniel and Evia. In a fit of anger and despair, Tabor stood, grabbed the slaughtered Passover lamb from Saul's hand and threw it with all his might at the plain stone outer wall of the city, splattering it with the lamb's remaining blood, before it fell to the rocky ground.

# CHAPTER 12


*Thursday, March 21, A.D. 26*

Under any other circumstance, Evia and Daniel would have been in awe to be walking through the halls of Pontius Pilate's magnificent fortress. But after being kidnapped by Roman soldiers and led through the palace corridors like animals by rope, with their hands bound, all they felt was terror.

Their captors eventually brought them into a room where three more soldiers sat at a table drinking Roman beer. The children did not understand the Greek conversation, but could tell they were being handed off to the oldest man in the room, who smiled and nodded with approval at the sight of the two Jewish youths.

Having been yanked and pulled, abused, put upon and frightened to the core for hours, Daniel and Evia, now, could only stare straight ahead in shock. The two soldiers who brought them to this place unbound their hands and left the room, while two other soldiers stood from their seats and guarded the door.

The oldest guard walked slowly around the terrified children, laughing at his own words, which caused the other two guards to laugh in response. From behind, he tore Daniel's robe in one forceful motion and let it fall to the floor. Daniel instinctively turned to confront the man, but the other two guards quickly thrust the metal point of their spears at him as a warning.

The three Romans laughed after Daniel turned back around. When he ripped off Evia's robe, she didn't even gasp. After the old guard pulled off their remaining undergarments, he examined the naked children for blemishes or disease. As he ran his hands over Evia's body, she began to tremble, still in shock, barely oblivious to the men in the room or her surroundings.

When she smelled the rancid, beer laden stench of the guards breath, as his mouth came near her own, her trembling became convulsive, followed suddenly by spontaneous vomiting, which splattered and soaked the guard's uniform.

Shouts of anger were immediately followed with a strike from the back of his hand beneath her eye, sending her to the floor where she stayed, cowering, pulling her knees toward her chest.

After a few more choice words for the guards, the fuming brute left the room and the two remaining guards stood Evia next to Daniel before pulling two white tunics over them both. Daniel pushed his arms through the sleeves of the robe, but Evia stood motionless, as state of shock persisted. One of the guards begrudgingly pulled her arms through the sleeves of her robe, before leading them back out of the room.

Saul went to Bethlehem and returned with Miriam to Tabor's home. For three days, Ruth would only eat or drink what Miriam fed her. Naomi refused to return to Bethlehem, choosing instead to stay with Ruth and Miriam. Passover came and went with no sign of the children. In their home, there was no Passover meal. No singing or dancing. All that marked this family's holiday was tightly clenched fists and long hours of waiting, interspersed with silent, streaming tears.

Tabor sat by the fire after dark, sharpening the points of short spears, before lashing feathers to the back of them. Koda sat near his brother, watching quietly, as did Saul.

"I'm going with you," Saul said, finally breaking the silence.

Tabor continued his sharpening without a response.

"I know the Romans. I know how they think. *You* do not."

Without looking at Saul, Tabor finally said, "Tell me everything you know, Saul. Everything that palace guard told you."

Even though the three women were in the house, he still lowered his voice before asking, "Are you sure, Tabor? Sometimes it is better to be ignorant."

"I'm sure, Saul."

Saul looked over to Koda, who merely nodded in agreement.

After taking a deep breath, Saul said, "Young children make the best slaves. They can be intimidated or threatened to do their master's bidding. But lately, in the past few years, the very young are used as *more* than servants."

Saul paused, before expressing the worst of what he was being compelled to say to his closest friends. "Young, attractive children, more often than not, are sent to Caesar Tiberius himself. The guard confided in me that Caesar surrounds himself with young sex slaves who perform for him day and night. They are taught that Caesar is a god and that it is their duty to please him, which comes from Tiberius' depravity and sexual perversions."

Turning to Koda, Saul added, "Caesar himself prefers young boys. Those who do as they are told will live. Those who rebel will die, and be used as examples to the others."

Tabor stopped sharpening the small spear in his left hand, and let out a beleaguered sigh. Saul walked over and sat next to him by the fire—uncomfortable about following through with his friend's request for information, yet loyal enough to finish.

"Once Tiberius tires of the children," he continued, "or if any of them make an effort to escape, they are executed in any manner that feeds Caesar's perverse desires. Generally, they're thrown from a cliff known as *Tiberius' Leap,* or from a tall tower, to their death."

One after the other, Tabor carefully rolled the tip of each short spear in the fire to harden them.

Saul concluded, "They are told if they please Caesar, they will be sent home, but if they fail, they will die. None have ever returned."

"Have any ever escaped?" Koda asked.

Saul shook his head. "Caesar has exiled himself to the Island of Capri. There is no way off the island."

"Are they already on a ship?" Tabor asked.

"They were taken to Pontius Pilate's palace at Caesarea Maritima on the coast to await transportation to Capri. It's the only fortified Roman outpost in Israel. A supply ship goes once a month from there to Rome and then back again. My guess is—that is where they'll be kept until the next transport."

Tabor pulled a spear from the fire and felt the hardened point. "I'm going alone."

"No, Tabor! I know this fortress and I know the Romans. I speak

Greek better than you and can hold my own in a battle."

"I'm going, too," Koda joined. "It is *my* son they hold, along with Evia."

Tabor looked at both men for the first time since Saul had sat down. The fire reflected in his eyes, echoing his resolve. He pointed the short spear at Saul and said, "You will go with me," before pointing to Koda, "and you will stay here."

Before Koda could protest, Tabor insisted, "Koda, I promise you, we will bring Daniel back or die trying. If we all die, there will be *no* one to care for the women. I need you to do this for me, brother. I need to know you will care for Ruth, Naomi, and our mother if I do not return. *Please*, promise me."

The room the children were led to was filled with multi-colored pillows strewn about the floor and strips of sheer white lace draped from the ceiling. In the center of the room was a large bed, covered with burgundy red silk and more pillows.

The guards shoved both Daniel and Evia to the tile floor, and then left as quickly as they'd come in. Looking around the room, the two youths saw a number of other children—each older than them by at least a few years—lying about on the floor or on pillows, some seemingly asleep. For their own safety, Daniel and Evia huddled together against a wall, not knowing what to anticipate.

Both of them immediately recognized that all six of the other children were dressed identically with the same white togas as they were now wearing. *Four boys and two girls,* Daniel thought. *I have to find a way to get Evia out of here.*

The only other people in the room were two large eunuchs, each of whom held an intimidating sword in his folded arms, with a *pugio* dagger strapped to his hip.

Daniel left Evia by the wall for a few moments, making his way toward a bowl of fruit on a nearby table against an adjacent wall. While eyeing the two guards to see if they were going to prevent him from taking food from the bowl, he lifted an apple and came back to Evia's side. Holding the apple in front of her, he immediately grew concerned, since she seemed unaware of even his presence.

"Evia, if you don't eat, you will lose your strength," Daniel whispered. "We *are* going to escape this place, but you won't make it if you're too weak."

Daniel held the apple again in front of his cousin, who moved her eyes to focus on the fruit. With a new sense of determination, she took the apple and bit into it. Within moments, she began ravenously tearing into it, each bite quicker than the one before, until the entire apple—core and all—was consumed. After pulling her hand across her mouth to remove the fruit's juice, she gave him a determined look and said, "More."

With a slight grin, Daniel then moved to the bowl to get more food for both of them to share. Upon returning to her side, he whispered, "Good, Evia, keep eating. Soon, we will be with our family again. You'll see."

Evia didn't respond, but started devouring another apple, having been stirred by Daniel's words of hope.

Suddenly, the door to the room swung wide open and the two eunuchs each took one side step, protecting the doorway. A moment later, a man entered the room, walking between the eunuchs, who immediately closed the door and returned to their posts, blocking the only exit.

The man seemed old to the children. He wore the same white robe as they did, and appeared quite small in stature. None of them had ever seen someone so clean shaven before—even his very pale head and his eyebrows were shaved. After spotting Daniel and Evia holding their knees against their chests in an effort to hide inside their robes, he smiled and clasped his hands, "Ah, my young lovers," he began in perfect Aramaic. "I see we have two new, adorable pets."

Daniel and Evia looked at each other, realizing the man had focused on them the moment he'd entered the room.

The man clapped his hands twice before becoming more serious, saying "Come, my pets, show our young lovers what we do."

Daniel and Evia watched as all six of them, at his command, began kissing and caressing each other. The old man sat on the end of the bed to watch the children do as they had been taught. Then he looked across the room to Daniel and Evia, who had not yet received his lessons in what he considered the art of love. "Come here, young ones," he beckoned with a wave of his hand. "Come, sit beside me. I won't hurt you."

Daniel and Evia held hands as they stood and walked around the others, who embraced each other passionately on the floor. As they got within arm's distance of the old man, he smiled and said, "My, you two are so young and tender. Caesar is going to just eat you up."

With a surprisingly clear tone of voice, Evia spoke her first words since being kidnapped. "Why are we here? I want to go home."

"Oh, dear, dear," he responded in a mocking, syrupy sweet voice. "Don't you know? You are home."

"She means our *real* home with our family!" Daniel said forcefully.

"Oh, my dear boy. In time, you will come to love your new home. You two have been chosen from all the children of Israel to meet the king of Rome, Tiberius Caesar Augustus himself. Isn't that thrilling?"

"But I don't want to meet Caesar," Evia responded tearfully. "I want my family."

"Trust me, child. Your parents are going to be so proud when you go home after meeting Caesar. They will be showered with gold and jewels. I'm quite certain by now, they know exactly where you are and are praying that you will do as you're told, so you'll bring honor to your family in the very best way."

Through their tears, neither Daniel nor Evia noticed the sixteen-year-old boy who managed to work his way on the floor next to one of the eunuchs. In less than two seconds, the boy jumped up, grabbing the dagger from the eunuch's belt—only to fall back to the floor with blood pulsing from the fresh opening in his throat. The eunuch showed no emotion, as he folded his arms once again, holding the sword that now dripped fresh blood.

Evia screamed, burying her face in her hands. The old man used the youth's gory death to clarify his lesson to the children. "There now, you see?" pointing to the lifeless body lying in a pool of blood. "That is what happens to a child who doesn't do as he is told. Now, he will never see his family, and his parents will be executed for his indiscretion." Raising his voice to speak to all of the children, he yelled, "Let this be a lesson to all of you! You can do as I say—or you can die. The choice is yours!"

# CHAPTER 13


*Sunday Morning, March 24, A.D. 26*

Ruth moved her sheepskin-wrapped arm toward Tabor's shoulder. Storm cautiously stepped forward, clasping her arm first with one claw, and then the other. "Take her inside, Ruth. I don't want Storm to follow us."

Without uttering a word, she did as she was told. "Ruth thinks I'm leaving her," Tabor said to Saul, as the two men stood outside gathering their supplies. "She thinks I'm committing suicide over the loss of Evia."

"She's right, you know," he replied. "The Roman palace at Caesarea Maritima, where Pontius Pilate lives, is protected by an entire legion of Roman soldiers. Two Jewish shepherds stand no chance against such an army."

"I promised Ruth I would return *with* our daughter and nephew. I feel it strongly, Saul—God is on our side."

"And if we die instead?"

"Better to die standing—than to live on your knees."

Koda and Miriam came out—without Ruth—to see the two men off. Koda embraced Saul and said, "God be with you." He smiled, and then kissed the cheek of the man who had been so much like a father to him.

Next, Koda moved to embrace Tabor. "Remember, brother. You

are not going to seek revenge. You are only there to bring our children home." Holding him close, he kissed his brother on the cheek.

"I will remember, Koda. Thank you for taking care of our families and our herds until we return."

Tabor looked to the door of his home, hoping to see Ruth step out, but the doorway remained empty. Neither Ruth nor Naomi could bear to see them leave. Even Miriam had no parting words. With tears in her eyes and sobs in her voice, she could only stroke the beards of each man for what she feared would be the last time.

On the road to Caesarea Maritima, both men seemed inconspicuous. Two Jewish shepherds walking alone, like the countless other travelers who entered and departed the city on business. Increasing numbers of homes and shops lined the streets, all of which became more congested as they entered the city by the sea. Fishing boats and trade vessels dotted the horizon within the bay near the mighty fortress.

"Do we have a plan yet?" Saul asked Tabor.

Tabor looked at the solid stone walls of the palace, which stood as tall as four men. There seemed to be a constant stream of soldiers and horses entering and exiting the heavily guarded palace gate. Roman soldiers walked the top of the walls, as well, crossing each other in military fashion.

"Let's go up the hill, south of the palace, to study it," Tabor finally responded.

Hidden by cypress trees and large boulders, the two men took the next few hours to survey the palace and the movements of the soldiers within it. That evening, as torches were lit, they continued watching, doing what they could to learn the patterns of the change in guard. The next day, the two shepherds began formulating their plan.

"Obviously, we can't attack. Even if we could kill three or four soldiers, they would overpower us immediately," Tabor concluded.

"I agree," Saul replied. "And I think, now, there is only one way. We must become Roman soldiers ourselves, so we can move freely among them."

Tabor looked at Saul, trying to determine if he was seriously suggesting they join the Roman army.

Saul gripped his iron dagger and began sharpening it on sandstone. Tabor watched as Saul put the knife to his own throat, and began scraping his skin to remove his beard. When his face was clean-shaven, he continued skillfully moving the blade, and soon a pile of hair was on the ground, the result of his having swiftly cut his hair short.

Even though Tabor watched Saul transform himself, it was difficult for him to recognize his companion. For the first time since the children were kidnapped, he couldn't help but laugh at Saul's appearance.

"Alright then, my friend. Laugh all you want, but now it's *your* turn." Saul held out the dagger to Tabor, who suddenly stopped smiling, realizing he too would soon look just as strange to Saul. Shaving his beard and cutting his hair was a detestable, sinful act for a faithful Jew, but Tabor knew it was necessary, if he wished for a chance of entering the palace without drawing attention.

"The skin on your face, where your beard once grew, is lighter complexion," Tabor observed.

"We will move under darkness," Saul replied. "No one will notice."

While Tabor shaved, he asked for more detail, "Even without our beards, how are we going to look like Roman soldiers?"

Before answering, Saul paused to make sure he had Tabor's complete attention. "We knew when we came here that blood would spill." Tabor didn't seem clear about the direction of his friend's statement, so Saul solemnly asked him, "Tabor, are you prepared to kill a man?"

Tabor tossed a handful of his own hair into the pile before saying, "I take no pleasure in it, but I am willing to kill every man in those walls, if that is what it takes to free Evia and Daniel."

Drawing upon his training as an elite guard to Herod the Great, Saul took time over the next hour to teach Tabor everything he could about fighting soldiers. "When you fight, you must never hesitate. You want to kill a man with a single blow. Cut his throat like you would slaughter a sheep, or stab him through the heart. Anything else will afford him the chance to cry out."

Tabor nodded his understanding, while he continued to shorten his hair.

Switching to Greek, Saul said, "And another thing. Every soldier in there speaks Greek. From now on, that is all you and I will speak."

Replying in Greek, Tabor said, "Understood."

"Un-der-stood!" Saul responded with a better enunciation. "We are going to have to work on your accent, if you don't want to appear as a Jew who wandered out of the hills into the palace of a Roman governor.

"*Un-der-stood*," Tabor responded, carefully forming the word to precisely mimic the sound he'd heard from Saul.

"Do you see the last soldier on the wall nearest the sea?" Saul asked, pointing at the palace. "He is the *only* one who does not walk the wall, passing another guard. He is constantly watching the port and the ships as they move. He is our first target. We will kill him and you will wear his uniform."

"I will wear his uniform," Tabor responded, this time with better diction.

"After you are in uniform, find a guard who is alone and out of sight. Kill him and bring me his clothes. When we are both in uniform, I will flank behind you to kill anyone who considers you suspicious. Remember, your mission it to find the children. My mission is to protect you."

Tabor nodded, letting his eyes roam from one side of the palace to the other. He felt an immediate sense of dismay as he surveyed the vast complex of buildings he would have to search. *God of Israel,* he prayed, *how will I find Evia and Daniel—are they even alive?*

Saul continued, "If one of us gets killed, the other must move on and proceed alone. After you are dressed as a Roman, you mingle with the other soldiers. There are so many of them, a stranger's face will not alarm anyone. Try to walk quickly, as if you have a purpose, and don't get pulled into a casual conversation."

"But, how do we find the children? That palace is like a small city."

"We'll need to use our instincts—and pray to God for guidance," Saul offered. "We must be flexible, and adjust our plan to the changing situation. The only hope we have for success is if we remain undiscovered. Once they realize we have breached the palace walls, we will be captured or killed within minutes."

Throwing down the last clump of his own hair, Tabor asked, "How do I look?"

Saul grinned at the sight of his friend's face. Reaching over, he slapped Tabor's bare skin and said, "There is certainly a reason God covers a man's face with a beard." Both laughed quietly, for a moment, breaking the somber mood.

"So we go now?" Tabor asked.

"Patience, Tabor. We'll go under cover of the deepest darkness." Saul began digging a small hole nearby with his dagger. "Help me bury this hair. If they discover it after we're gone, they will know they're looking for a Jew without a beard. For now, we sleep. Tonight will be a long night."

Looking over at the cold stone walls of the Roman fortress, Tabor suddenly felt Evia's presence. "They're alive," he whispered. "I know it." So many nights, when Evia was a young girl, Tabor had chased away her fears of darkness with the words of a reassuring prayer. This night, he sent her his most heartfelt blessing: *As the sun fades, and the day slips away, may the Lord watch over you. I promise you, Evia, we will be together again.*

Sleep came hard for Tabor. When the darkness of nightfall finally settled in, he managed some short naps, only to be awoken as his mind raced with every scenario imaginable that would lead to his capture, or worse, the death of Evia and Daniel.

"Tabor," Saul whispered, gently nudging his shoulder. "It's time."

Tabor realized he must have been asleep, even though he was certain there would be no sleep for him this night. "I'm ready," he whispered back, sitting up to see the torches burning on the palace wall.

With a quick drink of water and eating of a few dried figs— which they both knew might be their final meal—the two men quietly approached the seaward end of the palace wall under the darkened sky of a moonless night.

Communicating with hand signals to avoid being heard talking, Saul handed his iron dagger to Tabor and showed him the best place to scale the wall. Tabor held the blade of the dagger between his teeth, and carefully climbed his way up the jagged stone structure. Clinging to the top of the wall and cautiously lifting his head over it, he saw a guard to his left, the one who watched the sea. None of the others were visible in the torch-lit walkway that passed between two waist-high walls.

Without a sound, he breached the wall and let himself down to the walkway, crouching below the wall. After a moment of silence, he stealthily walked right up behind the unsuspecting guard and quietly grabbed the wooden handle of Saul's dagger.

*Pull the animal's head back to expose its neck,* he remembered his father instructing him before his first kill. *Draw the blade from one side to the other, cutting deep, so it will die quickly and painlessly.*

Tabor quickly visualized his daughter in Roman hands. The soldier's life, his family and children were of no concern to him. *This man's death is a necessary means to bringing Evia home.*

As he had done so many times before, this slaughter would be from behind, without looking into his victim's eyes, without watching death claim yet another life. With one swift movement, Tabor grabbed the man's forehead from behind, snapped his head back and drew the blade swiftly and deeply across his throat.

The man dropped his spear and reached for his neck, as the gurgling sound of air escaped, along with a surging current of blood from his body. He turned to see the face of his executioner before dropping to the hardened walkway, where he had stood for countless nights in his duty as a Roman soldier.

The sheath holding the soldier's sword struck rock as he collapsed, releasing a faint ring in the stillness of the night. Tabor looked around for movement from other guards, but saw nothing.

Quickly, he disrobed the dead soldier and dressed himself in the blood soaked garments. The skirt-like *pteruges* left his legs exposed, so he pulled his mantle high under the Roman breastplate, in order that his Jewish robe would not be exposed under the vertical leather straps. After donning the bronze helmet over his freshly cut hair, he wrapped the belt around his waist, which held the soldier's sword and sheath.

Saul clung to the rock ledge at the top of the wall, watching Tabor don the soldier's uniform. Although he had observed what looked to be a clean kill, Saul was distressed to see Tabor with his back to the walkway, where the other guards continued to walk their posts. Unable to call out to Tabor to turn and watch for the other guards without giving away their position, all he could do was watch the guards to see if any saw the clean-shaven Jewish man disrobing the body of a Roman guard.

Saul's training as a palace guard allowed him the discipline to remain silent, when he saw a young Roman soldier preparing to throw a spear at the back of the man who was standing over the half-naked body of a dead guard. Instinctively, Saul leapt over the wall and stood himself between the flying spear and Tabor.

Hearing a thump behind him, Tabor quickly turned around. He saw a spear head protruding from a man's back and watched as the man turned before falling to the stone walkway.

Tabor immediately turned further, toward the commotion behind him and saw a Roman guard jumping over the man lying on the ground, clutching the handle of a steel sword, prepared to strike. Tabor tightly grasped the spear he held in his own hand, taken from his victim, and lunging forward, thrust it deftly into the abdomen of the charging soldier.

With the razor-sharp steel of a Roman *pugio* taken from his first victim, Tabor cut the throat of the guard, who now stood with both hands clutching the shaft of the spear impaling his body.

In seconds, the plan for Tabor and Saul to free the kidnapped children had turned to chaos. "Saul!" Tabor called out in a frantic whisper, lifting his friend's head to rest on his thigh, as he knelt beside him. Realizing Saul had taken the spear that was meant for him, Tabor could only cling to his mentor as he lay dying in his arms.

Blood sprayed from Saul's lips when he coughed, yet somehow he managed to smile and grasp Tabor's hand, as it supported his head. "Tabor, at last, God has forgiven me."

"Hold on, Saul, I'll..."

"No, Tabor!" Saul whispered. "Do not let my death be in vain!" Coughing up more blood, he said, "Find them—save them."

As Saul's last breath passed between his lips, Tabor laid the man's head down gently, before standing to survey his surroundings. *This soldier I killed will be expected to walk past another soldier in a matter of moments. That soldier, too, must die*, thought Tabor, *or else he will alert the other guardsmen to his missing comrade.*

Now dressed convincingly as a Roman soldier, he retraced the steps of the guard who killed Saul, Tabor approached a burly soldier who was walking toward him along his assigned post. Before the blood finished spurting from the man's severed throat, Tabor had sent his body over the outside of the wall, so it would remain hidden in the darkness until morning.

Looking one last time at his friend's lifeless body, Tabor knew there was no time for grief—that would have to come later. Saul's earlier warning flooded his mind: *If one of us gets killed, the other must move on and proceed alone.*

Drawing in a deep breath, Tabor turned fully around contemplated his next move. Staring down from the top of the wall, he studied the buildings within the compound of the palace. *Somewhere, hidden within a room of those buildings*, he thought, *Evia is waiting for me, and I will find her.*

# CHAPTER 14



*3:00 a.m., Wednesday, March 27, A.D. 26*

Only minutes had passed since Saul had been killed protecting Tabor, who now stood on the stone walkway at the top of the palace wall, feeling uncomfortable in the Roman uniform he now wore. The sandals were laced tightly up his calf, exactly as they were on the man who wore them last. The bronze helmet was clumsy, and the heavy leather armor draped over Tabor's hidden mantle was obviously made for a much smaller man.

While he carried the sword in its sheath, Tabor chose to leave the spear and shield lying next to the soldier's body, so his hands would remain free to use the sling he had tucked in his belt, in combination with the handful of smooth river stones and three short spears stowed in the pouch he'd always worn.

Following Saul's instructions, Tabor spoke in Greek, as he took a deep breath and whispered a prayer to God, just loudly enough to give himself strength, "Protect me, Lord. Make me invisible to my enemies and lead me to my daughter. If she is already dead, then give me the strength to kill a hundred Romans before I die."

As he climbed down the ladder from the outer wall, Tabor heard the words of his friend, as clearly as he did when Saul first explained their invasion plan to him: *Remember Tabor, once you put on the Roman uniform, you must become a Roman soldier. Walk as if you are walking amongst your own sheep. Do not look frightened or confused. Your eyes will give you away.*

Passing by the stables, a similarly dressed soldier walked past him, gesturing a salute by forming a fist with his right hand and using it to tap his chest. Tabor mimicked the salute, tapping the breast plate covering his heart. Though his pulse quickened, his eyes remained focused ahead, and the two men passed each other indifferently in the stillness of the night.

Rounding the last stall, he stopped short at the sight of a large, bare-chested man, who stood near a young boy dressed in a white tunic. The boy was urinating against the wall of the stable, while his escort waited. When he finished, both of them turned and walked toward a large building with two tall pillars framing the entrance.

Tabor followed the pair into the building, passing through the main entrance behind the stone columns. The passage was dimmer than the torch-lit compound, but oil lamps hanging on the walls gave off enough light for him to follow at a safe distance along the corridor.

The boy and his escort eventually turned to pass through a doorway, flanked by two guards, both holding spears. Tabor continued walking past the large wooden door, which he noticed was covered with gold plates embossed into depictions of sexual acts. As he passed, one of the guards spoke a single word in Greek, "Helmet!"

Tabor quickly assessed the man's intent when he noticed that neither guard wore a helmet. Realizing he was being corrected for a uniform infraction, he quickly pulled his helmet off and responded in Greek, "Thank you!"

As he continued to walk the wide corridor, he turned the corner at the first adjoining hall. There he stood, momentarily allowing himself to breathe heavily as his heart demanded. *What now, Saul?* his racing mind asked.

Tabor knew he had no plan, but years of shepherding practice kicked in and he loaded his sling, preparing to clear the guards from the doorway.

Following a high-pitched whistling sound that lasted only a second, one of the guards twisted before falling to his side. In the dim light, the remaining guard could not see the blood that hemorrhaged from the man's temple, as he knelt beside his fallen comrade. Once again, he heard the short whistle, but never saw the smooth river stone that cracked his skull, directly above his left eye.

Tabor crouched next to both motionless men and looked around to ensure the sound of their falling to the floor had not aroused any attention. With the hallway quiet, he grabbed the spear leaning against the wall near one of them.

Tabor realized he did not know five seconds into the future what he should do; his only plan was to keep pressing forward until he found Evia, or die trying. Either way, nothing prevented him from opening the immense, salaciously decorated door.

Walking into the room, he passed between two large eunuchs, one of whom he recognized as the man he had followed into the building.

Standing merely a body length beyond the two men guarding the inside of the room, Tabor could see sleeping bodies everywhere, lit only by oil lamps mounted on two opposing walls.

"What business brings you here?" one of the eunuchs asked in a threatening tone.

Tabor turned and said, "My apology, I believe I entered the wrong room." Turning to exit between the two guards, he lowered the spear he carried and rammed it through the heart of the man on his right. The other eunuch pulled his large blade sword from its sheath, but failed to swing it even once before blood from a swift and deep gash in his throat rained onto the floor in front of him.

Wakened by the disturbance, the room's occupants began screaming and scurrying away from the horrifying scene. Most had been scattered around the room on the floor, but in the center of the room, on a large bed, a man shrieked in a voice high enough to be a woman's, before calling out, "Guards! Help!" However, the two lifeless guards in the corridor would be of no more help to the frightened man than the two lifeless eunuchs, whose lifeblood was now draining into a pool next to the opened door.

In a single, fluid movement—one he had practiced a thousand times before—Tabor loaded his sling with one of his three short spears and launched it, piercing the eye socket of the terrified man before coming to a rest against the back of his skull.

Tabor stood motionless, surveying the room, looking for a sign of anyone who wanted to challenge him or alert the palace guards. Those remaining in the room huddled next to each other in dread, watching every move of the man who was dressed as a Roman guard, fearing his killing spree had only just begun. When he called out, "Evia!" the short gasp of a young girl crouched against the wall to his left, drew his immediate attention.

"Evia, Daniel, is that you?" he called out in Aramaic, pushing his eyesight into the dim corner of the room. But his plea remained unanswered.

Stepping toward the sound of the girl's gasp, he spoke again, now realizing she would not know him without his beard and certainly not in the uniform of a Roman soldier. "Evia, it's me, Tabor, your father. Are you here, my daughter?"

Several seconds passed before he heard the unmistakable voice of his child, "Papa?"

With certainty, he ran a few steps to embrace his daughter, who was wearing a thin white tunic. Pulling her to her feet, he lifted her face to let her see his eyes. "You have my father's voice, but..."

Tabor persisted, "Evia, I have come to take you and Daniel home. Home—to your mother, Ruth. Home—to Storm."

Weeping now in her father's arms, she was finally able to acknowledge, "Papa, it is you—it really is you. Not just a dream."

The boy who had done his best to protect Evia throughout the ordeal, and who had been holding her tightly up to the moment Tabor discovered her, stood next to Evia. "Daniel." Tabor exclaimed with an excited whisper, immediately recognizing his nephew. And although both children wept and sobbed with relief in Tabor's arms, he quickly realized his mission was only half-over. *Somehow, I have to get the children past the outer palace wall without being discovered.*

"Come, we must hurry." Tabor said, releasing his hold on the children. "Do *exactly* as I say and God will deliver us."

As they approached the door, Tabor told them, "Evia, wait here. Daniel, help me drag the guards into this room so we can close the door."

Daniel and Tabor each took an arm of one guard and drug his corpse along the floor, through the pooled blood of the eunuchs and well into the room. Then, they went back into the corridor and did the same with the other. "Daniel, I want you to wear the guard's uniform. Get it off of him and dress quickly."

Evia helped Daniel remove the guard's uniform and in a matter of minutes, dressed Daniel, while Tabor watched through the slightly opened door for signs of movement.

"I'm ready." Daniel said in a loud whisper.

Tabor looked back to inspect the newest Roman soldier, but instead saw a boy who could barely keep the armored vest from slipping past his narrow shoulders. Any other day, he would have laughed at the sight, but now he feared Daniel's childlike appearance would alert even the most unsuspecting eye. He moved quickly to pull down the silk sheers that dangled from the ceiling, ripping them into pieces to stuff under Daniel's uniform.

After adding enough padding to the helmet to keep it from dropping over Daniel's eyes, he told the children, "Now listen carefully, both of you. We are two Roman soldiers taking a female slave from the palace. We must believe it if we want anyone else to believe. Do not say a word. I will do all the talking. Do you understand?"

"I do, Papa," Evia replied.

"Yes, Tabor. I understand," Daniel said.

Tabor ran to the lifeless body of the old man and pulled his short spear from the man's skull. Returning to the children he said, "Evia, you walk before us. Walk across the compound toward the stables, as though you need to relieve yourself. Daniel, always stay by my side, *no matter what*. And remember, if I get stopped or go down, you two run as fast as you can to escape and never look back."

Tabor turned to see the other children in the room still terrified and confused by the Roman soldier who left five bodies in the room and was now taking two of their own away. Knowing the chance of their own escape was near zero, he wished he could bring the rest of the children out, but knew that he couldn't. "God forgive me," he said before stepping into the corridor with Evia and Daniel.

Tabor quietly closed the door behind them and guided them down the corridor. His heart pounded loudly in his ears with each step they took. What had begun as a battle to stay alive in the center of a heavily guarded Roman fortress was now twice as difficult with two children in tow. His mind raced to devise an exit plan that would get the three of them past the heavily guarded walls.

Going out the way he came in was not possible. Even if they were able to make it onto the wall undetected, he could not expect the children to scale the outer wall as he and Saul had done to get in.

Eventually, they began crossing the compound, with Tabor acting as though he and his companion were purposefully escorting a young slave from one place to another. Once the three stepped into the shadows of the stable, protected by the sounds and smells of the horses, Daniel asked in a whispered voice, "How are we going to get out?"

Tabor looked at the gate, where he could see a number of guards walking their post, and said, "We are going right through the front gate, Daniel."

Two horses were tied to a post, fully saddled. Seeing the horses were unattended, Tabor asked, "Daniel, can you ride a horse?"

With youthful confidence, he replied, "Yes, I think so."

Tabor found a long rope hanging from a nail and proceeded to bind Evia's hands by tying the rope around her wrists in front of her. "Remember," he said tenderly to the daughter he'd feared he would never see again, "you are a slave and I am a Roman soldier taking you with me. You must walk until we get past the gate."

"I will, Papa. I trust you."

Tabor unhitched both horses and boosted Daniel onto the saddle of the smaller of the two. After mounting his own steed, he turned toward the gate, and slowly led them forward, holding the loose end of the rope with Evia following behind, as he had seen Roman soldiers do many times before.

Reminding the young boy—who was nearly as terrified by the horse between his legs as he was of any encounter with a Roman—Tabor said, "Remember, Daniel, not a word. I will do the talking."

As they approached the closed gate, the horses stopped walking, as they had done every day before, just with different riders.

Two guards stood at the gate. A third, an obese man who obviously outranked the others, rose from a bench beside the gate, approached the riders, and asked, "Where are you going and by whose authority?"

"We're taking this slave girl to Herod," Tabor replied, hoping desperately his accent would not make his Greek difficult to understand.

The commander walked behind the horses to the young girl wearing a white slave's tunic. Running the palm of his hand across the young girl's face and then down her back, he questioned the mounted soldier further, "And why would you be transporting a slave in the middle of the night?"

"I'm told Herod is going to trade five young boys for this girl. I suppose Caesar does not want his entire empire to know his preference for boys."

It was no secret amongst the guards in the palace that Tiberius Caesar Augustus lustily preferred boys, but rarely did they speak of it for fear of following the young slaves to their death. The guard stopped caressing the young girl before letting out a hearty laugh, "Caesar can have his boys! I'll take a whore like this one any day!"

Before releasing the soldiers, he pulled the back of Evia's hair downward to lift her face up, kissing her forcefully on the mouth. His breath tasted of rotted flesh, from years of decaying teeth. With his tongue, he pushed through the girl's clinched lips, passing the foul taste to her vulnerable senses. "There, give my kiss to Herod."

Evia knew better than to spit out the foul taste, so she hung her head low to let the grotesque saliva from the man's tongue drool from her lower lip.

Of all the men who died by Tabor's hands that night, this guard who fondled his daughter was the one he wanted to kill more than any. *Remember, brother. You are not going to seek revenge. You are only there to bring our children home.* Koda's words replaying in Tabor's head were the only thing that kept him on his horse.

"Open the gate!" called out the guard, and moments later, the three of them passed freely through, moving forward into the night.

# CHAPTER 15

*4:30 a.m., Wednesday, March 27, A.D. 26*

Darkness soon hid the travelers from view of the guards stationed on the wall above the huge wooden gates, as the two men on horses, followed by the barefoot slave girl, walked away from the torch-lit palace.

"Hold up, Daniel," Tabor said, once he knew they were safe. "Evia, come here."

Tabor lifted his daughter to the horse and sat her in front of him, finally safe. "I prayed for this moment, when I would once again hold you in my arms," Tabor whispered as he untied her hands, "and God has answered my prayers. Thank you, o' merciful One."

She embraced her father and clung to him. Before moving on, he turned his horse to look once more upon the walls of the Governor's palace, and then back around to the road that disappeared in the black of night.

With Evia no longer walking behind, they could now push the horses to a much faster pace. "Keep up with me, Daniel," he said, tapping the sides of the horse with his heels. Tabor knew galloping would be too risky in the dark, so they moved at the pace of a slow trot, following the road out of Caesarea Maritima.

The sound of the horses' hooves clapping against the occasional section of cobblestone along the way was their only assurance they were still on the road to Jerusalem. Tabor kept his gaze fixed on the silhouette of the distant hills outlined against the dark sky in the pre-dawn hours. Trusting the horse's instincts as much as his own, he kept them all moving forward as the port city faded behind the three riders.

As they neared the foothills, Tabor stopped and turned his horse back toward Caesarea Maritima. The torches burning around the city blurred into a singular dim light, yet in the stillness of the early dawn, Tabor heard a faint sound from the valley below. "Wait, Daniel. Did you hear that?"

Daniel stopped and turned his horse to stand next to Tabor's. "I don't hear anything."

"Shhh, quiet. Listen." The three sat quietly, chilled by the night air of the desert, hearing only the sound of their horses blowing heavy gusts of air from their nostrils. A moment later, they all heard the sound of horns blowing from the city below. Tabor studied the terrain of the mountains that parted on either side of the road to Jerusalem. "Our secret is out," Tabor said. "Get down, Daniel. We travel on foot from here on out."

"But we have a good lead." Daniel protested. "We can stay ahead of them on horseback."

"And when word spreads of two Jews dressed in Roman uniforms with a Roman slave, riding on stolen Roman horses, how long do you think it will take them to find us?"

Daniel reluctantly dismounted the horse and waited for Tabor and Evia to do the same. Tabor turned both horses toward Jerusalem and smacked them on their rumps, followed by a loud yell, startling the horses into a gallop away from the soldiers' presumed direction.

"Follow me," Tabor said. "We have to get off this road."

Tabor led them up a small hill, where they found a wide-sweeping view that improved with each passing minute, courtesy of the rising sun. When they crested the summit and the road was no longer in sight, they sat hidden within some brush.

"Let's get these uniforms off," Tabor said to Daniel, pulling the brass vest over his head. "Keep the sandals on, but cut the straps off, so they don't look like Roman sandals."

Tabor's mantle covered his body relatively well, once it was unbound from the bulky uniform and armor. Daniel looked much more like Evia, now that they were both covered with the thin white tunic characteristic of Roman sex slaves.

The Prefect, Augustus, walked swiftly through the outer chamber toward the inner chambers of Pontius Pilate, Governor of Judea. To report such a breach in security would surely cost him his rank, but failure to do so would certainly mean his death.

Pilate was already up when Augustus entered his bed chamber, awakened by the horns that warned every Roman soldier within the palace of imminent attack. Two servants were hurriedly dressing Pilate in battle armor with military precision. Pilate stood watching from his balcony, as scores of soldiers ran through the compound, taking their assigned places along the palace walls.

Without turning to confirm it, he knew the Prefect was behind him, down on his left knee with his right fist over his heart and his head bowed. "Report!"

Augustus rose to his feet and began conveying the facts as he knew them. "My lord! We are under attack."

"From the land or the sea?"

"By land, sir. Three guards dead on the south wall and two more in the servant quarters." He knowingly referred to the slaves as "servants," in accordance with palace instructions, even though everyone in the compound knew these were sex slaves who were being "conditioned" within the palace.

"What?" Pilate erupted. "There are invaders *already* inside the walls?"

"My lord, we believe they have fled the palace. We found the body of one of them on the south wall, but a search has turned up nothing of more invaders."

"Prefect, are you telling me some plebeian raiders got past your guards, entered the very heart of these palace grounds, killed five men and escaped *without detection*?"

Knowing he was signing his own death sentence, the Prefect bowed his head slightly and said, "Sir, the guard commander at the gate reports two mounted soldiers led a slave girl through the front gate by your order. They were told she was to be delivered to King Herod."

Pilate screamed at the top of his lungs, *"I gave no such order!"*

Turning his back on Augustus, he stepped out onto his third floor balcony. "Prefect, come here."

"My lord?" Augustus asked, approaching and standing next to Pilate.

"Look at these men," Pilate said, motioning with his hand out onto the palace grounds, as soldiers lined the walls and others searched every room of the buildings below. "Tell me what you see, Prefect."

"Roman soldiers, my lord."

"That's correct! Roman soldiers, the best trained soldiers in the world—who allowed *raiders* to pass through their ranks, *kill*, and then walk right out the front gate. Roman soldiers who are no better than their leader." With that, Pilate put both hands on Augustus's back and flung him over the railing.

From his balcony, Pilate called to a soldier who had stopped to look at the man whose body landed on the ground next to him, "You there!" When the soldier looked up to the balcony and saw Pilate calling to him, he stood at attention with his right fist against his breast plate.

Pilate issued his order, "Take that man's body to the desert. Feed it to the wolves and vultures."

Within the hour, the guard commander at the gate was stripped of his uniform and nailed through the wrists to the outside of the gate. Pilate ordered that his body be left there to decay, until his bones fell to be trampled into the dust.

---

"Tabor, how long will we have to stay here?" Daniel asked, as they peered over the mound at the road to Jerusalem.

"Until they stop looking for us."

"Did my father come with you?"

"No, Daniel. Koda is younger than me, so it was my decision that he would stay to protect your mother, Ruth, and Miriam. If the Romans find out who I am, they will try to kill the women as punishment against any Jew who would stand against them."

"So you came alone?"

Suddenly, Tabor remembered the man who was like a second father to him. "No, Daniel. I was never alone. Saul came with me. He led me to you, in fact. But he lost his life to a Roman spear, protecting me so I could live long enough to rescue you and Evia."

Overhearing the conversation, Evia gasped. "Saul died? Papa— Saul is dead?"

Tears swelled in Evia's eyes, as she moved closer to her father, showing emotion for the first time since they'd escaped the palace. Tabor put an arm around her and held her tightly. "Saul is the reason the three of us are together. He died, so we could live."

"Are *we* going to die, lost here in the desert?" Daniel asked, looking for words of reassurance from his uncle.

"I promised Saul, before he died, I would deliver you both to your homes, and I intend to keep my promise."

The morning sun rose as the crimson wisps of clouds gave way to blue sky, heating the cool desert floor to become a parched bed of hot sand and stone. All afternoon, soldiers rode back and forth along the road. Some were in full gallop, while others walked their horses at a slow pace, looking for signs of hoof prints that may have left the road.

"There..." Tabor said in a whisper. Daniel and Evia both climbed the short distance to lie next to Tabor. All three peered over the sandy crest at the two horsemen leading two riderless horses back toward the palace. "They know we're on foot, now. We can't stay here. They'll soon begin searching the hills."

The three backed down the hill, out of sight from the road. "This will not be easy," Tabor said. "We will stay off the roads, traveling mostly at night. Evia, do you think you can keep pace without sandals?"

"I will keep pace, Papa."

"And she can wear my sandals when her feet begin to hurt," Daniel offered.

Motioning for them to join hands with him, Tabor closed his eyes and turned to God for deliverance. "God of Abraham, God of Moses, God of Israel, lead us through the wilderness and deliver us from our enemy."

Just as they released hands, Evia screamed as an arrow flew silently past her and found its mark, piercing Tabor's back below his left shoulder, the metal point coming to rest deep within his muscles. In a split second, he had crumpled to the ground. Both Evia and Daniel stood frozen and wide-eyed, their mouths dropped open in horror.

Turning over to face them, he commanded the children, "Run! Leave me! Run, now!"

Evia dropped to her knees next to her father, but Daniel knew he had to follow Tabor's order. Grabbing Evia by the arm, he pulled the barefoot girl to her feet and ran in the opposite direction.

Again, Evia shrieked, as she and Daniel ran directly into the arms of two Roman soldiers. "Well, well—what do we have here?" said one to the other.

A third soldier came up running, stood over Tabor—who remained motionless on the ground—and held his sword to the fallen man's neck. Tabor squeezed his eyes, disgusted with himself, as he watched two soldiers bind Evia and Daniel at the wrists and ankles and lead them back up the hill toward him.

Blood soaked Tabor's back, and the wound from the arrow protruding from his shoulder was already beginning to ache severely. Defeated and in excruciating pain, all he could do was wish for a swift, fatal blow from the sword hovering above his neck.

Once the three soldiers were together, with Evia and Daniel in tow, Tabor heard them discussing his fate. "Pilate wants them alive. We can take the slaves back, but what about this Jew with the arrow? Can he walk?"

"We'll find out," the soldier who stood over him said. "Stand up, you Jewish dog!" he demanded, while yanking hard on the arrow in his shoulder to inflict pain. The metal barbs of the arrow point dug firmly into the muscles under the socket of his shoulder.

Tabor cried out, as his body lifted in response to the arrow pulling through his flesh. Evia and Daniel stood facing him, but shuddered as they watched. Tears fell from Evia's eyes, while watching her father's blood drip from the fingers of his hand.

"Why don't we kill him and take the children with us?" suggested one soldier.

"Pilate wants to make an example of him," replied the one who seemed to be the leader. "This man has killed our comrades and deserves to die as an enemy of Rome."

The lead Roman soldier motioned for him to walk in front of them, as the others led the children from behind. Only Tabor recognized the shadow that moved across the ground in front of him. Carefully, unnoticed by his captors, he removed his sling and wrapped the strap around the palm of his hand.

Again, the shadow slithered along the ground, larger this time. Tabor lifted two stones from his pouch, hidden by his body from the soldier who carried a spear pointed toward his back. Still, he waited for the signal. As they crested the hill, the cry to attack came from above. The screech of an eagle diving into battle drew the attention of the soldiers.

Tabor's sling was in motion when the lead soldier felt the piercing pain of the mighty bird's talons sink into his eye sockets, instantly blinding him. Tabor's first stone found its mark on the forehead of the soldier walking behind Evia. The third soldier thrust his spear into the air toward Storm, who flapped and screeched slightly out of reach, giving time for Tabor's second stone to deliver a debilitating blow.

With renewed zest, Tabor slit the throat of both soldiers who fell to the ground, spilling their blood on the desert soil. As the third soldier screamed and clutched at his eyes after Storm's attack, Tabor pushed his dagger under the man's breast plate into his intestines. The man stopped screaming and lowered his hands from his eyes to his abdomen, exposing the blood that streamed down his cheeks like tears. Twisting the dagger to slice through the man's intestines, Tabor waited for death and gravity to pull the man's body free from the weapon he'd wielded so deftly.

Evia cried and trembled at the blood and death surrounding her. Still tied to Daniel, he tried to pull her away from the horrifying spectacle.

Tabor sat beneath a willow tree, exhausted from the fight and his own loss of blood. Storm landed on a branch above him, moving her head in quick movements, ever vigilant as she watched for more soldiers. As his breathing slowed, he looked at the bird above him and asked, "So what took you so long?"

Responding to the sound of his voice, Storm spread her mighty wings, opened her beak and let out a short screech.

Daniel and Evia joined Tabor in the shadow of the tree, where they untied the rope from their wrists and ankles.

Tabor looked at the children, now rescued from Roman tyranny a second time in a single day, and tried to ease their fears. "I think next year for Passover, we should stay home and count our sheep."

Suffering severe shock, Evia managed to repeat the one word that broke through her fears, "Home."

"Daniel," Tabor said, "I can't reach this. You cannot pull the arrow out from behind. You will have to push it until the arrow point passes through."

"Tabor—I can't. It could kill you!"

"I'll die if you don't."

He rose to his knees and wrapped his arms around the trunk of the tree for support. Before he put a stick in his mouth on which to bite in order to dampen his scream, he told him, "Hard and fast, Daniel. Push it through on your first try, with all of your might."

Daniel stood behind his uncle. Even though Tabor was on his knees, the height of the arrow was well above his waist. After several false starts to grab the arrow, he finally reacted perfectly when Tabor grunted, "Do it! Now!"

Daniel pushed the arrow with both hands. Using all his strength and body weight, the arrow moved forward until his hands could go no further after stopping against Tabor's back.

Tabor's head lifted and he couldn't help but cry out in agony, before dropping face down onto the ground beneath the tree.

Evia jumped back, holding both hands over her mouth, a helpless witness to her father's writhing pain before her. Minutes later, once the bulk of his suffering subsided, Tabor was able to look at his left shoulder and see the steel point of the Roman arrow, now finally exposed. Carefully, he managed to sit up before complimenting his nephew, "Good, Daniel. You did good."

Tabor could see Evia was deep in shock, as her hands trembled profusely in front of her face. "Once more, Daniel. I need you to break the shaft of the arrow behind me."

Cautiously, he grabbed the shaft where it entered his uncle's shoulder, prying down on the back of it with his other hand until it snapped. Tabor nearly blacked out from the pain, but he held back his cries in fear of alerting more soldiers. With a single thrust, he grabbed the arrow shaft near the point and pulled the broken arrow from his body.

# CHAPTER 16



*Saturday, March 30, A.D. 26*

Koda tended the flock, while Miriam, Naomi, and Ruth sat by the cooking fire in front of the home Jonas had built. "Ruth, please eat," Miriam implored, holding a piece of bread out to Ruth.

Rocking back and forth, Ruth stared into the fire, shaking her head to refuse Miriam's request. "He's not coming back, I can feel it," she said in a mournful voice.

"Ruth, don't say that!" Naomi snapped back. "It's only been seven days."

Ruth continued rocking, as though in a trance.

"We must have faith, Ruth," Miriam said, trying to reassure her. "Faith that God will lead Tabor and Saul to our children and return them to us."

"God doesn't listen to the likes of me," Ruth said. "It's all my fault. I wasn't watching Evia and Daniel—and now Tabor and Saul have been captured or killed. Tabor would still be alive, had I never been born."

"Ruth!" Naomi said sharply. "Tabor and Saul *will* come back and, God willing, bring our children home, too. You'll see. But my dear, you must eat, so he doesn't come home to find his wife *dead*. Now, eat, or I will feed you like a child."

Ruth glared at Naomi, angered that Naomi seemed more concerned about her health than the family they had all lost. Grudgingly, she took the morsel of bread from Miriam's hand and bit a piece, holding it in her mouth to soften.

Ruth was the first to recognize the distant screech of Storm. Looking over her shoulder, she could see the outstretched wings of the mighty bird riding the warm air current rising up from the heated desert and mountains below.

Throwing the remaining bread to the ground, Ruth stood up and began hysterically screaming a ghostly cry, tearing at her own clothes. Miriam and Naomi both jumped up to grasp Ruth's arms in an attempt to keep her from hurting herself.

"Ruth! What is it?" Miriam asked. "What's wrong?"

Pointing to the eagle in the sky, Ruth hollered, "It's Storm. Don't you see her? I sent her out three days ago to find Tabor, and she has come back alone. They're gone. They're all gone."

Miriam and Naomi watched, as Storm began circling overhead. With the completion of each circle, she descended toward the only place she knew as home. Suddenly, something moving in the distance caught Miriam's eye. In the valley below, she noticed what appeared to be a figure walking with a long stick. Releasing her hold on Ruth, who continued to weep on Naomi's shoulder, she ran quickly forward in the direction of the moving figure and finally allowed herself to believe what her eyes were showing her. "Ruth! Naomi!" she called out. "Come here and look!"

Naomi gently pushed Ruth away from her shoulder, as she too saw someone approaching from afar. When Ruth also turned to look, she saw a man, and now the tops of two more heads, all walking directly toward them.

Naomi turned and ran a few steps to face the meadow where she knew Koda was tending the sheep, screaming at the top of her lungs, "Koda! Koda!" Returning to the two women, who were now frozen in place, Naomi stood watching the advance of a tall man with two children. She put an arm around Ruth, who bent forward and allowed the air that had been trapped in her lungs to escape with a scream.

Miriam turned to the two with widened eyes and then became the first to dare utter the names held tightly within the lips of all three women. "Evia! Daniel!"

Ruth and Naomi began running toward the man and two children. Catching sight of their mothers, both children ran into embraces they had feared they would never feel again.

Both Ruth and Naomi could barely see through the blurred vision of their tears, so neither recognized the stranger who stood between them. Miriam walked at her quickest pace with Koda's help and was the first to realize the tall man without a beard, wearing a robe half-stained with dried blood, was her first born son.

Ruth looked to the stranger to thank him for bringing her daughter and nephew home, but could only stare at the man with short hair and a beardless face. With a smile, he spoke directly to her, "Hello, Ruth."

"Tabor," she whispered, recognizing the voice of her husband before she could discern his face. "Tabor!" she said again, reaching one arm for her husband's neck, unable or unwilling to take both arms off Evia. Tabor's arms embraced Ruth and Evia, as the three clung to this precious reunion.

Koda left his mother where she stood to join his brother and family. Through tears of gratitude, he wrapped his arms around his son and wife who were locked in an embrace and offered a prayer from his heart, "Thank you, God! Though they are weak and thirst, and though their lips are bleeding through cracks blistered by the desert sun, they're alive. They are home, and they are alive."

Miriam stood frozen in the moment, covering her mouth with both hands, as she watched the families unite.

Storm flapped her mighty wings twice, slowing her descent to land on a high branch of the willow tree in front of the family home.

Ruth quickly began helping Evia change into her Jewish robe, while Miriam burned the thin smock used by Roman slaves. Before the sun had set, Evia's and Daniel's hunger and thirst had been fed and they both fell into a deep sleep.

Tabor struggled to stay awake, while Ruth wiped olive oil on his cracked lips and cleaned the infected wounds where the Roman arrow had passed. It was Miriam who first asked about the friend she had known since Tabor was very young, even though the answer was already clear. "Tabor, what happened to Saul?"

"Saul saved me, mother, *and* Evia and Daniel, and he made his peace with God. When he took his last breath, he was happier than I had ever known him."

Tabor slept all that night and the next day. Two days passed before he was able to talk about the details of the rescue. Neither Evia nor Daniel would ever fully disclose the events of their harrowing ordeal. What little they learned from Evia was enough to convince the adults that Daniel had done everything he could to protect his cousin.

When his strength returned, Tabor stepped outside his home, retrieved his shepherd's stick from where it leaned against the wall by the door, and recited the *Shema* as he did every day—but this time, the words carried meaning he had never before felt. "Hear, O Israel, the Lord our God, the Lord is One."

Soon, Tabor was up the hill and nearing the flock his brother was tending. When he was within earshot, Koda yelled to Tabor, "Are you well enough to work?"

Tabor didn't answer immediately. He approached and stood next to his brother, and they both watched Storm circling in a wide pattern high above, signaling no danger. The flock grazing on the hillside was larger than ever before, now that Saul's sheep were part of their herd, as both knew Saul would have wanted. The bandages Ruth regularly cleaned and changed nonetheless made it difficult for Tabor to raise his left arm, but his right arm easily rested on his brother's shoulders. Seemingly out of nowhere, he smiled and said, "I'm ready, Koda."

"You *must* stay near your home, though," Koda warned, "out of sight from anyone, until your beard grows."

"I am not going to cower in my home for fear someone will see me without a beard."

"Tabor. Hear me." Koda persisted. "Word has already spread from Jerusalem about a raid on Caesarea Maritima. The Romans are not stupid, Tabor. They know it was Jews who perpetrated the raid. We must assume they know from Saul's body that the Jews had cut their hair and shaved their beards. It is said that Pilate is furious, and is threatening to kill a thousand Jews if the marauders are not turned over to him—and *soon*."

"Caesar won't let him do that. Look, the tension around town will settle with time."

"Maybe. But there is fear all around that a Jew with short hair might find himself being captured and handed over to Pilate, along with his family."

Tabor paused and thought about Koda's warning.

"*Please*, Tabor. Stay here, out of sight for the next six months.

You saved our children and for that I am eternally grateful. Now let me protect you. I will bring you everything you need from Bethlehem. Fortunately, few knew about Saul outside of our family. If anyone asks about him, we will tell them he took his flock and relocated to the north."

Eventually, Tabor smiled and put his hand back on Koda's shoulder, "I will do as you say, Koda. Go with Miriam and your family back to Bethlehem. We should all appear as though our lives have been untouched by these Roman pigs."

Herod's entourage included twenty servants, eight of whom carried the King of Judea on a chair between two sturdy poles. The three senior advisors who accompanied him to Caesarea Maritima walked behind the servants. Before the palace gate opened, Herod covered his mouth to protect his senses from the smell of the two half-decayed bodies nailed to the large wooden gate—one, that of an incompetent Roman soldier and the other, that of an elderly Jewish man with short hair and no beard.

"Pontius Pilate," a Roman guard loudly announced to those gathered in the Hall of Justice, where the Roman Governor presided. "Provincial Governor of Judea and servant only to Caesar, I present King Herod Antipas."

Herod walked toward the chair where Pilate sat—several steps higher than Herod—and stood, but refused to kneel. "King Herod, I presume you know why I have summoned you?"

"I believe I do, Pilate. Something about a little skirmish you had here a couple of weeks back, I presume." Herod taunted the Roman Governor who he saw as a lower dignitary than Pilate tried to project.

Pilate well understood Caesar took favor with Herod and the Jewish people. Sitting high in his chair to increase his stature above Herod, Pilate said, "Now, you listen to me, Herod. As long as I am forced to govern this rancid cesspool on the outer corner of the Roman Empire, I *will* maintain order."

Herod stood silently, while Pilate held him in his gaze.

"I want the men who invaded my palace, killed my guards, and stole my property. These men *will* be brought to justice, where I will make a public example of them—in such a way that no Jew will ever again raise so much as an eyebrow to Rome. Caesar is angered by the report I sent him and he himself has instructed me to execute the raiders in any way I see fit. Do you understand my demands, Herod?"

"Perfectly, Pilate. But if the great Roman Governor of Judea cannot find these men, what am I, a mere Jew living in this rancid cesspool on the outskirts of the Roman Empire, to do?"

Infuriated, Pilate called out, "Guard! Escort this *Jew* from my sight and out of my palace!"

# CHAPTER 17



*Summer, A.D. 28*

"Grandmother?" Evia began, as she and Miriam walked the Bethlehem road toward the deep well, each carrying an empty clay pot. "Do you think I will ever have a husband?"

Miriam smiled as she considered Evia's words. "My—has my fifteen-year-old granddaughter grown from the little girl who used to chase lambs and wrestle young goats? Has she become a young woman, right before my eyes? Yes, Evia, of course you will have a husband one day."

Evia walked beside her grandmother, searching for the strength within to speak honestly of a matter she could never divulge, even to her own mother. Two years had passed since her capture. In her heart, she knew that every child in the room where she was enslaved those dreadful days in Caesarea Maritima, with the exception of Daniel and herself, was surely dead by now, or wishing to be so.

"Would a man take a woman as his wife, if her virginity cloth remained pure white?" Evia asked, while tears pooled in the corners of her eyes.

Miriam stopped walking, and set her water pot on the street. Taking Evia's pot from her and doing the same, she embraced her granddaughter tenderly. Together, the two wept, oblivious to the passersby who gawked and whispered behind their hands.

Stepping back just enough to look Evia in the eyes, with her arms still securely around her back, Miriam explained, "Hear me, Evia. What happened to you in the hands of those Roman animals was in no way your fault. Give your guilt and shame to God. He will take your burden from you, so that you may live the life He intended for you."

Evia wiped the tears from her cheeks. "But how, Grandmother? I cannot undo what has already been done."

"God will show you the way, my love. *And* with a little help from an old woman." Miriam smiled.

"Old woman?"

"Me, my dear." Miriam lifted her eyes to the sky for a brief moment and then continued, "When the night arrives for you to consummate your marriage, your mother will hand you a virginity cloth, as white as a newborn lamb. You will wave it high in the air for everyone to see. Then, just before you go inside with your new husband, you will hug me and I will hand you a second virginity cloth, red with fresh blood from the palm of my hand."

Evia backed away from her grandmother's embrace with her hand covering her mouth, looking side to side as though someone may have heard her grandmother's suggestion. "Isn't that deceitful, Grandmother? Isn't that lying to my husband?"

Miriam smiled at her granddaughter's innocence. "Evia, believe me, you will not be the first, nor will you be the last. There are many women, even in this town, who bare the scar across the palm of their hand from a time when they bled into a young bride's virginity cloth. Trust me, every heart has its secrets."

The two women embraced, and Miriam held tightly the young woman so cherished and beloved since the moment of her birth.

<hr>

At the well, as they drew water to fill their clay pots, both Miriam and Evia smiled at each other, realizing their relationship had moved into one of greater openness and trust.

Miriam looked at the faint scar in the palm of her left hand, then to her granddaughter pulling a rope to lift a water-filled bucket. In that moment, Evia became her mother, sixteen years earlier, drawing water from the very same well, where the young girl in love had confided in her shame.

*"Miriam," Ruth had begun nervously, breeching the matter that had weighed heavily on her youthful heart, "if I do not bleed for your*

*son on the night we lay together, will I be stoned in the morning?"*

*Miriam had studied the fear in the young girl's eyes before asking, "Ruth, have you been scarred?"*

*Unable to look Miriam in the eyes, she sat the bucket on the ledge surrounding the opening to the underground pool of water, "Twice before."*

*Miriam sat on the ledge and took Ruth's small, tender hand in hers. "Tell me, Ruth. I swear by all that is holy, I will carry your secret to the grave."*

*Ruth managed a forced smile before nodding to accept Miriam's promise. "When I sleep in the stables, I try my best to hide under hay or cover myself with animal blankets, anything to avoid notice from the men who come to the stable at night. More times than I can remember, I have been awakened by a man who knows I have no one to protect me."*

*Miriam gasped at the thought of the defenseless child, terrified in the dead of night.*

*"I have always been able to kick or scream to escape," Ruth continued, "except for twice. The first time, I was hit so hard that I lost consciousness. When I woke up, my clothes were torn and there was blood where he had entered me."*

*Miriam squeezed Ruth's hand, while tears fell from her own cheeks. "The second time was a Roman in the light of day. He took my arm in one hand and held my hair with the other, walking me through the streets until we were well outside the city. So many people saw, but no one stopped him."*

*Miriam stood and pulled Ruth into her arms. As she embraced the girl who was to become her daughter, she whispered in her ear, "On your wedding night, I will give you two virginity cloths. One will be as white as a newborn lamb, and the other wet with my own blood. When you wake the next morning, you will show your husband, and all who care to see, a blood-stained virginity cloth."*

*Ruth embraced the woman who was already more of a mother to her than her own ever was.*

"Grandmother—grandmother? I hear horses." Evia's observation brought Miriam back to the present as the distant sound of measured, deliberate horse hooves drew nearer.

Three soldiers on horseback approached at a slow and steady pace toward the center of town. Even though many women were near the well as the horsemen came closer, the lead rider spun his horse around until he found a man who was quickly walking out of sight. "You there!" he called to the villager in Aramaic.

The man stopped and turned to face the Roman without responding.

"Who is the village elder in this town called Bethlehem?"

The frightened villager looked from side to side to make sure he was the one being spoken to. "The Rabbi, sir—Rabbi Asher."

Evia nervously moved to hold Miriam's arm, instinctively frightened at the sight, or even the thought, of a Roman uniform.

The Roman removed his bronze helmet as a sign of trust and requested in an authoritative, yet nonthreatening tone, "Would you be so kind as to bring Rabbi Asher to me? I assure you, I mean him no harm."

The villager nodded and ran toward the rabbi's home.

Evia was not the only woman at the well that day who stared at the young soldier. Unlike any man she had seen before, Roman or Jew, this man looked like no other. His hair was lighter than the desert sand and longer than the style worn by most Romans. Without a single curl or wave, his hair moved easily with the wind. She moved cautiously behind Miriam, frightened by the Roman uniform yet focused on the man's peculiar features.

Peering over Miriam's shoulder, Evia's attention was focused on the eyes of this man; as blue as the sky and crystal clear as a mountain pool.

"Grandmother," Evia whispered, staring at what she saw as an oddity. "Is he a demon—or a messenger from God?"

"He's neither," Miriam responded as she turned and pulled Evia back toward the well where they would blend into the crowd. "He's a Roman. Nothing good can come from a Roman."

While Miriam struggled to coax her granddaughter to back up, the hood from Evia's mantle dropped from her hair, exposing her youthful appearance. In contrast to the fair-haired soldier, Evia's wavy black hair glistened under the afternoon sun.

As Evia watched the unhelmeted man on horseback from a safe distance, his two companions took notice of her.

Within moments, Rabbi Asher arrived on the scene, walking behind the villager who was dispatched to retrieve him. Even though he was one of the oldest men in town, and certainly one of the heaviest, the rabbi still managed a decent pace as he approached the men on horseback near the well.

As the lead horseman dismounted, meant as a sign of trust, he motioned to his guards, who were tasked with his protection, to do the same.

"Yes, yes, I am Rabbi Asher," the rabbi said, pausing to maintain a reasonable distance between himself and the Romans.

"Rabbi, my name is Thaddeus," the soldier began. "I am an architect and translator on assignment from Rome."

The crowd gathered in a half-circle to hear the young Roman, with the rabbi and Thaddeus facing one another in the center. Thaddeus turned to address the entire crowd, not solely the rabbi, and with raised voice, continued, "I bring you good news from the Great Caesar."

As the crowd tightened to hear the announcement from Rome, the two guards, Cyrus and Kennan, began circling behind the crowd toward Miriam and Evia, much as wolves do when stalking their prey in a herd of sheep.

"The money you pay Rome in taxes," Thaddeus yelled, "is being returned to you in the form of roads and water."

"We already *have* roads and water," replied a faceless voice of dissent from the crowd. "Give us our money back and we'll call it even."

Thaddeus smiled at the heckler and responded to the entire crowd, "Rome is going to build a road paved with stone from Bethlehem to Jerusalem, exactly as we have done for other towns and villages. Clean water will be brought to you in Roman aqueducts."

"No doubt built on the backs of Jewish slaves, with Jewish blood to mix their mortar," hollered back a different voice.

Evia watched the young soldier with fascination, less interested in what he had to say than how he said it. Every challenge to the soldier's speech was returned with a smile and ever more reassuring response.

"To the contrary," Thaddeus replied loudly. "Rome will hire every man who wants to work, paying a fair wage along with a midday meal."

Evia felt a forceful pull on her arm, as Kennan tugged her backwards before wrapping his hand around her waist and covering her mouth with the other.

Miriam screamed, because Evia could not, frantically trying to pull the soldier's arm from her granddaughter. Cyrus, easily twice the size of either of the women, knocked Miriam to the ground with a single shove to her shoulder.

Those nearest the commotion watched, but did not step forward to fight or defend her for fear of retaliation from a Roman sword or dagger.

When Thaddeus noticed the crowd's attention drift from him to the ruckus near the well, he stopped speaking and rushed to see why the crowd had circled his two guards. When he saw the old woman on the ground and the young girl terrified in the soldier's clutch, he stepped forward three paces and slammed his fist against Cyrus's face, delivering a loud crack to the man's jawbone, followed instantly by a spray of blood and two teeth.

Kennan, whose arms were wrapped around Evia, held her now more as a shield. Thaddeus pulled his sword from its sheath and angrily uttered a single command in Greek. Knowing better than to challenge an officer in combat—for such an act was punishable by death—the soldier released the girl and lifted both hands to show he was not making a move to pull his own weapons. Thaddeus held his sword intently at the soldiers in a threatening pose, until they returned to their horses and began walking them out of town.

Thaddeus returned his sword to its sheath and immediately knelt next to Miriam who was clutched in Evia's embrace.

"This is what our taxes buy us," a man from the crowd yelled. "We pay Rome to rape and pillage. Don't do us any more favors, Roman!"

Without his guards to protect him, Thaddeus was vulnerable to the temperament of the crowd, yet he remained vigilant in caring for the two women. "Are you hurt?" he asked first of Miriam, as he and Evia helped her to her feet.

"I—I'm not hurt," she responded, more shocked by the gesture of kindness from a Roman than the aggression of the two guards.

"And you?" he said, turning his attention to Evia. "Are you harmed?"

Evia looked into the deep blue waters of the Roman's eyes. The sincerity of his kindness was unmistakable, but within Evia exploded a flood of emotions as the memory of being forcibly held in a Roman soldier's grasp returned her to the last Passover she attended in Jerusalem when two soldiers had captured her and Daniel. The horrific visions of her captivity rose up and tortured her mind, terrifying her into believing she was once again captured.

In sheer terror, Evia screamed as she turned away from the handsome soldier. In a panic, she stood and ran, struggling to stay on her feet, through the streets of Bethlehem toward the home Miriam shared with Koda and his family.

Miriam stayed at the well as she watched Evia flee to safety.

With the skirmish now over, the crowd dispersed, leaving Thaddeus and Miriam, who were eventually joined by Rabbi Asher. "I am very sorry for what my men did, Rabbi," Thaddeus said. "I assure you, they will be punished when I return to Jerusalem."

"This is why there can never be peace between Rome and Judea," Rabbi Asher replied, lecturing the young Roman officer. "We have no rights under Roman law. We don't even have the right to exist. We are less than beasts of burden in the eyes of Rome."

Thaddeus had no defense to Rabbi Asher's accusations, and so remained silent as the rabbi turned to walk away.

Thaddeus and Miriam stood alone, as he said once again, "I am truly sorry for what happened to you and your daughter."

Miriam pulled her headdress forward to cover her neck before responding, "She's my granddaughter, and I accept your apology."

"Would it be possible for me to apologize to your granddaughter, as well?"

Miriam considered his offer before shaking her head and replying, "I don't think that would be wise. She..." Miriam thought carefully about what or how much to say. "My granddaughter is terrified of Rome. The sight of a Roman uniform such as yours is more than she can bear." Without another word, she lifted both water jugs and turned to walk back in the direction of her home.

Miriam walked into Koda's home and sat both water jugs on the floor. Koda and Daniel were tending the herd, but Naomi greeted her at the door with a kiss on her cheek. Speaking softly, Naomi motioned to Evia, who was crouched in a corner of the room with her arms wrapped around her knees, staring ahead with a blank expression. "She came running in here about an hour ago and has been like that ever since."

"I know," Miriam responded.

"What happened?"

"I'll tell you later." Miriam walked across the room and knelt next to her granddaughter. Whispering back to Naomi, she said, "For now, I need to speak with Evia."

Taking the girl's hand in hers, Miriam said, "Evia, everything is fine now. We're safe. No one is going to harm you."

Naomi kept her distance with her hand covering her mouth, wondering what dreadful thing had happened to  cause her niece to tremble with such fear.

Evia continued staring at the door, but finally managed to ask, "Are they gone?"

Relieved to hear Evia speak, Miriam squeezed her hand and simply said, "They're gone."

Evia turned her head as if in a trance, to look into Miriam's eyes. "I want to go home, now. I don't feel safe here. My father isn't here to protect me. Storm isn't here to watch over me. I don't feel safe without them."

Miriam nodded. "I know, my dear. I'll take you home. Please, come sit at the table and drink some water first."

Miriam held her granddaughter's hand firmly, as she helped her stand and move to a chair at the table. While Evia sipped fresh water from a cup, Miriam stood near Naomi and said, "I'm going to take her home, and probably stay with Tabor and Ruth for a few days. I think I need to be with Evia until she's feeling better."

Still unclear of the details, Naomi asked, "Do you think she will eventually be well?"

"Yes, I believe so."

Naomi hugged her niece as she left with Miriam. "Safe journey, Evia. God is with you."

As they stepped from Koda's home out onto the streets of Bethlehem, Miriam hesitated a moment, but then said, "Evia, there is someone I want you to meet. Will you trust me?"

Evia reached her arm around her grandmother's and said, "I trust you."

Together they walked arm-in-arm through the streets, past the vendor stands and through the crowds. "Sometimes," Miriam began, "things aren't as they first appear."

"What do you mean?"

"I mean, sometimes," Miriam continued, as they approached the well, "you realize someone you thought you could trust is a wolf in sheep's clothes."

The pair walked toward a man who stood next to the well, where only two hours earlier, they were both assaulted by Roman soldiers. The man, whose head was covered, wore a white mantle with two maroon vertical stripes.

"And sometimes," Miriam added, as she delicately squeezed Evia's arm, "you realize someone you feared, was really a sheep in wolf's clothes."

Gently, the man began to speak, turning to face the women. "Hear, O Israel, the Lord our God, the Lord is One." While he spoke, he pulled the headdress of his mantle, revealing hair the color of desert sand and eyes as blue as the morning sky.

Evia froze, as she stared at the man. "The *Shema*," she whispered.

# CHAPTER 18

*Summer, A.D. 28*

Evia watched Storm circling high overhead, as she and Miriam approached the path at the foot of the hill leading to Tabor's home. From the pattern Storm flew, she knew their imminent arrival was being announced to her parents, well before they could see her.

When the two walked through the open front door. Ruth kissed Miriam's cheek first, then Evia's. "I'm glad you're home, Evia," she said to her daughter, "but I thought you wanted to stay with Miriam all week."

Miriam leaned over and kissed Tabor—who was seated at the table—as did Evia, before sitting down and settling in. In reply, Evia blurted out, "Something happened while I was in Bethlehem."

Ruth looked quickly to Tabor and then back to Evia before asking, "Something good or something bad?"

Miriam patted the empty chair next to her, indicating to Ruth she might want to sit down before Evia began telling her story.

Evia recanted that day's events, describing especially clearly the Roman architect who had ridden into town with two of his soldiers, all on horseback. Miriam filled in the details about Rome's plan to build roads paved with stone and aqueducts to bring fresh water. Evia was afraid to tell the details of the attack, so Miriam explained what happened without getting too graphic. When she hesitated to continue,

Evia finished by telling of the heroic act of the Roman architect who came to their defense and promised swift punishment of the two guards who had attacked them.

"Romans!" Tabor yelled, stepping away from the table, picking up a grinding stone and repeatedly pounding it against a larger stone of the wall. "Why won't they leave us in peace?"

Ruth laid the palm of her hand against Evia's cheek, and the other hand on Miriam's arm, scanning them both before asking, "Are you alright? Were either of you harmed?"

"We're fine, Mama," Evia said. "But there's more I must tell you."

Tabor dropped the stone and moved closer to his daughter. Looking down at his hand, he realized he had smashed a finger between the stones. The finger started to throb, as blood began oozing from under his fingernail.

"Tabor," Ruth said, concerned her husband's anger might lead him toward thoughts of vengeance, "please, come sit with us. Evia has more to tell."

When Tabor was seated, Evia continued, "The Roman architect's name is Thaddeus. He is Immunes, which means he holds special status and does not fight or kill Jews. He was quite angered by what his soldiers did, and asked Grandmother if he could apologize to me."

Miriam said, "Evia had run back to Koda's home, so Thaddeus talked with me as I walked. I told him he could not meet Evia wearing a Roman uniform, so he bought some proper clothing and dressed like a Jew. I agreed to arrange a meeting with him and Evia in the public square *on the condition* he would back away, never to return if Evia was not comfortable with him."

"If he had been caught without his uniform on, he could have been executed," Evia added. "He risked his life, simply to apologize for what his soldiers had done to us."

"Good!" Tabor replied. "So we will put this behind us and thank God nothing worse came of it."

"But Papa, there's more." Evia announced. "Thaddeus and I talked, all afternoon, with Grandmother nearby, of course."

Ruth patted Miriam's hand to thank her for keeping a watchful eye.

"He is *nothing* like any of the other Romans," Evia explained. "He doesn't even look like them. He asked if he could see me again and I told him..."

"*I* told him," Miriam interrupted, "that we would need her father's permission first."

"No!" Tabor shouted as he stood, unable to keep his seat for even a single moment. "Absolutely not. You will never see this *Roman* again."

"But Papa! Thaddeus is *not* a Roman. At least, not like the *others*."

"How could he not be a Roman if he wears a Roman uniform?" Tabor snapped back.

"He's Jewish!" Evia shouted. Tears filled her eyes, as she saw her father pulling away, ignoring her plea for him to understand. "That is, he's half-Jewish. His mother was Jewish and his father was a Roman slave, captured from a Nordic tribe before Thaddeus was born. So he was born a slave to parents who were Roman slaves."

"He wears the Roman uniform!" Tabor countered. "He commands Roman soldiers. He sounds like a Roman to *me*."

Seeing Evia's dismay, Miriam said, "Tabor, he wears the Roman uniform because children of Roman slaves can serve ten years in the military to buy their freedom. Believe me, I would not have allowed him to talk to Evia if I did not trust who he is."

"Better to die a slave than to live as a Roman." Turning his back on the three women, he walked out the door and left to tend his sheep, shouting, "This matter is closed! I have made my decision. We will never speak of this Roman again."

"Papa!" Evia's sobs fell onto her mother's shoulder. With the yelling now stopped, Ruth began caressing her daughter's head. "Evia, this is too much for your father to handle all at once."

Miriam added, "Tabor protects us and cares for us. He can no more give his daughter to a Roman than he can give one of his sheep to a wolf. If his mother, wife and daughter can't reach inside of him and pull out the good heart we all know is there, then we will simply have to be patient—and persistent."

Evia wiped her tears and looked at her mother on one side and grandmother on the other. "Then you both think I'm right?"

Ruth smiled and ran her fingers through her daughter's hair. "We must always honor your father's decision—but after he's had time to calm down, he may be willing to look at what's in your heart. I watched your eyes light up when you were telling us about Thaddeus, and I saw a glow in you I have not seen for years. In time, your father will see it, too."

<hr>

Few words were spoken in Tabor's presence for over a week. The women went about their work, carefully obeying his edict to remain silent in regards to the Roman who captured his daughter's heart. The air was thick with tension and eyes quickly dropped to the ground when he passed nearby.

Tabor was slow to return home one evening. As he approached the front door, he thought, *I cannot bear the thought of Evia in the arms of a Roman, but if they persist, what chance have I against the will of three women?* After dinner, silence once again dominated the evening conversation. Tabor had decreed the subject closed and off limits. None of the women wished to anger him further, or worse, to hurt him. So they waited.

Tabor sat outside by the fire, listening to the sounds of the night, sliding the bronze blade of his dagger along the shaft of a wooden stick. Content to be silent, even with the three women present, he sat with them beneath the stars, carving off slender fibers of wood that curled before dropping to the ground. Every stroke made the shaft smoother and straighter. After carving one end into a point, he hardened it in the fire, exactly as Saul had taught him so many years before.

Around the same fire, the three women patiently watched him carve, each of them on the alert for a sign.

Without looking up from his work, he finally broke the silence. "You think this Roman saved your life—don't you."

Evia looked at her mother, who motioned her head toward Tabor, indicating it was time to answer. "Well, he didn't break into a heavily armed palace and take on a good portion of the Roman army, like the man I will always love above all others, but he *did* knock the teeth out of the Roman who pushed Grandmother to the ground."

Miriam looked across the fire to make eye contact with Ruth. Both women gently nodded their approval of Evia's response. Silence returned to the evening fire, broken only by crackling embers, which launched sparks into the starlit sky.

Miriam's seniority gave her the fortitude to reminisce aloud, "Ruth, did I ever tell you what I did the first time Tabor told me about you?"

Ruth pretended she hadn't, merely to hear it once again. "No, I don't believe you did, Miriam."

"I was sitting in this very spot," Miriam began. "And it was a night, not unlike this one. I listened as Tabor told his father about a young, homeless girl with no family, living on scraps and sleeping with the animals. I swarmed in on him like a field of locusts and forbid him from ever seeing that girl again."

"However, his father thought differently and decided we would meet this girl before making any decision. So, after a rough start, his father and I fell in love with this homeless girl with no family, and we *became* her family. One year later, she rewarded us with the most beautiful granddaughter I could have ever dreamt."

Evia took Miriam's hand in hers, while Tabor quietly ignored them. Turning suddenly toward his mother, he said, "It's not the same, and you know it. Ruth was not part of an army that wanted to enslave or kill your family."

The distant call of a wolf reminded Tabor he needed to relieve Koda from watching the herd. After standing and leaning the sharpened shaft against the stone wall, he turned to face the quiet women and said, "If God had intended for Romans and Jews to live together in peace, He would have told Moses to deliver the Commandments to the Romans, too. But He didn't! He chose our people for a reason."

If Tabor expected an argument from any of the women, he was surely disappointed, as all three offered only their silent attention.

"If a lion pretends to be friends with a lamb, it is only so he can eat the lamb when he is hungry."

The tender, tearful eyes of his daughter reflected the dancing flames of the fire between them. Tabor struggled to find the words that would end the one-sided discussion. He had every intention of holding fast to his earlier decision, but found himself instead saying, "If I grant you my permission to see this Roman again, it must be on my terms—agreed?"

"Agreed, Papa," Evia replied, sitting up straight to show her respect and attention.

"You must never be alone with him. Miriam, Ruth, or Koda must be within sight of you at all times. Agreed?"

"Yes, Papa."

"He can never be near you wearing his Roman uniform, agreed?"

"Yes, Papa."

"You must never tell him anything about me other than my being a shepherd, agreed?"

"Yes, Papa."

"You must never bring him here or tell him where you live, agreed?"

"Yes, Papa."

"Most importantly, above all else, you must never, *ever*, mention anything that would lead him to suspect that you and I were in Caesarea Maritima. Agreed?"

"Oh Papa—agreed."

Tabor lifted his shepherd's stick from where it laid against the wall and said, "My sheep need me."

Evia stood and ran to her father, hugging him tightly and saying, "I will always need you, too, Father. Thank you for trusting me and giving me this chance."

Tabor kissed Evia on the top of her head and started to walk toward the darkness, but Miriam replaced Evia's embrace with her own, saying, "Your father would be so proud of you right now, as am I."

He kissed his mother on top of her head as well, and turned to walk toward the flock, when Ruth stepped in front of him to throw her arms around his neck and kiss him on his left cheek. "That is for your strong hands." Next, she kissed him on the right cheek and said, "That is for your soft heart." Then, after a tender kiss on his lips, she said, "And that is for the man I love."

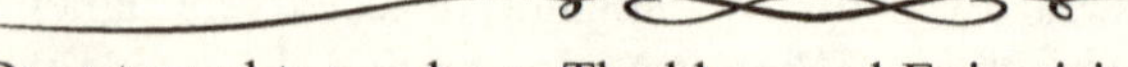

Days turned to weeks as Thaddeus and Evia visited with one another on the public streets of Bethlehem, always in the mindful presence of a member of her family. When work began on the road and aqueduct though, Thaddeus wore his uniform while directing the construction efforts. On these days, Evia was nowhere to be seen.

When weeks turned to months, the topic of a formal commitment naturally arose.

Early one morning, after milking the goats, Evia said, "Papa, I have followed your terms regarding Thaddeus for the past six months without ever breaking my promise."

Tabor finished tying a bundle of wool, turned to his daughter and replied, "And?"

"*And* I have a favor to ask of you, which you may consider against our agreement."

"So, what is this favor?"

"Thaddeus is being recalled to Rome. He has been ordered to design the new residence of the governor. My favor is his request to meet you before he leaves."

"If he leaves, then there is no reason for us to meet."

"*Please*, Papa?"

Tabor shook his head and sighed, staring at his daughter, who was quickly becoming a woman before his eyes. "On *my* terms."

"Oh Papa! Thank you. Yes, anything you say."

"I will meet him the day after tomorrow, one hour before sunset, south of Bethlehem, near the rock that looks like a snake's head. He must come alone, without weapons or uniform."

"I will tell him, Papa, and he will be there."

As Tabor neared Snakehead Rock, he gave a short, loud whistle, followed by a long whistle that increased in pitch. Storm, who had been perched on his shoulder, leaned forward and extended her wings, pushing away from him to begin moving skyward. Soon, she found the currents that carried her aloft to where she could glide in a high search pattern and see the movements on the desert below for a great distance.

With smoldering coals carried from his home, Tabor started a fire on the desert floor, burning a stack of dried brush he'd gathered along the way. Not long after he'd gotten the fire going, he saw a man walking through the desert in his direction. Sitting on his mat by the fire, he waited motionless while the man approached.

"Peace be with you, Tabor of Bethlehem," the man called out from a distance. Tabor immediately noticed he was wearing a traditional Judean mantle.

"And with you, Thaddeus. You came alone?"

"I did, indeed, with nothing but wishes of peace and God's blessings upon you and your family."

"Then sit with me by the fire."

Thaddeus unrolled a mat and sat facing Tabor on the other side of the small, but brightly burning fire. When the two men were seated, Tabor offered Thaddeus water and dried figs, which he graciously accepted.

"And for you, my friend," Thaddeus said, offering Tabor an intricately carved wooden bowl made by Roman craftsmen.

Tabor raised his hand with his palm facing Thaddeus, denying the gift. "I don't have any Roman friends."

Thaddeus set the bowl by his side and said, "Tabor, if there is anything you wish to know about me, you have only to ask."

"I already know all I care to know," he replied rudely. "What is it you wish of *me*?"

"Tabor, I fell in love with your daughter the first day I met her, and my love has strengthened every day since. As you know, I am being reassigned to Rome, and I would like to take Evia with me as my wife."

"How does Evia feel about your plans?"

"She said she would miss her family and home, but would be happy wherever we live."

"That's because Jewish women are taught to respect their husbands, unlike Roman women."

Thaddeus did not take the bait to enter an argument. Instead, he tried to distance himself from his Roman life, "Tabor, I am half-Jewish, but in my heart, I am a Jew. I have one and a half years of service left to Rome before I can buy my freedom. I promise you, as I have already promised Evia, when the time comes, we will relocate back to Jerusalem to spend the rest of our lives in Judea."

"Evia doesn't like Jerusalem—and neither do I," Tabor responded coldly.

"To Bethlehem, then. I promise you, we will return to Bethlehem once my terms are fulfilled with Rome and I am granted my freedom."

"There *is* something I want to ask you, Thaddeus. How did a Jewish slave become a Roman officer?"

"I was fortunate to be assigned as an assistant to one of Rome's top architects. I worked extremely hard serving him, and in return became his apprentice. When he died, there was really no choice other than to promote me, since no other man possessed his knowledge."

"So you serve the enemy of the people you claim to love?"

"I do not fight, though I am well prepared to defend myself. I have never killed a man and I have been able to use my rank to save the lives of many Jews."

Tabor studied the face of the fair-skinned Jewish Roman soldier who professed to love his daughter. Above Snakehead Rock, Storm flapped her wings to ease her descent to land. In the final moments of sunlight, both men paused and watched her silhouette, a majestic sight to behold.

An awkward silence lingered between them. Finally, Tabor said, "Thaddeus, I believe I understand what Evia sees in you. I have a tendency to judge people from the outside, which is why I have been so against her knowing a Roman. My daughter is more like her mother, and sees people from the inside. I believe I may have misjudged you."

Thaddeus held himself from replying, waiting respectfully for Tabor to continue, if he had more to say.

"I will not grant your request to marry Evia and take her to Rome. In my eyes, it would be as if I sold her into slavery. However, I will give you my word she will remain unwed for two years. If you return within that time, a free Jew without ties to Rome, I will grant you my blessing."

Thaddeus moved himself so as to sit more upright, saying, "But if I..."

Tabor shook his head, stopping the suitor's protest against an offer that was not negotiable. "Thaddeus, if you profess yourself a Jew, then honor Jewish customs. If you take Evia against my will, you bring shame to your family and mine. But if you honor my decision, you will be right in the eyes of God."

Thaddeus lowered his shoulders and took a deep breath before responding, "I will respect your decision, Tabor. I love Evia enough to wait ten years times two. I will be back in less than two years, standing before you a free Jew to ask for your daughter's hand in marriage."

Tabor smiled and looked at the intricately carved wooden bowl. "Now, I accept your gift, and am proud to say I have a Roman friend."

# CHAPTER 19



*Sunday, March 26, A.D. 30*

"He sent for me specifically?" Rabbi Asher asked the temple priest for the third time.

"We must hurry." was the priest's reply, being a younger man who was flustered that the rabbi's age and weight made him as slow as an old donkey.

Rabbi Asher stood in place at the bottom of the mountain of steps leading to the great temple in the heart of Jerusalem. *This climb is certainly daunting*, he thought, yet all around him, men his age and older climbed and descended in constant motion.

With his walking stick leading the way, the rabbi—with the priest by his side—progressed one step at a time, pausing frequently for the old man to slow his breathing. Midway up the second tier, the priest himself stopped and said, "We wait here."

Descending the steps, an entourage of five priests, all adorned identically in black robes, approached the pair. Two of the priests walked past them on their left, and two passed on their right. The fifth stopped two steps higher than where the rabbi stood.

"Rabbi Asher," Chief Priest Joseph Caiaphas began, "I have asked you here to discuss a matter of great importance."

"Me, o' Great Caiaphas? I am but a humble teacher from

Bethlehem. There are many, more qualified than me, to serve you right here in Jerusalem. How can I serve one so holy as yourself?"

"Walk with me," Caiaphas responded, seeking privacy on the steps to the great temple. "Rabbi, I am told the man who led the raid on Caesarea Maritima four years ago may have taken up residence in your little town."

"With all due respect, I have no knowledge of this man of whom you speak. And if I did..."

Caiaphas raised his hand to interrupt. "Rabbi, I am not on a quest to destroy this man. To the contrary, I seek a man of such talents for a matter of extreme importance to the future of Israel. Please, Rabbi, return to Bethlehem and bring the man to me. No harm will come to him—*or* you, for that matter."

Suddenly, Caiaphas stopped walking and turned to face the elderly teacher, "Rabbi, my need is urgent and my intentions honorable."

Bowing to the priest as he turned to leave, Rabbi Asher replied, "I will do my best, Chief Priest."

---

Ruth pounded the soap-root into a white froth on the rocks at the edge of the stream, cleaning weeks of sand and sweat from Tabor's clothing. She pushed her husband's woolen mantle back and forth with both hands over the coarse sandstone, while a ribbon of white suds meandered along the cool creek water. Her focus on the laundry and the babbling sounds of the stream kept her from noticing a man approaching. "Hello, Ruth, how is God treating you this day?"

Ruth turned to the man's voice. "Rabbi Asher! What a nice surprise."

Realizing quickly that her head was uncovered, she pulled the hood from her mantle over her hair and dried her hands on her robe, before reaching both hands to grasp the rabbi's fingers. "What brings you so far from Bethlehem, Rabbi?"

"Shepherds aren't the only ones who must count their flock," he responded in a cheerful voice. "Rabbis travel great distances to find their lost sheep, as does your husband."

Ruth smiled and nodded, waiting for him to explain.

"Tell me, Ruth, is Tabor nearby? I have a serious matter to discuss with him."

"Oh yes, Rabbi, yes. Please come to our home and I will find him." Ruth started to gather the wet clothes from the bank of the creek, but decided instead to leave the bundle for later, so she could walk the rabbi up the hill to her home.

When seventeen-year-old Evia saw her mother walking with the old man, slowly ascending the well-worn path up the hill, her shyness pushed her back into the shadows of the doorway to their home. As they approached the entrance, Ruth called out, "Evia!" knowing her daughter was there. "Go find your father and bring him home. Tell him Rabbi Asher has come to visit and needs to speak with him."

Without pausing to politely greet the rabbi, Evia ran past her mother toward the hill where she knew her father had moved the flock. As she quickly closed the distance to him, she yelled, "Papa! Papa!" Breathless when she finally reached him, she steadied herself by holding his arm, unable to complete a sentence.

"Evia, what brings you running out here like a frightened rabbit?"

"Mama sent me for you. Rabbi Asher is with her in our home and wants to speak with you."

"Rabbi Asher?"

Evia nodded her head. "Yes, Papa. I hope no one is ill. I hope no one has died."

Tabor smiled to reassure his daughter. "No, I'm sure he simply came to lecture me for tending my sheep on the Sabbath again. For some reason, he thinks sheep should rest on the Sabbath, just like everyone else."

With a sigh of exasperation, Tabor relented. "I suppose he will not leave until he gets what he wants, so I may as well go see the good rabbi." Handing his shepherd stick to Evia, he instructed her, "Evia, watch the flock until I get back."

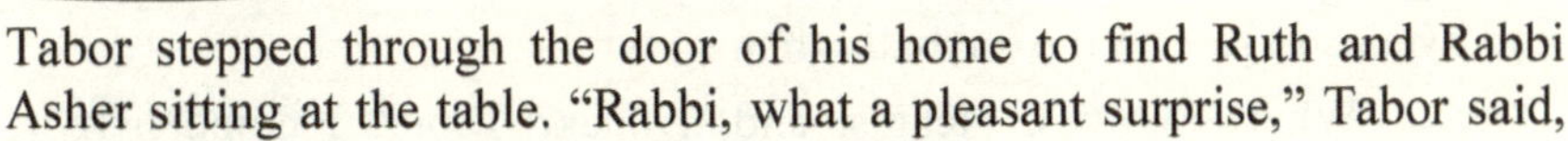

Tabor stepped through the door of his home to find Ruth and Rabbi Asher sitting at the table. "Rabbi, what a pleasant surprise," Tabor said, grasping the rabbi's right hand with both of his.

Gesturing to the vacant chair, the rabbi welcomed him to sit. "Greetings, Tabor. Please, sit with us. I have news for you, such wonderful news."

Tabor sat down at the table, casting a glance to Ruth, who he could tell was unable to offer any explanation as to what the Rabbi's news might be.

"Yes, Rabbi? What is it?"

The old rabbi who had performed Tabor's circumcision as an infant, married him and Ruth, and blessed the birth of Evia, was not about to jump directly to the point of his visit. "I tell you, the world is changing all around us. A man can't feel safe in his own home anymore."

"Are you hurt, Rabbi?" Ruth asked. "Did someone harm you?"

"No, no, no, Ruth, I'm fine," the rabbi said, reaching across the table to pat her hand to thank her for being concerned.

"The Romans," he continued, "they ride through our villages, take our animals, and tax our people."

"Have the Romans hurt someone, Rabbi?" Tabor asked, trying to decipher the Rabbi's message.

"No, no, no, Tabor, everyone is fine."

"Then what is it, Rabbi?" Tabor asked, slightly annoyed.

"Israel is suffering, Tabor. God freed us from slavery and bondage in Egypt and led our people to this land. But still, we suffer." Leaning forward to emphasize his point, he lowered his voice as though he might be overheard. "I tell you truthfully, Tabor, we have never known freedom."

Tabor looked over at Ruth, who tried her best to keep from laughing. "But Rabbi Asher, you said a moment ago you had good news, yet all I've heard so far is about pain and suffering. What is the good news, Rabbi?"

"Ah, yes, yes, Tabor, I must tell you very few men have an opportunity in their lives to do something great. We're born, we work, and we die. What decides whether or not that life was a good one or a bad one is how well we serve our God while we are here."

"Rabbi," Tabor asked, "is this about me herding my sheep on the Sabbath again? As I said before, when you can get the wolves, jackals and hyenas to rest on the Sabbath, then so will I."

"What? Wolves, jackals, and hyenas? Tabor, I come here to discuss something with you of great importance to Israel, and you want to talk about wolves, jackals and hyenas?"

"I'm sorry, Rabbi. Please, continue."

"Wolves, jackals, and hyenas," he repeated. "No, Tabor, I'm talking about Caiaphas, the chief priest."

"Has Caiaphas been hurt?" Ruth asked, trying to link the rabbi's messages together.

"No, no, no, God forbid," the rabbi responded, again patting

Ruth's hand in appreciation for her concern. Turning toward Tabor, he said, "No, it's you, Tabor. Caiaphas wants you."

Tabor nervously leaned back in his chair, as a wave of dread rushed over him. "Rabbi, why would Caiaphas want *me*? What could he want with a poor shepherd? How would he even *know* of me?"

"I returned from Jerusalem two days ago, after being summoned to the temple by Caiaphas himself. He specifically asked for me, Tabor. And he wants me to return to Jerusalem with *you*."

Looking at Ruth, who shared his fear of discovery, Tabor turned back to the rabbi and pointedly asked, "But why *me*? Why did Caiaphas *specifically* ask for *me*?"

"Caiaphas is seeking the man who raided the palace in Caesarea Maritima, back four years ago. I may be an old rabbi, Tabor, but I am not so blind that I didn't notice Saul's disappearance at the same time as word spread about the raid."

At these words, Tabor stood quickly, knocking his chair over behind him. A twinge of pain in the old arrow wound on his left shoulder caused him to wince. "No, Rabbi, you have the wrong man. I am not the man he seeks."

Ruth stood to be next to Tabor, wrapping an arm around his waist for fear he could be taken from her again.

"Please, please, sit, both of you," Rabbi Asher requested. "You don't kick your dog when it is barking at a wolf. Caiaphas is not interested in hurting you. If he was, would he send an old man like me to find you? He has many temple guards, if he wanted to capture you, Tabor. Caiaphas only wants to speak with you. He believes you can help him."

Sitting back at the table after picking up his chair, Tabor asked in a cautious voice, "Help him do what, Rabbi?"

"I don't know, Tabor. He wouldn't tell me. But I tell you this, his need for you is larger than us. I could see fear in his eyes and he believes you are the man he needs."

Tabor drew in his breath, while Ruth could not contain the tears pooling in her eyes. Letting out a long sigh, Tabor relented, saying, "Alright, Rabbi, I will go with you to Jerusalem. I will meet with Caiaphas."

# CHAPTER 20

*Wednesday, March 29, A.D. 30*

Tabor centered the faded wool blanket on the back of his donkey by the pen in front of his home. As Koda approached, he turned to his younger brother and said, "Watch over Ruth and Evia while I'm away, Evia will help you with the flock. She's becoming quite a shepherd in her own right."

"I will, Tabor," Koda replied, but with hesitation in his voice. "I still wish you would stay here, though. We could even relocate to another village where no one knows you. I have a bad feeling that if Caiaphas knows your name, then he knows more about your involvement in the raid than we realize."

"I would never do anything to risk bringing harm to our families, Koda, but as Rabbi Asher said, if Caiaphas wanted to hand me over to Pilate, he would have sent temple guards for me, not an old rabbi."

While Tabor continued securing water bags and food for several days' travel to the back of his donkey, Ruth stepped out of their home, followed immediately by Rabbi Asher.

The morning air was already warm and dry, as though readying the land for the scorching day ahead. "Thank you, Tabor, *and* Ruth," Rabbi Asher began, "for opening your home to a weary old rabbi."

Ruth smiled at the humble man and replied, "It is a blessing upon our home for a rabbi as kind as you to stay the night."

Greeting the elderly sage with a smile, Tabor said, "Come, Rabbi, you will ride, while the donkey and I walk."

"Yes, yes, yes, Tabor. But first a blessing for our trip," replied the rabbi, who took a few short steps toward the donkey, then rested a hand on its back. "Woe is me and my years."

Looking skyward, he began, "God of our fathers, God of Israel, guide and protect us on our journey. Give this donkey the strength it needs to carry this old teacher of your Word, and if it stumbles and falls, may I land in a field of clover. Amen."

Tabor opened his eyes, bowed slightly in thanks for the prayer, and then helped the rabbi up onto the back of the donkey. Ruth hugged Tabor and kissed him before saying, "I will never let you leave me again without a kiss." She ran her fingers through his thick beard and reminded him, "Try to hold onto your beard this time."

Tabor laughed and said, "I will. I promise. I should be back in two or three days."

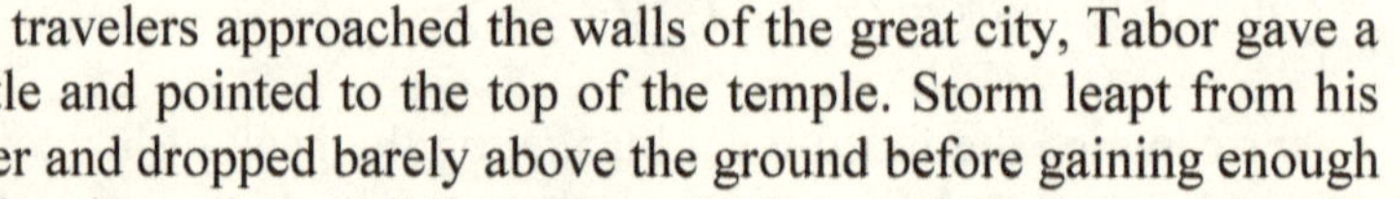

As the two travelers approached the walls of the great city, Tabor gave a short whistle and pointed to the top of the temple. Storm leapt from his left shoulder and dropped barely above the ground before gaining enough speed to flap her wings, gliding along higher and higher, eventually riding the noontime heat that reflected off the desert floor. The old rabbi watched in awe as the eagle flew directly to the highest spire above the largest dome, where she perched, looking as though she were a statue of great dignity and beauty.

Tabor passed through the southern gate entering Jerusalem, leading a donkey that carried Rabbi Asher as others passed on either side, all going about their own business. Throughout the city, Roman guards stood on street corners and in front of buildings, maintaining order and showing the strength of Caesar's rule.

Helping the rabbi down from the back of the donkey, Tabor turned around and tied it to a post near the bottom of the steps that led to the temple. "Let me do the talking," Rabbi Asher told Tabor, as they approached a temple priest near the first step.

"Rabbi Asher of Bethlehem to see Caiaphas," the normally talkative rabbi said in a concise business tone.

The priest looked at him and quickly turned his attention to Tabor, who wore a dusty robe and sheepskin vest. "And who is this *shepherd*, who smells of sheep dung?"

"This is Tabor of Bethlehem. We were both summoned by Caiaphas."

After another moment of studying Tabor, the priest said, "Follow me." Instead of proceeding up the steps toward the temple, they were led around the side into a room with a pool of water.

"The shepherd will need to bathe and put on a clean robe and sandals." Motioning toward several white robes that hung from nails on the wall, the priest added, "You will be able to retrieve your clothes when you leave. Wait here until I return."

Tabor did as he was instructed, somewhat embarrassed, but not surprised, for being singled out for his appearance. Every Passover he had attended in Jerusalem had begun much the same, but with public baths outside the city walls.

As promised, the priest shortly returned to the bath house and, after a quick inspection of Tabor's dress and somewhat less offensive aroma, again said, "Follow me."

After walking up the first flight of stairs toward the temple, the priest approached another priest dressed in an identical black robe and cap. The two exchanged a few words. The first priest then started down the stairs without acknowledging the visitors, and the second priest, looking them over, said, "This way, Rabbi."

After climbing the remaining stairs, they were led to an intricately carved wooden door and handed off to a priest and two temple guards, who led them through a massive room.

Tabor was in awe, as he tried to absorb the majesty of the carvings and paintings within the inner maze of the great temple—a site few, if any, shepherds had ever witnessed.

Down a side corridor, they were taken into a chamber, which had pillows strewn against two walls for reclining and a table that was generously prepared with food, water, and wine.

"Please relax and eat," the priest requested. "Someone will be with you soon. The guards will be outside your door should you require anything."

Before the door was closed, Tabor began picking through the food, sample tasting the wide variety of fruits, breads and meats, the likes of which he had never before experienced. "You see, Tabor? *Nothing to fear*. This is not the way prisoners would be treated," Rabbi Asher assured him.

"I have never seen such bounty," Tabor replied. "Caiaphas lives like a king on the sweat and taxes of his flock."

Several minutes later, the priest reentered the room and said, "Rabbi, please come with me." Turning his attention to Tabor, he added, "You will remain here. Someone will take you to meet Caiaphas shortly."

Tabor looked at Rabbi Asher, concerned they were being separated. In response, the rabbi said, "Nothing to fear, Tabor. What Caiaphas wishes to talk to you about is a private matter. I will see you after your audience."

The priest said nothing to either confirm or deny the rabbi's assessment. He merely followed Rabbi Asher out of the room and closed the door behind him. Tabor continued eating the delicacies provided him, but his growing sense of apprehension raised his concern for the situation. Standing alone in a room protected by guards made him feel more like a trapped animal than a welcomed guest.

Silently, he waited. His sling and stones were with his clothes in the bath house. Storm waited on top of the highest spire above the great city. For what seemed like hours, he contemplated all the worst case scenarios he could imagine. If the door opened and Caiaphas entered, then all would be well. But if soldiers entered, he knew he was defenseless.

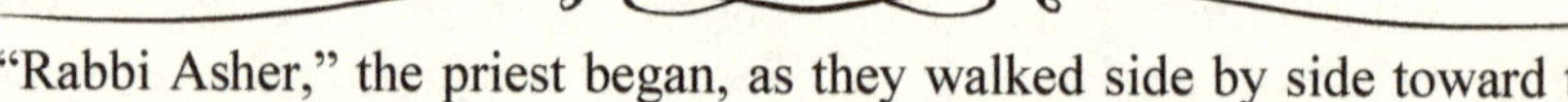

"Rabbi Asher," the priest began, as they walked side by side toward the entrance of the temple. "You will return to Bethlehem with your donkey. Tabor will remain here."

"No, no, no, that is not what I was told."

The priest stopped and said rather sternly, "Tabor of Bethlehem will remain here to serve Chief Priest Caiaphas, until such time that his services are no longer required. You will return to Bethlehem and speak to no one of this, beyond his family. For their sake, Tabor's sake, and Israel's sake, they *too* will also speak of this to no one. Do we understand one another?"

The rabbi nodded and began walking further ahead with the priest. Then *he* stopped and asked, "May I assure Tabor's family no harm will befall him?"

"You may tell his family that Caiaphas has need for Tabor, and that he will return to them in the glory of the Lord God Almighty."

From the top of the stairs leading to the temple courtyard, the priest watched as Rabbi Asher led the donkey toward the city gate.

Walking alone through the halls of the temple, a priest stopped at the door flanked by two temple guards. Opening the door, he spoke directly to the man who waited inside, "Tabor, follow me, please. I will escort you to the Chief Priest."

Tabor walked behind the priest through halls decorated with both carvings and murals depicting scenes of Jewish ancestry. Behind Tabor walked the two temple guards. At the end of the hallway was a large opening, sealed by two wooden doors. On either side of the great doors, two more guards stood.

The guards moved to open both doors as the priest approached. Tabor followed the priest into the large room, flanked closely by the two guards who were still escorting them. As the two doors closed behind them, the guards took positions on either side of the doors in the great room. The priest stopped in the center of the room, as did Tabor. "Chief Priest Caiaphas," the priest began, "I present to you Tabor of Bethlehem."

At first, Tabor did not see anyone else was in the room, but after the priest's presentation, he saw a heavy man with a white beard wearing a black robe and very tall headdress step out from behind a nook at the side of the room.

Tabor stood in an attitude of respect, bordering on reverence, realizing he was in the presence of the leader of his spiritual faith. Silently he stood behind the priest, as the two men waited for the Chief Priest to walk up three steps to a podium, where he sat on the tallest of five chairs.

Caiaphas motioned with both hands for the two men to be seated. Tabor followed the priest's lead by sitting on a pillow near the base of the podium.

After studying Tabor for a moment, he asked, "You are Tabor of Bethlehem?"

Tabor nodded and responded, "I am."

Caiaphas nodded slightly, but seemed subtly taken aback at Tabor's lack of formality.

The priest corrected Tabor in a subdued voice, "Your Holiness."

Tabor restated his response, "I am, Your Holiness."

Caiaphas nodded again, acknowledging he would overlook the shepherd's uneducated reply.

"Tell me about yourself, Tabor of Bethlehem."

"Your Holiness, I am Tabor, son of Jonas and son of Bethlehem. I am but a mere shepherd with a wife and daughter."

"Are you faithful to the God of Israel, Tabor, son of Jonas?"

"I am, Your Holiness."

Caiaphas paused, again studying the man before him. "You have put me in a very difficult position, Tabor of Bethlehem. For the past four years, I have had Herod and Pilate badgering me for the names of the men who invaded the palace at Caesarea Maritima. Sources who are faithful to me tell me that I am speaking to one of the men who Pilate seeks."

"Me, Your Holiness?"

Tabor suddenly felt his heart pounding so hard, the sound he heard seemed to echo from the walls with every passing beat. A sudden rush of nausea pushed beads of water through his skin in a quick cold sweat.

"I will not ask you to confess to this crime against Rome, but I do ask you to deny it if I am speaking to an innocent man."

With a moment to contemplate his response, Tabor replied, "I do not deny it, Your Holiness."

Caiaphas leaned back in his chair with a slight smile, satisfied that he was indeed speaking to one of the men who dared to carry out a midnight raid against Pilate. "Your secret is safe with me, Tabor of Bethlehem, provided you will keep my secret, as well."

"I do not know any such secret, Your Holiness, but I assure you, I would never betray you or the Temple," Tabor said, realizing his life continued only because Caiaphas had not divulged his name to the Roman occupiers.

Caiaphas leaned forward in his chair and spoke solemnly to Tabor. "Believe me, Tabor, I hate every Roman I see. I pray daily to God Almighty that he cast a plague on those Romans who set foot on Israeli soil. When I heard that Jews had successfully raided the Roman fortress, I thanked God for the men who were brave enough to attempt such a deed."

Lowering his voice, Caiaphas asked, "Tell me, Tabor, why would a small band of Jews raid a Roman stronghold?"

Tabor looked over to the priest who sat quietly next to him, before returning his attention back to Caiaphas. "Perhaps, Your Holiness, such men would kill Caesar himself, if necessary, to free their children from being used as Roman sex slaves."

Caiaphas stroked his beard, as he contemplated Tabor's response. Nodding his head, he replied, "Yes—I see. Yes, Tabor—indeed. So the 'property' Pilate keeps raving about being stolen from him was—Jewish children?"

"The father of children who were kidnapped from these very walls of the Holy City, during the week before Passover, would be a man who would risk his life to get them back."

"Here? In my city?" Caiaphas cried, distraught at the callousness of the Romans to kidnap Jewish children from within the walls of Jerusalem. "So you went to Caesarea Maritima and..." Caiaphas didn't finish the sentence that would have implicated Tabor. Instead, he contemplated the bold and daring rescue by a distraught father.

Turning to the priest seated next to Tabor, he shouted, "Do you see, Malachi? *This* is why I asked for this man to be brought to me. He has as much reason to hate the Romans as *I* do!"

# CHAPTER 21

*Friday, March 31, A.D. 30*

"What has become of Rabbi Asher?" Tabor asked Malachi, the temple high priest, as they walked together, escorted by the same two guards, back to the room that would serve as Tabor's chambers.

"The Rabbi has returned to Bethlehem with instructions to inform your family that Caiaphas has need of your services."

"What is this need? He never said what he wanted of me."

"He will tell you when he is ready, not a moment sooner or later. You are free to walk about the temple with the guards, Tabor, but please do not leave the temple. Your presence here must be kept secret from the Romans. Their soldiers move freely about the city, but they are forbidden from entering the temple."

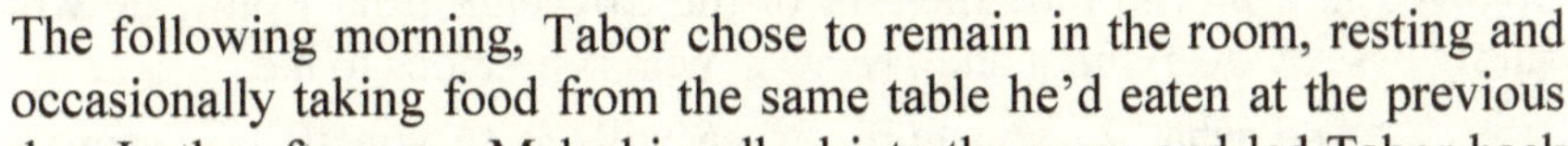

The following morning, Tabor chose to remain in the room, resting and occasionally taking food from the same table he'd eaten at the previous day. In the afternoon, Malachi walked into the room and led Tabor back to the large chamber where he'd first met Caiaphas.

"Tiberius Caesar desires more from Israel than our children," Caiaphas began, briefly glancing out a large window into the hot sunny sky. "He has a strong interest in our culture and is said to even respect our faith in God, as opposed to the Roman worship of many gods. As such, Caesar collects artifacts that belong to Israel. Herod is a Roman puppet, who lets Caesar deplete our heritage and resources. For the most part, I am powerless to stop the carnage—but from time to time, we manage to hide a precious artifact in a place the Romans will never find."

"Yes, Your Holiness," Tabor acknowledged.

"*Recently*," Caiaphas continued in a more agitated voice, "Caesar sent word through Pilate to Herod, *and now to me*, that I am to hand over the Ark of the Covenant. The audacity! The arrogance of Rome to claim the most beloved treasure of Israel! The very *cornerstone* of our faith. And to imagine that Herod would simply roll over the way he did. I am *alone* in my sanity!"

"But I was taught," Tabor replied, "the Babylonians took the Ark when they destroyed Solomon's Temple, *hundreds* of years ago."

"True, Tabor. By fabricating the demise of the Ark, we have protected it by hiding the Ark along with the jar of manna, a jar containing the holy anointing oil, and the rod of Aaron, *under this great temple*. But now Caesar's advisors have convinced him that the Ark is in Jerusalem. So once again, we must move the Ark of the Covenant and hide it from Rome's grasp."

"*This* is where I have need of you, Tabor. *This* is my secret I entrust to you the way I keep yours. I want you to lead and protect an expedition of my best guards and priests to safeguard the Ark of the Covenant. You must keep it from Roman hands at all costs."

"Your Holiness, I am but a simple shepherd. What chance have I against the will of Caesar?"

"I am not asking you to wage war with Rome, Tabor. I merely need you to lead my men through the wilderness, avoiding Roman eyes. In a few days, soldiers will come here to take the Ark in Caesar's name. To preserve the existence of Israel, they must not find it."

"I'm sorry, Your Holiness," Tabor responded. "I am not afraid for myself, but the risk to my family is too great. If Pilate discovers I am involved in a plot to hide the Ark of the Covenant from Rome, he will surely destroy everything and *everyone* who is precious to me."

"And what do you think Pilate will do to you if he discovers your involvement on the raid of his palace four years ago?"

Tabor hesitated, realizing he was being coerced by the Chief Priest. "You would hand me over to Pilate?"

"I would hand my own brother over to Pilate, if it meant keeping the Ark out of Roman hands," Caiaphas said bluntly. "For your service to the preservation of Israel, I will pay you thirty pieces of silver. Think about that, Tabor. That is more than a shepherd can earn in ten years."

"Keep your money, Chief Priest," Tabor replied, offended that Caiaphas would offer to buy his loyalty. "In return for my service, promise me you will guarantee the safety of my family until I return, or provide for them if I do not."

"You have my word, Tabor." Caiaphas eased himself into his chair before continuing, "Malachi has assembled a team of four priests, in addition to himself, to carry the Ark, along with six servants and fourteen of my most trusted guards. Including you, Tabor, the expedition will consist of twenty-five men. All twenty-five must take a vow to God that he will take the hiding place of the Ark to his grave. You leave tonight, under cover of darkness."

"Tabor, it is time," Malachi whispered as he opened the door to the room where Tabor slept.

"Good, the sooner we do this, the sooner I can get back to my home."

As the two men walked from the temple, only then did Malachi begin to reveal details of his plan to Tabor, telling him only what he needed to know. "Two days ago, shortly before you arrived here, we moved the Ark to a safe location near Bethany. We will travel in pairs, so as not to raise suspicion from the Romans."

"Give me a fast horse," Tabor suggested, "and a cart to carry the Ark, and I will have it secured in two days."

"Tabor, the Ark is not a box of trinkets. There are rules and rituals that govern the movement of the Ark. It can only be carried by priests who have been ordained to do so. It must never be opened, except by the Chief Priest, and only then under the strictest of sacrament."

Tabor proceeded to the bath house where his robe and sheepskin vest still hung. After dressing in his clothes and securing his sling, along with a pouch that held numerous stones and six short spears, Malachi handed him two iron daggers in sheaths, which he secured about his waist.

"Is that all you carry?" Malachi asked.

"I have one more weapon. I never find her, though. She finds me."

"She?"

"Yes, she," he smirked. "Temple priests aren't the *only* ones with secrets."

Within a few hours' walk from the walls of the great city, Tabor and Malachi approached the slow moving caravan, which was already in motion, traveling toward the morning sun, along with pack animals equipped with food, supplies and the mysterious, veiled container.

The two stopped alongside the road, as the caravan moved before them. "The Ark of the Covenant is contained within a wooden sarcophagus underneath the blue veil," Malachi explained to Tabor, pointing toward the large box-like structure suspended on two poles, resting on the shoulders of four priests. "The Ark is a chest ornately embossed with gold, designed and constructed to precise dimensions as given by Moses, and within the Ark are the Ten Commandments, etched in stone by the finger of God, delivered by Moses."

Tabor replied, "Three days ago, I was leading my sheep into the hills to find higher grazing. Today, I'm leading the Ark of the Covenant through the desert, exactly as Moses and Aaron once did." His tone of voice indicated the significance of his being involved with such an expedition was not lost upon him. As his eyes moved skyward, briefly looking for a sign of Storm, Tabor added, "Before today, it has all been words to me. Stories of heroic men in great battles. Conflict and triumph between man and God. That is, until now."

Tabor watched in awe as both man and beast walked past in two columns, none of which acknowledged him or Malachi. In this moment, as the Ark of the Covenant passed before him, Tabor saw and felt all of the ancient stories become as one—and for him, they were now real.

As he took his place near the front of the caravan, High Priest Malachi said, "Stay in front and lead us."

Drawing on the strength created by his previous encounter with Rome, Tabor nodded to Malachi and began walking to the front, gazing back to see the procession behind him, the priests surrounded by servants and temple guards, all of them walking in precise, tradition-bound formation.

For the next few hours, the two men walked separately, Tabor at the front and Malachi closer to the middle of the procession, just before the Ark. When the sun broke over the hills to the east, Tabor made his way back toward the caravan to talk with Malachi. Storm had returned and was now perched on Tabor's left shoulder, her head extending well above the top of his. "This is your secret weapon?" asked Malachi. "A hunting bird?"

"Storm is more than a hunter. She talks to me from high in the clouds, and shows me where predators are hiding."

"We're not driving a flock of sheep, Tabor."

"Romans are predators, too," Tabor snapped back. "When will you tell me our destination? It is hard for me to lead, when I don't know where we're going."

Malachi answered vaguely, "We're heading toward the Dead Sea. A vault in which the Ark will rest has already been prepared in a place so remote, not even the whispering winds will find it."

"That will take us five more *days* at this pace! Surely we could find a suitable hiding place sooner than that."

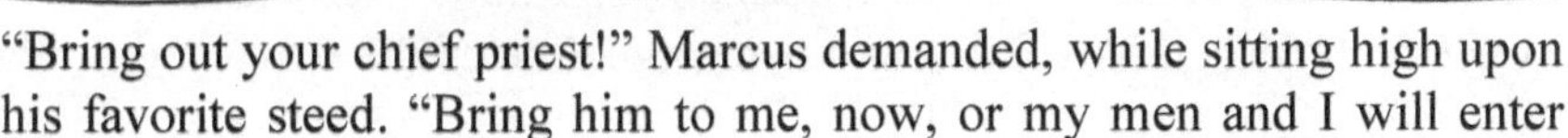

"Bring out your chief priest!" Marcus demanded, while sitting high upon his favorite steed. "Bring him to me, now, or my men and I will enter your temple!"

Political decorum demanded that Rome respect the sanctity of the Jewish temple in Jerusalem, but Pilate's new prefect was not known for his tolerance. A single warning was all he was ever willing to offer, before turning to force.

Sitting on his horse at the bottom of the temple steps, wearing full battle gear, Marcus's patience was thin by the time Chief Priest Caiaphas leisurely descended the stairs, two steps in front of six staff priests.

The priest walking directly behind Caiaphas spoke in a subdued voice, which only the priests could hear. "Six horsemen and twenty foot soldiers seems more like an attempt to wage battle than a man sent to retrieve what most Romans consider to be a Jewish box filled with ancient superstition."

"Caiaphas! You know why I have come." Marcus called out, as the Chief Priest continued his slow and methodical descent toward the Roman soldiers.

Caiaphas did not answer until he stopped seven steps from the bottom, which kept his head higher than that of Marcus. "No, Prefect, I do not know why you are here, or what gives you the right to interrupt our council meeting."

Lowering the spear he held with his right hand to point in the direction of the seven priests lined across the steps in front of his soldiers, Marcus shouted, "Don't toy with me, old priest. Bring out this Ark of yours. This temple, this city, and everything you have belongs to Caesar!"

Caiaphas raised his hands to calm the Roman soldier. "I know, I know—Caesar rules. But as I have told King Herod and Pontius Pilate, the Ark of the Covenant is not here. It was lost centuries ago. I don't know why rumors persist that it is hidden in this temple, but it simply isn't so."

"Herod has assured Pilate the Ark exists and is in this temple of yours!" Marcus hollered. "If you do not bring it to me in one hour, we will enter your precious temple and find it ourselves."

"Please, please, Prefect," Caiaphas protested. "There is no need for violence. If I had the Ark, I swear I would give it to you. It was probably melted into golden idols or jewelry, and the stone tablets most likely rest as paving stones in a Roman road built with the blood and sweat of Jewish slaves. I swear to you, the Ark of the Covenant is not here."

Undeterred by the priest's words, Marcus reiterated, "One hour!" Without the desire to debate the matter further, Marcus turned his horse and pointed his left hand to his left, and his right hand to his right. Immediately, the foot soldiers divided and ran in both directions to take positions around the temple, where they could watch all known exits.

In one hour's time, Marcus signaled his men to enter the temple. Every soldier had been briefed to look for a gold ornate box, about the size of a large rice basket.

"I protest such a gross infringement on the sovereignty of this temple!" Caiaphas yelled, as the impatient leader entered the temple behind his men. Marcus pushed Caiaphas aside, as though he was a street beggar who'd stepped in his path.

The temple guards who protected the entrances were easily cut down by the Roman soldiers, who'd been trained to do battle against far better warriors. Blood ran from every doorway, until the few temple guards left alive fled the temple grounds.

Priests and holy men gathered in corners, holding precious artifacts tightly against their chests, as they prayed for God's mercy and vengeance against the incursion. For two hours, noise of room after room being ransacked filled the once peaceful halls of the holiest of Jewish temples.

The priests and servants who protested lost their lives by Roman swords. Rabbis protected ancient scrolls and Torahs, while the soldiers pillaged gold and silver artifacts, but the Ark of the Covenant was nowhere to be found.

Stunned by the utter destruction and senseless loss of life,

Caiaphas stood at the bottom of the temple steps, watching Marcus mount his horse. With tears streaming down his cheeks, he said nothing to the Roman prefect. The desecration of the temple was like losing a loved one, and Caiaphas tore his robe in anguish, rage, and hatred. Marcus's callous expression showed his indifference.

# CHAPTER 22

*Saturday, April 1, A.D. 30*

"We'll stop here and make camp," Malachi announced to the priests carrying the Ark. The shadow from the mountains to the west had quickly descended upon the ancient road. An orange hue from the setting sun gave the distant hills a rusty tint, as if the rocks had suddenly aged beyond their years.

Once they'd received their instruction to make camp, every man other than Tabor began performing his part of the ritual to prepare the ground both physically and spiritually before the Ark could be allowed to rest.

"Why are you stopping?" Tabor shouted back to the entire caravan.

"The sun is setting," Malachi hollered back in reply.

"So the sun is setting. We still have plenty of light."

"Tabor, the sun is going down. The Sabbath is beginning."

Frustrated by the decision to stop the caravan, Tabor turned to look at the surrounding landscape. "Malachi, look around you. We are in a valley with hills on three sides. This is the worst possible place to camp, unless you *want* to be discovered. At least keep moving until we reach the foothills."

"We cannot go another step until sundown tomorrow. As I told you, there are strict rituals we must follow to move the Ark, and observing the Sabbath is actually the *first* rule."

"Tell me, Malachi." Tabor argued, "Which rule says we should die in the desert because we followed the *first* rule?"

Malachi looked at the impatient shepherd and lowered his eyebrows. "Don't blaspheme, Tabor. The Ark is safe, and God will guide us through the wilderness."

"If God is guiding us, then why am I here?"

"Because, Tabor, you are the one who God is guiding."

---

Marcus beat his right fist against his chest in a salute to his commander. "My lord."

Pontius Pilate turned to see his trusted prefect standing at the entryway to his chambers. "Well, Marcus? Did you bring me my Ark?"

Hesitating for a brief moment, he replied, "My lord, the Ark is not in the temple in Jerusalem. Caiaphas refused to present it to Caesar, so we searched the temple completely, but found nothing."

The purple cape Pilate wore rose behind him when he spun to yell at the soldier, "What? How dare you return to me with nothing but empty hands."

"My lord," Marcus quickly offered, "I have reason to believe the Ark was recently moved. We found a tunnel deep beneath the temple walls. At the end of the tunnel, it looks as if a wall was recently chiseled open to reveal a compartment that was large enough to have held the Ark, as you described it."

"Then why are you standing *here*, instead of pursuing the thieves who stole Roman property?"

"My lord, I need only your orders and permission to use any means necessary to find the Ark and return it to Rome."

"Listen to me, Marcus. Caesar ordered me to take possession of this precious Ark, in which the Jews put so much faith. If it were up to me, I would pound the stones into gravel, but Caesar sees possession of this Ark as a way to control the Jews. He is convinced that if the Ark is in Roman hands, the Jews will acquiesce."

"My lord?" Marcus questioned, waiting for some clear direction from Pilate.

Marcus knew that permission to use *any means necessary* was a clear directive to forgo any consideration of Jewish culture or life, meaning this Roman quest would certainly be marred with Jewish blood.

"Yes, yes! Do what you must, but do *not* return to me without the Jewish Ark. I'll be damned if I'm going to let Caiaphas get the best of me."

Nervously watching the horizon surrounding the caravan, Tabor felt as though the hills themselves had eyes, watching and waiting.

The pack animals of the caravan were led to a nearby stream, where they could find water and grass, but they would not be burdened with carrying supplies on the Sabbath. Priests and servants alike gathered together and shared the same food and water, as the rabbi began morning prayers.

"Tabor, come sit with us," Malachi said, smacking the flat boulder upon which he sat. "You pace like a nervous mother of seven children."

Suddenly realizing he had, indeed, been walking back and forth, from one side of the camp to the other, more times than he could remember, Tabor replied, "I truly don't like sitting out here in the open, Malachi. Something doesn't feel right. I'm going to scout around the area." With that, he strode over to the temporary corral, looked in on the camels, and then began to survey the wider area around the makeshift camp.

Malachi laughed and shook his head at this strange man who seemed more comfortable with his eagle, and the caravan's sheep and pack animals than he did the men with whom he was on this journey. However, as Tabor left the camp and moved toward the stream, he sensed the animals shared his uneasy feelings. Three sheep, each with a lamb that was eventually to be sacrificed, nervously formed an outer ring around their young. Seeing this, Tabor knew the sheep shared his feeling of being watched.

Tabor walked alone with the mighty eagle on his shoulder, away from the caravan—that now sat in silent reverence to the Holy Sabbath— toward the hillside the sheep and camels watched with cautious interest. Once he'd neared the base of the hills, he whistled twice and Storm took flight.

The ground pulled further and further away, her mighty wings lifting her into the clear blue of the morning sky. She continued toward the hills in the direction Tabor was walking before veering left. In a matter of minutes, Storm rested on the warm air currents that carried her high above the hills, unnoticeable to anyone except her loyal guardian.

Tabor continued his surveillance, steadily moving toward the hills, even though Storm was clearly circling over a ridge to his left side where three pigeons were suddenly startled, and took flight. He climbed the hill and came in behind the target upon which Storm seemed to be focused. *If luck is on my side,* he thought, *I can sneak in to get a closer look without being detected.* Peering over the crest of the hill, he saw three horses standing side-by-side, each tied to branches of the same bush. Above the horses was the crest of a slightly higher hill.

Tabor walked as carefully as he could toward the horses, suspecting the men who rode in on them were watching the caravan camp just over the hill. He began petting the horses, knowing that might help keep them from startling or making noise, alerting the men who were very likely nearby.

Tabor froze every muscle in his body when he heard a screech from Storm high overhead. Recognizing it was not like her to call attention to herself when she was stalking, he knew he was being warned. A split second later, he crashed to the ground under the weight of an attacker who dropped from the boulder above.

The surprise ambush sent both men to the rocky ground. Tabor used the momentum from the fall to roll out from under his attacker and spring to his feet. Spinning around, he saw he was facing a battle-hardened soldier with an iron dagger in his hand. Scars disfigured the man's face, indicating this was not his first fight. Without diverting his eyes from the menacing soldier before him, Tabor's hand swiftly reached to his side for the dagger in his belt.

Before he could find it, though, two men grabbed him from behind, securing his arms in their powerful grip. Tabor struggled to free himself, but the well-trained soldiers were simply stronger and had him immobilized instantly. "I'll give you only *one* chance to live," the aggressor who faced him said in Greek. "Where are you taking the Jewish Ark?"

As he tried to catch his breath, Tabor finally replied in Greek, "I do not know about this Ark of which you speak."

The soldier pushed his *pugio* against Tabor's neck, confident the other two soldiers were holding him securely. The grip on Tabor's arms tightened, as the men pulled his arms up his back, forcing him to bend at the waist to face the ground. The soldier with the *pugio* kicked Tabor hard in the face, splitting his lip and causing a stream of blood to flow. "You lie, you Jewish dog. I have seen what you carry. Tell me where you are headed and I will kill you mercifully. Tell me one more lie and you will die watching the vultures fight over your entrails, after I split your gut open and stake you to the desert floor."

Tabor pushed back against his captors, so he could stand upright to face the questioning soldier. He drew a breath, but instead of speaking, he spit the pool of blood in his mouth directly into the eyes of his accuser. Surprising the man, Tabor lifted his legs and kicked the soldier squarely and hard in the face, breaking his nose with a crack.

The other two soldiers quickly drew their daggers to kill this rebel who had more fighting spirit than they had expected. But before the soldier on Tabor's right arm could thrust his dagger toward his chest, he was suddenly blinded by large brown wings fluttering and flapping in his face, followed by excruciating pain as Storm's talons pierced his right eye and sank deeply into his flesh.

Both men released their grip on Tabor, instinctively defending themselves. Tabor pulled the steel *pugio* from the hand of the soldier trying to escape Storm's fury and passed the blade across the jugular vein of the soldier on his left as if he were a sheep being slaughtered.

The soldier with the broken nose crouched with both hands against his face, cradling his nose as blood ran between his fingers. Tabor lunged fiercely, stabbing the man where his armor left his belly unprotected, slicing upward until the blade met his bottom rib.

In one smooth motion, Tabor had his sling in hand. A single whistle told Storm to release her grip and move away from the blinded man. Then Tabor dropped him with a stone from his sling.

Exhausted, Tabor sat on the ground to recoup, not far from the three dead Roman scouts, their blood pooling near his feet before soaking into the sandy soil. Storm swooped down, and after landing on Tabor's left shoulder, stood on one leg and cleaned the blood from her talons with her beak and tongue. After a few moments of rest, Tabor joked to his feathered ally, "The worst part of this day is that we'll both be chastised by the rabbi for fighting on the Sabbath."

Before returning to the caravan, Tabor unsaddled the Romans' horses and sent them running north, away from the occupying forces. Storm stayed on Tabor's shoulder until the pair reached the edge of camp. Once again taking flight, she surveyed the surrounding area, and with no sign of imminent threat, began stalking a sizable desert rat.

As Tabor approached a circle of seated men from the caravan, Malachi stood and greeted him. Seeing their guide was stained with blood from head to toe, he asked, "How many were there?"

"Three," Tabor replied. "And there will be more. They know we have the Ark and they are determined to find us."

"Are we safe for now?"

Tabor looked toward the sky and saw Storm flying a random pattern, as she continued hunting for food. "Yes, but tomorrow we must get off the roads and travel through the hills."

"Travel through the hills with the Ark and pack animals?"

"Moses carried the Ark with animals and thousands of followers through the wilderness without a single Roman road to pave their way."

"Which is why it took him *forty years*," Malachi replied with a smirk.

# CHAPTER 23

*Sunday, April 2, A.D. 30*

Koda and Daniel walked up the hill to the home that Jonas built. Koda called out, "Ruth—Evia!" mainly to identify himself so he would not frighten the women who were unaccustomed to being left alone.

Ruth stood, having been on her knees scraping the remnants of flesh and fat from an outstretched sheep hide. "Any word?" she asked Koda, hoping for a mere inkling about her husband's whereabouts.

"Nothing yet, Ruth."

Evia kept her seat on the bench by the front door, working a handful of wool into fibers to be spun into yarn.

"Good day, Evia," Daniel said politely, approaching his cousin.

"Good day, Daniel," she replied, keeping focused on her task.

"We lost another one, Ruth," Koda said. "Looks like wolves again. There isn't much left of it."

Ruth looked down at the hide on the ground, calculating the loss of another sheep. "So we're down to twenty-eight?"

"I think so, yes. And truly to make matters worse, she was pregnant."

Ruth flung the hide scraper to the ground in frustration, "When is Tabor coming back? There's simply no way one man can handle this many sheep alone."

"Well, I've decided I'm going to start sitting with them at night. I'm not as good as Tabor, but if I see a wolf, I can chase it off with my sling—even if I can't kill it." Glancing back at his niece, he asked Ruth, "Do you think Evia might be able to help Daniel watch the flock during the day?"

Ruth looked over to Evia, who stopped working the wool when she overheard the conversation. Evia quietly nodded at Daniel and then her mother, acknowledging she would be willing to work with her cousin.

Ruth said, "We will do as you say, Koda. I only pray Tabor will return soon. My heart feels heavier with each passing day."

"Pontius Pilate, Provincial Governor of Judea, faithful servant of Tiberius Caesar Augustus," the palace guard formally announced, "the Judean High Priest, Caiaphas!"

Following his introduction, Caiaphas was allowed to enter the room where Pilate typically held court.

"Caiaphas!" Pilate yelled, even before the priest completed the walk to stand before him. "Give me my Ark."

Caiaphas lifted his shoulders and both hands, looking around the room with a dumbfounded expression. "Your lordship, I have already told your men who looted my temple and killed my guards, *I do not have the Ark*. It was lost hundreds of years ago, a tragedy that Israel mourns every day. From what I have heard, you should be looking in Babylon."

"You're lying to me, Caiaphas!" Pilate shouted back, louder than before, as he sat in the chair from which he had sentenced many men to their death. "You know it, and I know it. Caesar has decreed that the Ark is *Roman* property, which means anyone who is complicit in taking it is guilty of stealing from Rome. And stealing from Rome brings a sentence of death, even for the priest who planned the theft."

"Don't threaten me, Pilate!" Caiaphas lashed back. "You kill me and you will have to kill every man, woman and child in Israel, because they will not rest until they have their revenge on *you*."

Pilate stood swiftly and pointed down at the bearded, heavyset priest. "Hear me, old man. I will find your precious Ark, and when I do, I will crucify you, the men who serve you, and the families of everyone involved. There will be so many crosses with your bodies hung upon them that there won't be a stick of wood left in this Jewish cesspool."

Pilate then turned his back on the speechless priest and left the room without dismissing him. The frustrated governor returned to his chambers, committed to devising a scheme to recover the Ark. For years, he'd endured his assignment in Judea in order to earn points with Caesar, in hopes of being reassigned to Rome. Now, however, he could feel his career slipping through his fingers.

Standing on the balcony, Pilate watched as a mounted soldier led three unsaddled horses through the main gate. "Lord Pilate," came the familiar voice of his prefect from the entrance to his chambers.

"Yes, what is it, Marcus?"

"Lord Pilate, three of my scouts have been found dead, sir."

Pilate turned to face the soldier. "Those three scouts, where were they?"

"Near the road to Jericho, my lord."

Pilate smiled devilishly. "So they are pointing the way, Prefect."

"Yes, my lord. I believe they were murdered by the thieves who fled with the Ark. I have already assembled and dispatched two special troops, each comprised of twenty of your best men, with orders to stop at nothing to kill or capture the thieves and return the Ark to you, my lord."

"Excellent!" Pilate replied. "And tell that arrogant priest Caiaphas that I said he should choose the tree from which he wants to make his cross."

Marcus smiled, enjoying Pilate's satisfied mood, however momentary. "With pleasure, Lord Pilate."

Helping two of the servants, Tabor carried one of the lambs, being more accustomed to shepherding than leading a caravan. The tiny lambs were unable to keep even the relatively slow pace of the caravan as it traversed the rough terrain, and carrying them kept the adult sheep close to the men who cradled their offspring.

"Tell me, Malachi, what is it about this Ark that makes you believe it has the power to protect us?" Tabor asked, as the two men walked behind the Ark at the rear of the caravan.

"Finally curious about our Hebrew culture, eh?"

"The Romans have not given up yet. If we possess a weapon capable of defeating an army, I'd like to know how to use it."

"The Ark is not a weapon to make Israel great, Tabor," Malachi admonished. "The Ark is a gift from God to keep Israel holy."

"I *understand*, Malachi. But through the years, many men have lost their lives trying to capture this Ark. How does it triumph time after time, as it seems to do?"

"The Ark contains the Word of God, inscribed on stone *by* God. It is not the Ark itself, for the Ark was made by man. It is the contents of the Ark that blesses those who believe in the Word."

The two men stopped walking and stared silently at the sacred object being carried a short distance in front of them. Malachi continued, "The Ark was created according to a pattern given to Moses by God, when Israel was encamped at the foot of Mount Sinai. The chest was made of acacia and gold-plated with a crown of gold to adorn the lid. Four rings were attached to its four feet, and through these rings, wooden staves were inserted. The staves are used to carry the Ark and are ordained never to be removed."

"Why do you cover it with blankets and animal skins?"

"Moses instructed that it remain covered behind a veil at all times. The Ark is to be carried only by priests of the temple, yet even the priests are not permitted to lay eyes on the Ark. When we rest, we erect a tent we carry called the tabernacle, again according to the laws of Moses."

"And when we fight?" Tabor pressed. "How does the Ark protect us from our enemies?"

"The Ark does not protect *us*, for *our* lives are insignificant. The Ark protects *itself* from our enemies. It is indestructible in its own right. If someone handles it against the laws of Moses, or dares to look upon it, they will surely die."

"But didn't the Ark protect the Levites when they destroyed Jericho?"

"True," Malachi agreed. "The walls of the city of Jericho were shaken to the ground with no more than a shout from the army, immediately after the Ark of the Covenant was paraded around them for seven days. And when the Ark was borne by Levites into the bed of the Jordan, the waters parted as God had parted the Red Sea for Moses, making a way for the entire host to pass through."

"So will the Ark protect us from the Romans? Will it make us invisible or shield our bodies from their spears?"

"*No*, Tabor," Malachi replied, frustrated he was not getting through to him about the true purpose of the Ark. "*Listen*. We will follow God's path to secure the Ark in a safe place. If the Romans find us, then we will die, but the Ark will survive. *It* is eternal, Tabor, because *God's Word* is eternal."

# CHAPTER 24



*Sunday, April 2, A.D. 30*

"Centurion!" Marcus barked out, calling for the attention of his second in command.

With a quick salute, the centurion stepped forward in front of his leader, ready to receive his orders.

"Bring me two of the priests who follow Caiaphas around like dogs. Do it in such a way that Caiaphas does not know we have them."

Without a word of response, the centurion saluted once again and turned, signaling two other soldiers to follow him.

Within a few hours, the centurion provided Marcus with the men he sought, each tied to a different pole in a secluded field north of the walls surrounding Jerusalem.

"Good work!" Marcus said, complementing his subordinate while dismounting from his horse near the two priests. Four soldiers stood nearby, armed with spears in hand and swords at their sides, sweating profusely, as the midday sun poured down upon them.

Marcus approached the priests, who watched him fearfully. Speaking fluent Aramaic, though colored by his thick accent, he began his inquisition. "Names?"

"I must protest this unwarranted attack, Prefect, and all your brutal crimes against our temple." the first priest began. "Caiaphas will hear of this and have you stripped of your rank."

Marcus calmly nodded to the centurion standing at attention nearby. Instantly, he strode over to the boisterous priest and slammed his fist into the man's gut, causing him to wrench forward and pull against the bindings around his wrists behind the pole.

"Now, I will ask you only one more time," Marcus proceeded, "because I am not a very patient man—names?"

The second priest replied with a tremble of fear in his voice, "I am Hiram. I serve on the council to the chief priest."

As the first priest regained his composure, he reluctantly responded, "I am Joram."

"Well, well," Marcus began. "Hiram and Joram, I suppose you wonder why I have invited you here today."

Again, Joram lashed out, "I'm warning you, Marcus."

This time, with the back of his hand, Marcus hit Joram's face himself, as hard as he could, causing blood to spray from the man's mouth.

Hiram gasped and flinched, then briefly closed his eyes.

"Now," Marcus continued, "I believe you have something I need. The only thing I want is the names of the men who have stolen your precious Ark."

Hiram turned toward his fellow priest. Joram shook his head, while looking at Hiram, and said, "Keep your mouth shut."

Hearing Joram's order, Marcus drew his sword and promptly ran it through the middle-aged priest's abdomen. The weapon protruded out the man's back, as Joram looked into his executioner's eyes with absolute fright. Marcus then pulled the sword back out, but at a sideways angle and with a twist, slicing even more of the man's internal organs. Instantly, the lifeless body slumped away from the post to which it was tied.

Hiram screamed, "I don't want to die! Please don't kill me! I don't want to die!"

"Hiram!" Marcus yelled over the priest's cries and pulling his beard to direct his face at him. "Listen to me. You're *not* going to die. Your friend Joram had a bad attitude. But he did tell me one thing. He told me you have the answers to my questions, right? So you will *not* die."

With his eyes bulging in shock, Hiram looked at Joram's body and the blood covering the rocks around his feet.

"Hiram!" Marcus bellowed. "Tell me, my friend, what are the names of the men who took the Ark?"

Hiram's mouth moved, as he tried to form words, but managed to utter no sound.

"Hiram? Talk to me, my friend—who took the Ark?"

Hiram's shaky voice managed to whisper, "Temple priests."

"Yes, I know, temple priests," Marcus pressed. "But give me a *name.*"

"The High Priest, Malachi."

"Good, Hiram. Malachi—who else?"

After several attempts to speak again, Hiram finally said, "Tabor—of Bethlehem."

Hiram changed his distant gaze to look directly at Marcus. "Tabor is not merely a shepherd from Bethlehem. He is leading them."

"Tabor of Bethlehem," Marcus repeated. Smiling, he lightly slapped Hiram's cheek. "There now, Hiram. That wasn't so hard, was it?"

As Marcus walked toward his horse, the centurion ran up next to him and asked, "My lord, shall I free the priest?"

Without breaking his stride, Marcus replied, "Kill him."

The following morning, as the caravan moved through a valley, still two days from the Dead Sea, Tabor noticed a change in Storm's flight—the wide, slow circles were replaced with small circles of descent, followed by a rise in altitude to repeat the pattern—a sign of concern.

"Malachi, we're being followed," Tabor said, expressing a sense of dread. "If it is the Romans, then this will not be scouts as before."

"I am prepared to die," Malachi replied, "if it is God's Will."

"Maybe you are ready to die, but I'm not."

Scanning the hills on either side of the valley, Tabor spotted a large cave opening at the bottom of a cliff directly above a rise in the hillside. "There," he said, pointing to the cave. "Take your priests and the Ark into that cave and pray they have not seen us yet. Have your temple guards and servants continue on the same path we've been walking, bringing with them the animals and supplies. If they encounter Romans, they must kill every one of them or more will surely come."

Tabor turned to backtrack along the base of the hill, hoping to discover their stalkers before being seen by them. Malachi ordered the caravan to split up as Tabor instructed.

When he finally saw a number of figures off in the distance moving in his direction, Tabor stood behind a large boulder resting on the valley floor, hidden from sight. *I could let these soldiers pass and return to my family*, he thought. *If I stay and fight, Ruth and Evia will never know what became of me.*

The sounds of horses could be heard in the distance, along with men whose metal armor clanked as they walked. High above, Storm's circles were coming in closer, which Tabor spotted easily. *Do I really want to die a senseless death in a place where my bones will be scattered by wolves?* He wondered.

While watching Storm circle directly overhead, Tabor heard the hoof-beats and heavy breathing of horses closing in quickly. He moved stealthily around the boulder to stay hidden from the Roman Troop, who were so close he could see their shadows on either side of him as they steadfastly marched by.

When the troop had passed, Tabor realized he could run. *Return to Bethlehem undetected,* he thought, *into the arms of my family. Return to a flock of sheep I could lead to green meadows, instead of leading all those men to their deaths.*

"Tabor." The sound of his name came from behind him, as he hugged the side of the boulder, hidden from Roman sight.

Turning quickly, his back pressed against the boulder, Tabor tried to identify the man standing in plain sight on the hill. *How is it the Romans did not see this man?* Tabor thought to himself.

"Tabor," the man repeated, "you do not live so others may fight. You fight, so others may live."

The man's voice was suddenly familiar, as was his form, "Saul?" Tabor whispered, turning quickly to see if his voice caught the attention of the soldiers who had just passed him. Looking back to where he'd seen Saul, he realized his vision had passed, but the words of his mentor lingered in his heart.

The soldiers not far down the path through the valley walked in two columns, each man beside another. If one man fell, the one beside him would immediately notice. *They have to be taken down in pairs*, he realized, *but their heavy armor is surely impenetrable by mere sharpened sticks and hurled stones.*

Tabor followed as closely as he could, waiting for an opportunity. When one of the last two men removed his helmet to wipe the sweat from his forehead, a flying stone found its mark. The soldier beside him stopped abruptly to see why he had fallen. Kneeling next to his comrade, he looked directly into the path of a short wooden spear thrown with tremendous force deep into the man's neck.

The noise made by the Roman troop as they marched hid the sounds from Tabor's attack. Tabor ran from cover onto the path behind the Romans to the fallen soldiers, confirming they were dead and recovering the short spear protruding from the soldier's neck.

With two men dead along the trail, Tabor retreated to a hiding place behind some bushes, next to the rocky slope of the hill.

The remaining soldiers approached the valley where Malachi and the other priests hid in a cave with the Ark. Tabor decided to wait for the procession to pass through the valley before attempting further ambushes, but as the Romans entered the valley, the trumpeting call from a ram's horn could be heard far and wide.

Two scouts who had been watching the Jewish caravan from a ridge overlooking the valley—undetected previously by either Tabor or Storm—were alerting the Romans to attack. As the horseback riders called out instructions to the foot soldiers, both scouts continued blowing their horns while running down the rocky slope toward their comrades. The Roman formation began to split, per their strategy, but quickly realized two of their own were lying dead on the ground behind them.

Tabor watched from behind the bushes, as the infantry soldiers spread apart and surveyed the hills around them for any sign of the men who had already killed without detection. He was too far away to hear their conversation, but watched as one of the scouts approached the lead horseman and pointed toward the cave.

To his added horror, Tabor saw the second scout point skyward toward the eagle circling overhead. With a single shouted order from one of the horsemen, who also pointed to the eagle overhead, two soldiers stepped forward, each with a trained falcon perched on his left hand. The men removed the hoods from their falcons' heads and identified their target.

The two falcons flew together, quickly gaining altitude, until they were level with Storm. Being smaller and more maneuverable, each falcon took turns diving onto Storm's back and then flying up again. Tabor stared intently at this battle in the sky, fearing for his lifelong friend, while each passing strike seemed to cause her to stumble in the air.

Suddenly, using a maneuver Tabor had never seen before, Storm flipped over onto her back, catching one of the falcons with her mighty talons before rotating to level flight. With a crushing squeeze from her beak on the falcon's neck, she killed her attacker before releasing it to plummet to the ground below.

Taking advantage of Storm's being distracted, the second falcon flipped under the eagle's breast and grabbed deeply into the great bird with her talons and beak. Unrelenting, the two birds fell from the sky in a single mass behind the hill. Neither bird flew out. The falcon's death grip succeeded in bringing Storm down, where Roman soldiers had failed.

Tabor's heart was ripped apart by grief, watching Storm fall to her death. Determined to rush the soldiers, spurred with anger and vengeance, he stood in the open, hoping to take down at least two before he himself fell.

Again, the ram's horn trumpeted a call to battle, but every Roman's eyes were on the ridge across and away from Tabor's position. Looking up at the ridge, he saw the temple guards and servants lined side by side. Every man had returned, prepared to protect the Ark that was now trapped in the cave, its location now known to the Romans. An overwhelming feeling of awe and respect filled Tabor for the men who had returned to face their own mortality.

Fourteen temple guards and six servants prepared to take on the remaining twelve Roman soldiers and four horsemen. Tabor quickly assessed the situation and thought, *The numbers are in our favor, but the battle experience and weapons favor the Roman forces.*

The Romans stood ready, while the Jews ran toward them in a futile death charge. The horsemen remained mounted behind the soldiers, who stood in formation with shield and sword brandished.

From his position on the ground, Tabor saw an opportunity to pick off the horseman in the rear. Approaching from behind, he loaded a short spear in his sling and sent it flying toward the man's back. The spear found the intended target, but glanced off the soldier's armor without penetrating.

Turning toward Tabor, the soldier kicked the sides of his horse, launching him into a full gallop toward the man in the dirty white robe with a thick black beard who was frantically trying to load his sling with a stone. The horse easily trampled Tabor, rolling him several times before he came to rest on the rocky desert floor.

In and out of consciousness, Tabor could only watch moments of the battle. The modest body armor and brittle weapons of the temple guards could not withstand the superior weaponry of the Roman troop. In the end, all of the Jewish guards and servants lay dead next to the bodies of three Roman soldiers.

The Roman centurion who led the legion pointed his sword at Tabor, who lay motionless but breathing, ordering, "Bring that one to me."

Two guards lifted Tabor by his arms and drug his feet over the rocky ground to their commander, before dropping him on his back by the feet of the centurion's horse. "Shall I finish him?" the foot soldier asked, raising his sword above Tabor.

"No," replied the centurion, raising his hand. "This is the Jew who Prefect Marcus told me to capture. Pilate wants to send a message to any rebel who thinks he can challenge Roman authority. When I bring him the Jewish Ark *and* the Jew who stole it, I'll make Captain for sure."

Pointing to a scraggly tree, right below the cave, the centurion barked his orders, "Tie him to that tree and give him some water. I'm going to bring him back alive."

In the cave, Malachi and the other priests had prepared the tabernacle as well as they could, given the hardness of the cave floor, which had prevented them from driving spikes for the tent corners. All five priests knelt facing the Ark, devotedly reciting scripture in prayer.

Four Romans entered the cave, one carrying a lit torch, unsure if they were going to face resistance or were walking into an ambush. Swiftly the Romans beheaded the still praying priests, splattering their blood on the tabernacle. Once the cave was secure, the soldiers stepped outside to await further orders.

"Bring it out!" called the centurion.

From the tree where Tabor could not support his own weight without the ropes that held him up, he cried out in Greek, "It's a decoy, you fool! The *real* Ark is in Egypt by now. Pilate will *crucify* you when he learns what you brought him."

"Wait!" the centurion called to the soldiers.

"Sir?" a soldier on horseback next to the centurion questioned.

"Do you know how inept I would appear if I presented an empty box to my superiors?" the centurion explained. "Better to open it here than in front of Marcus or Pilate."

Dismounting his horse, the centurion rallied his remaining troops, "Four of you bring torches. The rest follow me. I want two sentries outside the cave standing guard."

Tabor watched the Romans enter the cave. Blood continued to trickle down his back from wide gashes from the horse's hooves, and he felt himself again slipping in and out of consciousness.

In a matter of moments, the mouth of the cave began to light up, taking on a bluish hue emanating from within. The light grew brighter, and swirling veils of blue-tinted mist flew from the mouth of the cave. Agonizing screams of men echoed from the cave entrance.

Believing their comrades were under attack, possibly from soldiers hiding within to protect the Ark, the two sentries rushed into the cave. One soldier emerged, stumbling around in terror. Tabor could see black holes where the man once had eyes. Suddenly, he clutched the sides of his head and dropped to the ground in merciful death.

When the cries fell silent and the blue light faded, the rocky cliff above the darkened cave began to tremble. Small stones shook loose, followed by larger and larger rock. In less than a minute, the rockslide and quaking stopped, and the cave entrance had completely disappeared. Tabor looked around and suddenly realized he was the only man— Roman or Jew—left alive.

As the dust began to settle, Tabor saw the figure of a man standing next to the place where the cave entrance had been. The white-bearded man appeared to be very old, wore a red and brown striped Jewish robe, and held a tall staff; without any words passing between them, Tabor knew he was looking at Moses, the architect of the Ark and patriarch of Israel.

Suddenly, he realized the significance of the odyssey in which he'd played a part and the sacrifice his brethren had made to protect and preserve the Ark of the Covenant. In that moment, Tabor understood what Malachi had been trying to teach him. *His people's reverence for God and God's Word within the Ark,* he thought, *was the basis of their belief. They knew. They all knew their lives would be given before we started.*

As the apparition of Moses lifted his staff, the bindings holding Tabor to the tree fell to the ground. When Moses lifted his other hand, desert winds began blowing through the valley, nearly pushing Tabor to the ground. While frightened horses fled in full gallop, all around him the sands carried by the wind buried the bodies littered across the valley floor.

In a matter of minutes, there remained no sign of battle and no trace of the mouth of the cave. Only a solitary man, battered, beaten and bewildered, standing in the midst of a desert valley remained. And then, as quickly as the mysterious figure had appeared, he simply vanished.

# CHAPTER 25

*Monday, April 3, A.D. 30*

Pilgrims crowded the Jerusalem streets as Passover approached. Cyrus and Kennan, once demoted by Thaddeus for attacking Evia, sat quietly on a bench in the shade, watching the shadow from the canopy move ever closer to their sandals, as the sun traversed the spring sky. "Isn't that...," Kennan started, slapping the back of his hand against his friend's arm. "Look at that Jew and tell me if we know him."

Cyrus stared across the street at the Jewish man wearing a white and brown striped mantle. "He doesn't look any different to me than any other Jew," he responded, watching the man pass through a crowd and eventually out of sight.

Kennan stood up so he could see the head of the unusually tall Jewish pilgrim moving with the others. "You didn't see his face, did you—tell me, Cyrus, how many Jews do you know with hair the color of sand and blue eyes?"

Hearing the description, Cyrus stood up next to Kennan and asked, "Are you telling me you saw Immunes Thaddeus, the architect, dressed as a Jew?"

"Not only dressed as one, but looking like one as well. He has a beard and his hair is longer, but I'm telling you, that's him!"

Cyrus smiled, revealing the hole that was once filled with two teeth. "Our old commander who fought his own men to protect a Jewish girl has returned to Judea to live with these desert rats?"

"Cyrus, I have dreamed of this day ever since he attacked us in Bethlehem. Come, let's take him out of town where we can show him how *real* Romans punish a traitor."

Cyrus grabbed Kennan's arm. "No, wait! Let's follow him. I'll bet a month's wages he's come back for that Jewish whore of his. If he leads us to her, we can finish what we started in Bethlehem, *and* pay him back him as well."

Kennan smiled as he punched his friend's breast plate, "You keep an eye on him. I'm going to tell the Centurion that we have a lead on the Jew he's been looking for."

Evia walked leisurely through the herd, dragging her hand across the back of each sheep she passed to feel the thick curls of wool pass between her fingers. The sheep grazed without fear, comforted by the touch of their protector.

When the ram lifted his head to look behind Evia, she stopped and turned to see a man walking the path directly toward her. "Papa," she quietly gasped, suddenly relieved to see her father. Running toward the man, expecting to be lifted by his powerful hands, she slowed to a stop when she realized the stranger was not Tabor.

The man lowered the hood of his mantle, exposing hair and a beard the color of desert sand as he spoke loudly to the girl who studied him from a distance, "Hear, O Israel, the Lord our God, the Lord is One."

"Thaddeus!" she called out, once again running to the man, who was no stranger to her.

Evia grasped his outstretched hands, staring for the first time in nearly two years, into eyes as blue as the morning sky. "You came back!" she said, barely able to contain her excitement.

"I came home," the freed Roman replied. "Home, to claim my mother's heritage as a descendent of Abraham. Home, to begin my life in Bethlehem."

After a reflective moment, Evia broke the silence, "Come, mama will be glad to see you."

Side by side the young couple walked the path to the hill that held her home. When she saw her mother, Evia could not contain her excitement as she ran ahead to announce the return of Thaddeus.

Ruth ground the grain as she explained Tabor's absence to Thaddeus while he helped Evia prepare the fire for cooking the evening meal. "For you, Ruth," Thaddeus said as he presented two pomegranates from the pouch that hung at his hip from a strap around his neck.

Ruth set the grinding stone in the bowl and accepted the pomegranates, taking one in each hand and briefly studying the firm, crimson spheres. With eyes closed, she held them below her nose to breathe the fruity scent. Slowly opening her eyes, she gasped, dropping the fruit to the ground when her hands began to tremble. With a terrified stare over Evia's shoulder, she whispered, "Evia, Thaddeus—run."

Both Thaddeus and Evia turned to look behind themselves to see a Roman soldier on horseback, moving at a slow pace toward them. It wasn't until Ruth repeated her instructions that they ran.

Thaddeus grabbed Evia's hand and ran to the left while Ruth ran to the right. All three quickly stopped and turned when foot soldiers enclosed them from all sides. Unarmed and trapped, the three captives turned, continually looking for an opening through which they could escape. Ruth looked at Thaddeus with stern determination, "Hear me Thaddeus—whatever it takes, you get Evia away and do not look back!"

"Thaddeus, my friend." Marcus called out in Aramaic as he approached the petrified three. "I can't thank you enough for leading me to Tabor's home. You truly saved me a lot of work."

Ruth and Evia both looked to Thaddeus as he responded, "What do you want, Prefect? We have done nothing wrong. You have no cause to be here."

Marcus dismounted and stepped forward, "Well now, Thaddeus—I see you've become one of them. Tell me, Immunes—what would make a man choose to live among Jewish filth after earning all the rights of Roman citizenship?"

Thaddeus stood quietly without responding.

Marcus nodded to the soldier standing directly behind Thaddeus, who swiftly clubbed the blonde man on the side of his head, sending him to the ground unconscious. Both Evia and Ruth jumped back and screamed. Evia quickly knelt next to him and felt blood pulsing from the wound on the side of his head.

In despair, Evia raised her head and cried out, "My father saved us from Pontius Pilate, and he'll save us from you, too!"

"Evia!" Ruth's effort to quiet her daughter was useless.

"Well, well," Marcus said as he realized the value of Evia's confession. "This day just keeps getting better."

After surveying the area, Marcus ordered, "I want one of them tied to the post in front of the home and the other tied at the bottom of the hill by the stream. These two women will be the bait we use to catch the thief, Tabor."

Cyrus stepped forward, grabbed Evia by the hair and started walking her down the hill. Kennan gestured to Thaddeus and asked, "What should we do with this one?"

Marcus looked at the unconscious man and said, "He earned his freedom and Roman citizenship, yet chose to become a Jew. I decree this man to be a traitor to the Roman Empire. If he wants to live as a Jew, than let him die as a Jew. Crucify him!"

Kennan saluted with pleasure, knowing he was clearly granted permission to satisfy his lust for revenge. With help from another soldier, he laid Thaddeus over his horse's saddle and led them to the stream, where Cyrus tied Evia to the trunk of a tree.

Cyrus started a fire for warmth and cooking while Kennan butchered one of Tabor's sheep. Both men removed their armor and weapons as they settled for what would be a long, chilly night.

After taking their fill from the slaughtered animal, Cyrus motioned to Evia who was barely visible by flickering firelight, "What about her? Prefect Marcus wants her alive until he captures the Jew, Tabor."

Kennan pulled some meat from the leg bone propped above the flame and carried it to the young girl sitting at the base of a willow tree with a rope binding her wrists behind her and around the trunk. Evia turned her head to the side when Kennan held the flesh near her mouth. "She's not going to eat," he concluded as he returned to the fire near Cyrus.

Above her left shoulder, on a thick branch that protruded from the trunk, Thaddeus passed in and out of consciousness, with his arms now hooked over a tree limb that stretched behind him. His wrists were bound by a rope that tightly wrapped his waist. With his feet unable to touch the ground, Thaddeus faced death by crucifixion.

Looking up the hill toward the home, Kennan saw two camp fires burning, but could no longer see the soldiers encamped or the tormented woman tied to the post near the front of the home. "Cyrus," he said in a subdued voice as though he could be overheard. "No one can see us."

Cyrus looked beyond the fire into the darkness and then revealed his toothless smile, "Finish what we started in Bethlehem?"

Kennan nodded, "We can *have* the girl and kill the Immunes, all in one night!"

Cyrus led Evia by the rope that now bound her wrists together, to the fire. In her state of shock, she could neither resist nor cry out, making it easy to lay her on the ground. Kennan pinned her shoulders to the ground while Cyrus pushed her tunic up above her hips, past her undergarments. Then, as if awakening from a trance, she looked into the eyes of the man's face nearing hers and screamed. Cyrus quickly silenced her with a blow from his fist to the side of her jaw.

Kennan laughed with nervous anticipation for his turn, as Cyrus forced himself between the young girl's legs. Suddenly, Kennan's laugh was silenced as he saw the point of a sword protrude through his chest, then he fell to the side as the sword was withdrawn from his back as quickly as it had entered.

Cyrus looked up to where Kennan had been kneeling, surprised to see a man with a rope hanging from his right hand and holding a sword. Thaddeus's thumb was covered with blood and torn flesh and had been dislocated, showing his determination to free himself from the tree.

"Get off of her!" Thaddeus said through gritted teeth.

The half-naked Roman was unable to reach his own sword before his head fell to the ground.

Suddenly relieved from the crushing weight of two large men, Evia scooted backwards until she was pushing against a large rock. Thaddeus dropped to his knees before her, exhausted by the ordeal. In the dim firelight, she saw the bloody sword in a man's hand and screamed once more.

Thaddeus covered her mouth, "Evia! Quiet!" He kept her mouth covered until she found the sense to recognize him. Cautiously he lowered his hand until he could be certain she realized she was safe.

The sword dropped to the ground as Thaddeus collapsed next to where she sat.

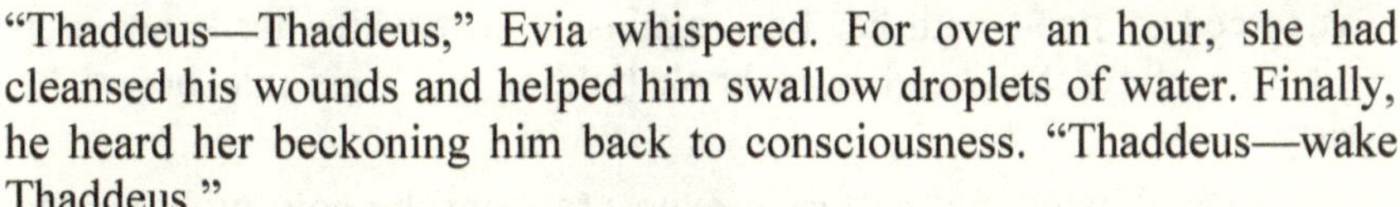

"Thaddeus—Thaddeus," Evia whispered. For over an hour, she had cleansed his wounds and helped him swallow droplets of water. Finally, he heard her beckoning him back to consciousness. "Thaddeus—wake Thaddeus."

In the stillness of the darkest hour, he eventually found the strength to sit up and eat remnants of the sheep leg that had fallen into the smoldering coals and burned on one side.

Even though they were blinded by the darkness, Thaddeus heard the horse standing near the camp and surmised the situation. Two bodies lay near them, though he had no memory of how they died. Camp fires burned on the hill near the home.

"Evia, we must flee."

"Not without my mother," Evia responded forcefully.

Thaddeus looked at the fires on the hill once again, knowing Marcus was camped with the rest of his soldiers where Ruth was held prisoner.

Shaking his head, he explained, "Evia, I can't. Even with all my strength, it would be suicide for me to attack Marcus and his men. I'm willing to die for your mother, but I'm *not* willing to let you die."

"I'm not leaving without her!"

Thaddeus rose to his knees to face the woman he loved. Barely able to see her face in the dim light, he laid his hand on the side of her face, wiping a tear from her cheek with his good thumb. "The last thing your mother said to me was to get you away from here. It is my intention to honor her wish, even if I have to carry you over my shoulder."

"If your father was here," he continued, "he would insist I protect you. Under Roman law, you and I are guilty of murdering Roman soldiers, a charge that will follow us for the rest of our lives."

Evia glanced at the two lifeless bodies barely visible as the coals burned dimmer.

"We will take this horse and ride north. But Evia..."

Thaddeus waited until she lifted her tear swollen eyes to look into his.

"It will be a very long time before we can safely return. For your mother—for your father, we ride like the wind."

Evia looked down for a moment, before nodding in agreement.

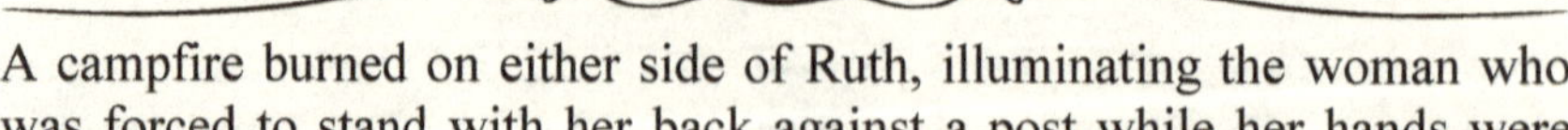

A campfire burned on either side of Ruth, illuminating the woman who was forced to stand with her back against a post while her hands were held high above her head by a hook holding the rope that bound her wrists.

Dehydrated and suffering exposure from the cold night air, her legs trembled to keep the weight of her body from pulling against the ropes around her wrists. In the stillness of the horrific night, her prayer was answered by God, who did not sleep like the soldiers scattered on the ground around her. From the stream at the bottom of the hill, she heard a lone horse gallop into the darkness.

# CHAPTER 26

*Tuesday, April 4, A.D. 30*

Mere moments passed before the hostile cries of battle, the rumble of a mountain landslide and the rush of supernatural desert winds ceased. The deafening noise surrounding him turned to utter silence. Tabor saw nothing of the bodies of the men he had come to know and respect on the Ark's final journey. Alone, in a valley filled with the palpable memory of blood and death, he decided to continue east in search of the animals from the caravan, hoping one or two of the servants may have stayed with them.

He did not have to travel far, though. As he cleared the summit, Tabor immediately saw the caravan had stopped in the valley below. *All gone*, he thought, surveying the camels and sheep standing together with no human caretaker. *God, would it have been too much to bring just one horse back for me?* he thought in prayer. After relieving the pack animals of their burdens and harnesses, Tabor set them free to wander loose; realizing most would become food for predators, yet silently hoping some nomad might stumble upon them and praise God for his good fortune.

After gathering as much food and water as he could carry for what he estimated to be a two-day journey home, Tabor gazed toward the afternoon sky. A wave of grief tore at his heart. *As Saul did before her,* he thought, *Storm sacrificed her life to protect me*. With no one left to hear, he threw his face into his own hands and sobbed aloud, falling to his knees and crying long and hard at the loss of his beloved friend. As his tears fell, he stood and looked toward the heavens. Suddenly, he drew a deep breath and let out a thunderous, heart-wrenching yell. The cry of Tabor's anguish echoed among the bleak, deserted hills, finding no ears but his own.

Bruised and battered, with three cracked ribs from being trampled, Tabor began his arduous journey home. For two days, he moved steadily through the wilderness toward his home near Bethlehem. Every breath was a new experience in pain, and every step was a moment closer to his family. Each night, he'd sleep near a fire he kept burning to ward off predators. Many thoughts plagued Tabor's mind as he continued onward. He battled guilt for leaving Ruth and Evia unprotected, and worried about their safety and well-being.

When he was able to lift himself from the torment of his thoughts, Tabor continually returned to practicing the story of the caravan's demise and the hidden location of the Ark that he would surely be presenting to Caiaphas in the days ahead. Meticulously, he memorized landmarks and stacked rocks in patterns that would help lead him back to the valley of the Ark's tomb.

On the second day, after the sun crossed its peak, Tabor found himself on familiar ground. *Beyond the next hill*, he thought, *I'll be able to see my home in the distance.* He reminisced about the many times he walked the same trail to be greeted by his wife and daughter, but his fears rose as he saw not one, but three columns of smoke rising beyond the only hill that stood between him and his home.

*Caiaphas swore to protect my family. If he is a man of his word, then the fires will be tended by palace guards.*

Instinctively, Tabor looked to the sky to study Storm's behavior, only to remember she would never again be his eyes. With only his own senses to call upon, he laid on the ground of the hill's crest to peer over the rise in order to study the situation around his home. As if a crushing stone had landed on his back, he was crushed beyond despair to find himself staring straight into his worst nightmare.

More than a dozen Roman soldiers walked the slope in front of his home. As he watched, two more stood upright after stooping to walk out the stone framed doorway. Some tended the fires burning out front, while others laughed at a young soldier chasing after one of his sheep. *Oh God*, Tabor thought, *please tell me Ruth and Evia escaped, and are somewhere safe. Caiaphas—where are the guards you promised would protect my home and my family?*

Backing down the hillside to avoid detection, he circled toward higher ground to get a closer look. Lying on his chest, gazing over a closer ridge, Tabor now had a better vantage and could hear the soldiers' voices. With horrified despair, he could also hear Ruth's occasional cries. After hearing her voice rise up, Tabor was finally able to spot her, tied to the pole he had used many times to gut and carve the meat from a slaughtered sheep.

Try as he might, Tabor could not hear or see Evia. Ruth's back was to the pole with her wrists tied to a hook above her head. She seemed barely conscious by her lethargic movements, with only a sporadic plea of "Please stop" in a language the soldiers surely didn't understand.

He could also see several soldiers further down the hill shooting arrows into one of his sheep, making a game out of seeing how many arrows they could put in the animal before it dropped dead. Purposely, they shot into the hind quarters of the sheep to watch it run in pain, taking pleasure in the animal's slow death.

Rage and anguish replaced Tabor's better judgment, as he left his protective cover to enter the new Roman stronghold. His first target was one of two soldiers who stood guard over the encampment above his home. With deft accuracy, Tabor flung the short wooden spear into the man's throat, preventing him from uttering a sound before death claimed him as one of its own.

The second guard fell in relative silence when Tabor's stone crushed the bone above his right temple. Tabor's third victim had carelessly left the protection of his comrades to relieve himself in semi-privacy and was cut down with ease.

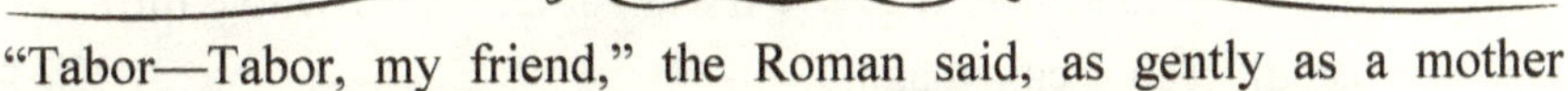

"Tabor—Tabor, my friend," the Roman said, as gently as a mother would wake her child in the early hours after a full night's rest.

Blurry strands of light temporarily filled Tabor's vision until he was able to focus on a steady stream of blood dripping from a bronze tipped arrow protruding through the front of his own chest. Air hissed around the arrow's shaft as it escaped his collapsed lung. The hands that gently slapped his cheeks to waken him belonged to the man calling his name.

Tabor realized he was facing the ground and that his arms were behind him, wrapped around the trunk of the tree that Storm once used to watch over her adopted family.

"Leave him alone!" Ruth screamed at the Romans who finally

held their prize. The desperation in Ruth's voice brought Tabor back to consciousness and he immediately tried to stand erect.

Realizing their prisoner was waking after an hour of unconsciousness, the soldier lifted Tabor's head so he could see the man's eyes. "Oh my goodness," the Roman taunted him. "That arrow *does* look painful. Would you like me to get it out for you, Tabor of Bethlehem?"

Tabor closed his eyes, refusing to acknowledge the Roman, but that didn't stop him from feeling excruciating pain when the soldier pulled hard on the shaft of the arrow, passing it through his body in the same direction from which it entered. Tabor grimaced and gritted his teeth, but kept his silence so as to deny the aggressor any pleasure of watching him cry out in anguish.

The soldier walked away from Tabor, holding the blood soaked arrow in one hand and repeatedly smacking it against the palm of his other hand. "Tabor, Tabor, Tabor—what am I going to do with you?"

Tabor used the rope tied between his wrists to pull himself up, realizing he was facing Ruth who was now conscious, yet severely weakened after two days of standing, suspended by the rope that held her arms above her head.

"Evia! Where's my daughter, you Roman pig?" Tabor asked, barely able to say three words between breaths from his remaining lung.

"*I* will ask the questions here, Tabor." the soldier in charge replied. "First, allow me to introduce myself. I am Marcus, *Praefectus Castrorum*, serving Pontius Pilate. Now you, my friend, are nothing more than a thorn in Pilate's side. Oh yes, Tabor, I have learned much about you in my short visit to your little cave dwelling here. Tell me, Tabor, what is it like to live in a cave like an animal your whole life?"

"Evia!" Tabor called again.

"Ah, you must mean that little Jew whore we found," Marcus continued, taunting Tabor with his sarcasm. Marcus turned and approached Tabor, so he could watch his reaction before continuing with a lustful laugh, "She ran away like a desert rat, preferring to die alone in the desert than to live with her family."

Tabor could not help but cry out, "Evia!"

"Oh, come now, Tabor. Don't make such a fuss. After all, Jew whores are around every corner. You'll find another one."

Through her pain and exhaustion, Ruth managed a slight smile when she whispered to Tabor, "She is safe."

"One very interesting thing, though," Marcus continued, still slapping the arrow he'd pulled from Tabor's chest against his hand. "Your daughter, who I must say Tabor, tasted sweeter than honey, told me a very interesting thing about your past. She told me you are the man who broke into Pilate's home and stole two of his slaves. Is that true, Tabor?"

Tabor struggled for each breath, never taking his eyes off of Ruth, knowing every breath might be his last.

More forcefully now, Marcus questioned Tabor, "I asked you a question, friend! Is it true you are the man who stole Caesar's slaves, thinking you could keep them for yourself?"

Tabor's silence angered Marcus, who hit Tabor's cheekbone with the back of his hand. "Stay with me, Tabor. I have many questions for you, and if you and your little Jew wife want to live another day, you're going to have to give me some answers."

Tabor turned his attention to Marcus for only a moment, before looking back on Ruth's large brown eyes. Speaking directly to her heart, he mouthed the words, *I love you.*

In response, while tears streamed down her cheeks, she returned the unspoken words.

Still, Marcus continued, "Now, Tabor, I could not care less where you get your whores. Frankly, I think it is disgusting when I hear the stories of what Caesar Tiberius does with little children. I mean, let them get a little older so they can enjoy it before he kills them, am I right, Tabor? I said, am I right?"

Tabor heard Ruth scream, "No!" but felt no pain from the next blow of Marcus's fist directly below his left eye.

"Now, Tabor, what I really want to know is where you hid the Jewish Ark. It's as simple as this, my friend. You tell me where the Ark is, and I will set your wife free. If you refuse, she will die. I'll let you think about that for a minute. You will make the decision whether your wife lives—or dies."

Marcus walked to stand next to Ruth, at which point he pulled out a steel *pugio*. Reaching the dagger above Ruth's hands, he laid the blade against the rope that bound her hands to the pole. "Tabor—does she live?" Next, lowering the blade to touch her throat, he continued, "Or does she die?"

Ruth's eyes widened, as she tried to pull her head back hard against the pole away from the cold steel blade.

"So I will ask you this question only once more, my friend Tabor. Where is the Jewish Ark you stole from the temple in Jerusalem?"

Tabor turned his attention from the calm, cold-blooded gaze of the Roman prefect to the panic-stricken look in his wife's eyes. "No!" Tabor yelled, searching desperately for the words that would satisfy his captor. "We took it into Egypt. I can show you where we buried it. Now let her go!"

"Ah, Egypt," Marcus replied. Slowly, he walked in front of Ruth, but as he passed, he pulled the blade deeply across her neck, letting her warm blood coat the dagger and the hand holding it.

Ruth's mouth opened, but she was unable to scream, as air from her windpipe made a hissing sound when it mixed with blood, pumped from the final beats of her heart.

Tabor neither cried out nor looked away. He could only stand captive, in shock, watching his wife's head ease down. No longer able to stand on her own, the rope around her wrists now held the weight of her lifeless body. From her neck to the ground, her mantle had turned crimson, as the last pulse of blood drained from her fatal wound.

Marcus continued his slow walk toward Tabor, where he wiped Ruth's blood from his hand across Tabor's face, "Her blood is on you, Tabor of Bethlehem. I know you did not go into *Egypt*. You and your band of Jewish thieves were traveling east."

Marcus walked away from Tabor, frustrated he was unable to get him to tell the truth about the Ark's location. While the prefect went about wiping the blood from his hand and cleaning his dagger, a centurion approached him and asked, "Sir, why did you kill her? Now he'll never talk."

Marcus chuckled and said, "Everyone knows you can take a Jew's family, and he will find another one. But if you touch his mother, he will crumble."

# CHAPTER 27

*Thursday, April 6, A.D. 30*

"I want this man kept alive!" Marcus warned the centurion. "Pilate is in Jerusalem for the Jewish Passover. If I can't deliver the Ark to him, I will deliver the man who *stole* it."

After saluting his commander, the centurion turned to pass on the order to his men. Within moments, he took two guards over to the tree to which Tabor remained tied and motionless, staring at his wife's body still hanging by the wrists. The ground at their feet had absorbed her blood and was now darker than the sandy soil around it.

"If I had my way," he said to Tabor in Greek, stepping in front of him to block his view of Ruth, "I'd gut you right here and let the buzzards have what's left."

Turning his attention to one of the soldiers who was with him, he ordered, "Cut him loose and tie him into the back of the supply wagon. This Jew gets to ride while we walk."

From a rope around Tabor's waist, the centurion saw a sling hanging by his side. Pulling at it with a swift tug, he dangled the sling in front of Tabor's face, "You won't be needing *this* anymore, will you now?" Tucking the sling into a pocket of his own uniform, the centurion knew it would bring a decent price when he finally got back to his barracks.

A bearded priest walked unusually fast through the halls of Herod's temple in Jerusalem, striding past the ongoing repairs and cleanup following the Roman pillage of the temple. Pulling open the heavy wooden door, the priest interrupted the Great Sanhedrin. The Chief Priest, temple priests, and local aristocrats all stared at him, annoyed by the disruption. "Caiaphas!"

"What is it?" the Chief Priest snapped back.

"My apologies, holy one, but the Romans just brought the shepherd Tabor into the city and took him directly to Pontius Pilate in the palace."

Caiaphas nodded, signaling he accepted the priest's apology, and with a simple hand gesture, motioned for him to stand and wait. Reflecting for a moment, he turned his attention to the Sanhedrin gathered before him. "My friends," he said, "we will meet again tomorrow. I have an urgent matter requiring my immediate attention."

The elders stood and bowed to Caiaphas before exiting the room. Not a word was spoken until the door was closed behind them. Once he was alone with the messenger, he asked, "Were any of our people with him?"

"No one. I watched with my own eyes," the priest replied. "At first, I didn't recognize him. He is wounded, severely beaten, and covered in blood."

"The Ark! Did they have the Ark?"

"Not that I could see. The column was led by Pilate's prefect, Marcus. There was only one wagon and it seemed to be carrying mostly supplies and the one man, Tabor of Bethlehem."

"If they don't have the Ark, and they brought Tabor back alive, that means they must not know where it is," Caiaphas reasoned. "Assemble my staff. I will go see Pilate at once and demand my right to talk with Tabor."

Bowing to Caiaphas, the priest hurriedly left the room.

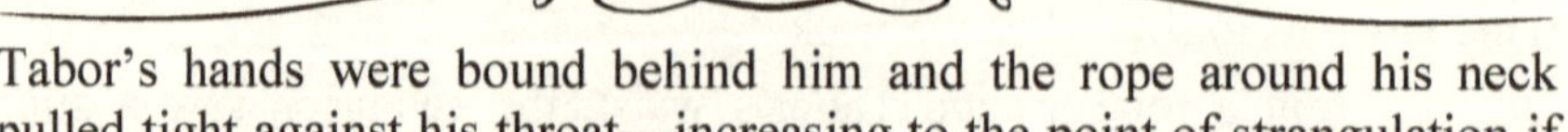

Tabor's hands were bound behind him and the rope around his neck pulled tight against his throat—increasing to the point of strangulation if he did not keep pace with the Roman guard assigned to lead him. With two more guards behind him, the four men made their way through the corridor. Eventually, all four entered the large hall where Pilate held court.

Marcus was standing before Pilate, having recently explained

Tabor's involvement in the disappearance of the Ark *and* the raid on Pilate's palace at Caesarea Maritima. When the guards stopped and saluted the Roman Governor, Pilate gave a halfhearted wave to acknowledge the salutes, but remained focused on their Jewish prisoner.

"This poor excuse of a man, this *plebeian*," Pilate began, as he stood from his chair and stepped down from the chair's pedestal, "is the one who broke into *my* home and stole *my* servants?"

No one in the room spoke, as Pilate circled Tabor, studying him from all angles.

"*This* is the filthy pig Caiaphas used to steal the Ark from Caesar?" Making a dramatic face for the others to see—as though he had bitten into a lemon—he added, "Ugh, he smells awful! It's a wonder the sheep don't run from him to find fresh air."

Two of the soldiers chuckled, but then immediately gathered themselves back into their proper military presence. Pilate didn't mind, however, and continued his dramatic interrogation.

Stopping behind Tabor, he spotted the hole in his robe where the arrow had entered his back, surrounded by a dark red blood stain. Pushing his finger deeply into the wound so as to inflict even more pain, Pilate asked, "So, Tabor of Bethlehem, what have you done with my Ark?"

Tabor grimaced, but said nothing.

"Marcus!" Pilate called. "You speak their language. Ask him where he hid my Ark."

Marcus took one step forward before addressing Pilate, "My lord, the Jew speaks Greek fluently. He's merely being obstinate."

Pilate retracted his finger from the hole in Tabor's back and walked around in front of him, addressing him face to face. "A Jew who speaks Greek. What next, I wonder?"

Tabor lifted his head to look Pilate in the eyes, so the Roman governor could see the hate in his face as he screamed, "You killed my wife!" Blood from Tabor's mouth sprayed Pilate's robe before his head fell back down to his chest from sheer exhaustion.

Turning away from Tabor, Pilate asked, "Marcus? Is this true?"

Again, Marcus stepped forward and replied by reminding Pilate of the orders he himself had issued, "*Any means necessary*, my lord."

Pilate took a second look at his prefect, while considering the extremes Marcus must have taken to capture Tabor.

Silence filled the room when Pilate stopped speaking. Purposely, he walked up the two steps to his chair where, when seated, he was still higher than the tallest man in the room. "Tabor of Bethlehem," Pilate began, announcing the formal charges against his prisoner, "you stand before me accused of breaking into Roman grounds, stealing Roman property, killing Roman citizens—the list goes on and on. I can have you executed for any one of these crimes. Do you understand these charges levied against you?"

Tabor remained silent, looking only at the floor.

Pilate looked over to his secretary, who meticulously made notes describing the proceeding. Now in Latin, he stated the formal charges against the accused for official recording, "Let the record show the accused admitted guilt to all charges by refusing to defend himself."

Addressing Tabor once again in Greek, Pilate continued, "Tabor, I'm sure you've had a bad day. I've had days so bad even *you* would agree your problems pale in comparison to mine. So here are my final terms. If you show me where to find the Jewish Ark, I will grant you a full pardon. You will be exiled from my territory, but you will be allowed to live."

Tabor made no effort to reply, so Pilate persisted. "Now, surely you can appreciate the magnitude of what I'm offering you, Tabor of Bethlehem. No man, not even a Roman, has ever been pardoned for crimes such as yours. I am offering you a chance to start your life over in a new land. All you have to do is tell me where you hid a little box. It isn't like I won't find it without your help, Tabor, but you *could* save me some time and trouble. In exchange, I am offering to spare your life."

Again, the room was filled with silence while Pilate waited for a reply.

Realizing he would need to use more forceful interrogation, he waved the back of his hand to the guard who was still holding the rope tied around Tabor's neck. "Take him to a cell," he ordered. "I will give him two hours to consider my offer."

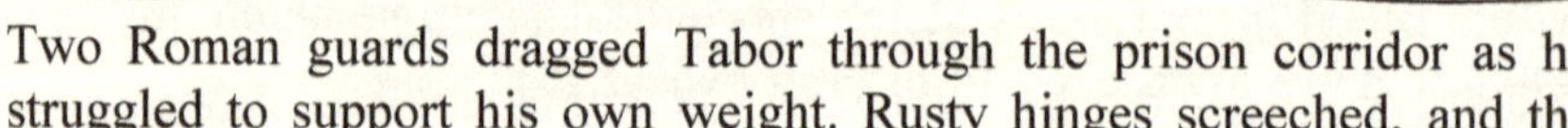

Two Roman guards dragged Tabor through the prison corridor as he struggled to support his own weight. Rusty hinges screeched, and the opened door revealed a cell void of light and filled with the stench of human waste.

"This is the end of the road for you," one guard said, "until you're ready to cooperate with Governor Pilate."

The other guard pushed Tabor from behind, and he collapsed face down on the floor. Underneath him was a floor made of stones that had been worn smooth from countless prisoners before him who had passed the hours pacing back and forth like caged animals. The heavy door slammed closed with the sound of thunder that seemed to echo the guard's warning. Slowly he rolled over to lie on his back, but his body weighed heavily against the one lung that still functioned. The heels of his bare feet found the edge of stones protruding from the floor, and he pushed himself backward until he found the wall behind him. With his remaining strength, he sat up and rested against it. The cool damp stones soothed the pain from the wound on his back.

Every shallow breath brought excruciating pain. The silence in the sealed room was almost deafening, making the sound of a heavy chain sliding over the cell's stone floor even more startling. His eyes were slow to adjust to the strands of light that crept past the edges of the door, but one thing was certain—he was not alone. Even so, the darkness of the prison cell offered a sense of isolation and solace. He closed his eyes in silent retreat and prayer. *All I desired was to live in peace, to love my family, and to tend my flock. What have I done wrong, Lord, that would make You punish me so?*

Tabor drew one hand across his face, wiping away the tears that came as he reflected on a life once worth living. Perhaps later, his fear and pain would give way to sleep and he would drift into blessed unconsciousness. Until he experienced that sweet relief, he must try to extinguish all thoughts of the anguish Pontius Pilate surely had planned for him in the morning.

From the darkest corner of the cell, where chains slid once again over the stone floor, came a question, "What's your name?"

"Tabor."

After a brief pause, the voice broke through the darkness, "Tell me your story, Tabor. Tell me what brought you to this fateful end."

"I don't feel like talking."

"I don't want to waste my last night sleeping," the man's voice continued.

Tabor contemplated the man's request. Thinking back over his life, everything was linked, like ripples in the desert sand. Pain yielded to memories, as he realized memory was all he had left. Finally, he reached the beginning that led to the end. "My story, as I lived these past thirty six years—began with a star."

Within the hour, Pilate was troubled once again, as he waited for word that Tabor wished to talk. "My lord," the Roman centurion said, upon entering the room.

"Yes, what is it? Is the Jew ready to talk?"

"No, my lord. Chief Priest Caiaphas has requested an audience."

Pilate rolled his eyes and shifted position in his seat before responding, "That's all I need! Caiaphas and his whining problems. Send him away. I don't have time for him today."

"My lord, he wishes to discuss the Jew, Tabor."

Pilate paused to consider the possibility that Caiaphas could work toward his advantage. "Fine, bring him to me."

The door to the court was opened and Caiaphas was formally announced.

"Governor Pilate," Caiaphas began, after approaching Pilate's dais. "You are holding the Jewish shepherd, Tabor, who has committed no crime against Rome. I demand to see him."

Pilate became enraged. *"Committed no crime?* You *can't* be serious, Caiaphas. This man has broken every law we have, and probably even a few that haven't been written."

"I wish to hear from his own lips what he has done against Rome," Caiaphas persisted. "Take me to him at once."

"Now you listen to me, old priest," Pilate retaliated. "You have *no* right coming into my court demanding *anything* from me. I am convinced this Jewish shepherd was involved in your scheme to steal the Ark and hide it before it could be turned over to Caesar. A crime, by the way, for which I will charge you, once I find where your thieves hid it."

Caiaphas lifted both hands palms up, along with his shoulders, to gesture his innocence. "Pilate, as I told your prefect before he ransacked and pillaged my temple, the Ark does *not* exist. It was lost over three hundred years ago. Caesar is chasing a ghost."

"You lie!"

"Let me talk to Tabor, Governor Pilate," Caiaphas insisted. "I will find out what he knows about this matter and report back to you. I swear it."

"You can talk to your Jewish shepherd in the presence of my prefect," Pilate compromised, gesturing toward Marcus. "He speaks your Jewish language as well as you speak Greek."

"Tabor will not talk if a Roman is present. I must speak with him in private."

"No deal!" Pilate snapped.

The heavy iron bar on the outside of the cell door clanked just prior to the doors movement. It opened momentarily as a guard sat a bucket of water on the floor of the cell before slamming the door closed once again.

"If I could move from this place, I would have had that guard in here with us, and his neck would have been broken before he could cry out for help," the man said at the brief glimpse of his most hated enemy.

"Is that why you're chained?" Tabor asked.

"Yes, they have good reason to fear me."

The chains rattled against the stones as the prisoner shifted position. "Tabor, can you reach the bucket? I'm thirsty."

Not realizing how stiff he had become sitting in the same place for so long, Tabor found it painful to cross the cell and to lift the bucket. After helping the stranger get some water, and drinking a few handfuls himself, he left the bucket next to the stranger and carefully returned to his place on the floor.

"Continue, Tabor. You were telling me how Jonas died."

The hours passed as Tabor continued telling the story of his life. Once again, the cell door came to life with the clank from the iron bar. The door stayed opened only long enough for a malnourished, wiry man to be thrust through the opening to land face first just beyond Tabor's feet. The man quickly stood and laughed hysterically as he turned and ran face first into the closed door.

"Who are you?" Tabor asked.

The peculiar man spun around at the sound of another's voice in the dark cell. "I'm Ishmael, who are you?"

"Tabor. What brings you to this fate, Ishmael?"

"I am to be crucified for stealing bread from a Roman guard who I found asleep on duty three days ago," Ishmael confessed. Then he cackled an irritating laugh.

Ishmael turned with a start when he heard yet a second man's voice. "Sit down and be quiet, Ishmael. Tabor is telling me his story, and I don't want to deal with interruptions from the likes of you."

Koda entered the small home in Bethlehem he shared with Naomi, Daniel and Miriam, only to be greeted by his panic-stricken wife. "Koda!" she screamed, grabbing both his arms. "It's Miriam!"

"What about her? Is she ill?"

"They *took* her, Koda!"

"Slow down, Naomi."

"Roman soldiers, Koda. Two days ago, right after you left to take the lambs to Jerusalem for Passover. Daniel tried to stop them, but they pushed him against the wall and held him there until they left with Miriam."

"Did they say anything? Did they say where they were taking her?"

"I didn't understand their language, Koda. The only word I recognized was *Tabor*."

"Tabor!" Koda cried. "Ruth—have you heard from Ruth?"

"No, Koda, not a word. Daniel wanted to go check on her, but I wouldn't let him go. Koda. I'm so frightened!"

Koda saw Daniel sitting alone in the back of the room, still shaken by yet another encounter with Roman soldiers. "Daniel, come with me. We need to make sure Ruth and Evia are safe. Naomi, you stay with friends tonight. I don't want you to be here alone. One way or another, we will be back before sunset tomorrow."

Tabor sat on the floor of the damp cell with his back against the wall, facing the cell door. The cool moisture from the stone against the wound in his back offered minor comfort when compared to the wrenching pain caused by his every breath, spreading infection, and the accompanying movement of his severely damaged lung and cracked ribs. Telling his life's story drained his energy while passing his final hours. "That is my story, from the Star of Bethlehem to the day of my death."

The stranger stood stepping into the dim light coming through the edge of the cell door. He was a short, burly, bare-chested man with tangled hair. His ankles were chained to the wall, which prevented him from crossing the cell.

"I am Barabbas, leader of the Jewish revolt. Given the opportunity, I would lay my life down for you, Tabor."

Tabor pulled in enough air to say, "And I for you, Barabbas."

Barabbas let out a hearty laugh that caught the attention of the guards in the outer room. "Quiet down in there," one of them hollered.

"We would have been great together, Tabor."

Yelling even louder to ensure the Romans heard him, Barabbas boasted, "My armies have killed a *thousand* Romans. If I am to die today, then it is a *good* trade. But to die a common thief is an insult to God!"

The iron hinges squeaked loudly, as it swung open. "Get in there," the soldier commanded, pushing a man into the cell with Tabor, Barabbas, and Ishmael, slamming the door behind him, followed by the sound of the iron bar that dropped into place.

Tabor watched as the man who had been shoved to the floor stood. "Another victim for a Roman cross?" Barabbas asked.

Without responding, the man turned his attention to Tabor and began looking him over, as would a shepherd inspecting a hurt sheep. After a few moments, he knelt beside Tabor and pressed the palm of his hand against the wound on Tabor's chest, who was too weak to resist. The warm flow of energy coming from the man's touch spread through his body, giving him a feeling of tranquil peace.

"Breathe," the man said, before backing away to sit against the wall opposite Barabbas.

Tabor's next breath filled both lungs. The pain in his lung suddenly vanished. He pressed his own fingers against the chest wound and took a deeper breath to feel the air rush in. Amazed and bewildered, he stared at the man who sat near him. "Who are you? Are you a messenger from God?"

"I am Jesus of Nazareth."

"But you healed me with nothing more than your touch."

"I healed you with faith," Jesus replied.

Tabor found the strength to sit up higher, pushing his back further up the wall. "Have you come to take me out of here? If you help me escape, I will kill Romans—I swear it!"

"I am not here to take life, but to preserve it," he said. "I can save you, if you are willing to die with me."

"I don't understand—how will you save me if I am dead?"

From across the cell, Barabbas listened to the conversation of the two men. "Don't listen to him, Tabor! I have heard of this man. He is a rabbi who believes he is the Messiah. He goes around telling those who will listen that the only way to defeat Rome is to live in peace with Rome. Well, I say kill them all first. Only *then* will peace come to Israel."

Jesus stood and approached Barabbas, who was now standing across the cell. "And I know *you*, Barabbas. Truly I tell you, God gives life to all men. It is to God, then, to decide when that life is to end—not man."

Barabbas moved toward Jesus, his chains stopping him directly in front of Jesus, their noses nearly touching. "For every Roman who kills one of our people, I kill ten Romans. *That* is what God demands of me."

"Put down your sword, Barabbas, and follow me," Jesus said. "When you die, your movement dies with you, but when I die, my movement will have only just begun."

Barabbas stared at the man who faced him without fear. Very few men, even his most trusted soldiers and confidants, had dared to challenge him as Jesus had.

"Why are you here with us?" Tabor asked. "Why would Rome want to kill a Jewish rabbi?"

Jesus returned to sit next to Tabor. "It is not what I have done, Tabor. It is what I am about to do. I am here to fulfill the prophecy."

Barabbas spoke with a mocking tone, "The prophecy to hand Israel over to the Romans, so we can live as slaves?"

"No, Barabbas, the prophecy that the Son of Man shall die and on the third day of death shall rise and live again, bringing the glory of God's Kingdom to *all* men."

"Dead is dead, Jesus of Nazareth," Barabbas taunted. "Before the sun sets, you will be a dead prophet and I will be a dead warrior. Who do you think better served Israel? A man who spent his life hiding from the Romans behind his faith or a man who gives his life in a fight for freedom?"

Calmly, Jesus responded, "Truly I tell you, Barabbas, this is not your day to die. While the Son of Man suffers on the cross, you will be given the freedom to choose between a life of sin and anguish or a life of redemption and forgiveness."

Quietly Tabor asked, "Jesus, why did you *heal* me if I am to die?"

"I healed your body, Tabor, and relieved your suffering, so *you* can heal your soul. Hear me, Tabor. You *will* die this day, as will I. What I am going to ask of you will require more strength than anything you could possibly imagine. If you do as I ask, however, then will you be truly free."

"Rabbi, what is it you ask of me?"

"When you are hanging on the cross, forgive the executioner

who will have driven the spikes through your hands and feet. And when you forgive that one Roman soldier, forgive *all* Roman soldiers."

Fury raged in Tabor's heart, as he lashed back, "How can you ask me to forgive even a *single* Roman? You cannot possibly know what they have done to me and my family."

"*That's* it, Tabor!" Barabbas yelled, applauding his response. "*Never* lose the hate. Without hate, we will lose the war."

Confused, Tabor looked at Barabbas to his right, from whom he heard the message of hate and revenge, but then turned to his other side, where, next to Ishmael, sat a man who delivered a message of peace and forgiveness.

Once again, Jesus put his hand against Tabor's chest, in the very spot the arrow had pierced, and said, "Tabor, love them—as I love you— and yours will be the Kingdom of Heaven."

The rusted hinges squeaked to life and the heavy door was flung open. "Come with me, *King*. Herod wants to see you," the guard mockingly told Jesus, roughly lifting him to his feet and tying a rope around his neck. A moment later, he was leading Jesus out the door and through the prison corridor.

Tabor watched as the enigmatic stranger walked away, the door clanging shut between them. Closing his eyes to escape the unbearable horror of Ruth's murder, he returned in his mind to the hills beyond Bethlehem. For the last hour of his last night, he found comfort in a vision with his father and Saul that broke through the darkness.

"*Father, the Rabbi bids me to forgive these murderous Romans.*"

"*I know, Tabor,*" Jonas replied as the three men walked the familiar path to his home. "*True forgiveness comes from deep within your soul.*"

"*Years ago,*" Saul added, "*your father found his strength when he forgave me for my involvement in the Bethlehem slaughter.*"

"*And when I forgave Saul,*" Jonas continued, "*it set my spirit free.*"

"*And by his forgiveness,*" Saul concluded, "*my spirit was raised on the wings of an eagle.*"

Suddenly, the door squeaked to life, pulling Tabor back to the dark prison cell. "Come on, you," the guard said, quickly looping a rope around Tabor's neck and pulling him to his feet. "Time's up. We have other ways to make Jews like you talk. Works *every* time."

"Never give up, Tabor," Barabbas yelled, as Tabor was led away. "As long as you have a single breath in your lungs, you still have a chance."

When Tabor moved from the dark confines of the basement prison to the brightly lit courtyard, his eyes needed time to adjust. His wrists were tied in front of him and pulled above his head. Next, the rope was secured through a metal ring above him on a tall wooden pole.

"Well, Tabor?" came the sound of Pilate's voice. From the shade of an awning, Pilate sat peacefully, surrounded by his staff and guards, including Marcus. "Have you decided to talk to me? This is your last chance to save yourself from a very painful death, I assure you."

Tabor looked up at the empty blue sky, his eyes having finally adjusted to the sunlight. In the courtyard, citizens from Jerusalem and countless Passover pilgrims gathered to watch the flogging of a prisoner, although few knew the charges held against him. Tabor had been resolute in his silence. Even Pilate realized he would never reveal his secrets, because his secrets were the only reason he was still alive.

"So be it!" Pilate yelled angrily. "But before you forfeit your life for the crimes you have committed, I have a little show for you to enjoy."

Pilate motioned toward the open courtyard where the crowds stood, forbidden to pass beyond a temporary barricade. Pushing his way to the front of the crowd, Tabor recognized Caiaphas and two of his priests, who were hoping to hear anything from Tabor that would offer a clue about the Ark's location.

A Roman soldier walked into the yard carrying a short-handled whip, its three leather tendrils tipped with lead balls and mutton bones, coiled in his hand. Behind him walked two more soldiers leading a Jewish woman with ropes tied tightly to her wrists. One soldier held the rope tied to the woman's left wrist, and the other soldier did the same with a rope on her right. The two soldiers separated once they reached the center of the yard, pulling the woman's arms straight out from her sides to prevent her from squirming.

The soldier with the whip walked up behind the woman and pulled the headdress of her mantle from her head, revealing her hair and face. Instinctively, she screamed, "No!"

Tabor's realization of what was coming was far more painful than if he were the one being whipped. "Mother!" he cried out.

Pilate looked at the anguish in Tabor's face before asking, "Shall we begin, Tabor?"

Hearing only silence from Tabor, Pilate nodded to the soldier with the whip. The soldier, experienced at inflicting maximum pain, cracked the tethered straps of the whip against Miriam's back, who yelped at the burn from the strike, much to the delight of the soldiers. The sight of this woman being flogged was too much for some in the crowd, who gasped at the cruelty and moved away from the courtyard.

The soldier with the whip looked to Pilate, who flipped his hand, indicating the punishment should continue. Two more searing cracks with the whip caused Miriam's knees to buckle, while she continued to cry loudly after each burning slash of her flesh. The soldiers holding her ropes increased the tension to help hold her up on her feet.

Pilate raised his hand to stop the flogging, giving Tabor time to consider what he was watching. "Well, Tabor? I understand you let your wife die to protect your crime. Are you going to let your *mother* do the same?"

Tabor turned to Pilate, then back to his mother. Sweat from the heat of the day dripped from his hair and streaked down his face. The thought of watching his mother die was unbearable, but the sounds of her suffering surpassed even that. His eyes were wide with fear and his breathing was rapid. Finally, he shut his eyes and prayed for death's release.

Pilate wickedly raised the stakes in response to Tabor's silence. "Turn her around!"

The two guards on Miriam's ropes traded places, turning her to face the soldier with the whip. The entire crowd gasped, as the soldier walked toward Miriam, who was now barely able to hold her head up, and ripped her robe open to her waist, exposing her breasts. Tabor watched as the first strike from the whip left a wide, red bloody wound from her left shoulder across her right breast.

Looking skyward for an answer from heaven, Tabor saw the silhouette of a large bird, circling high above the courtyard. No one in the crowd, nor any of the Roman soldiers, not even Pilate, knew what to make of Tabor's loud whistle scarcely before he yelled, "Storm! Miriam!"

In an instant, Storm tucked her wings and entered a dive, pulling out just in time to extend her claws and penetrate the soldier's face, forcing him to cry out as he dropped the whip. In a fluid motion, Storm circled tightly to attack the soldier holding Miriam's right arm, who dropped the rope when Storm dug her talons into his scalp. The other soldier, who held the rope on her left arm, released it to pull his sword, swinging it recklessly in the air, but nowhere near the great eagle.

As the three men fought the bird that hovered above them, screeching in anger, Miriam slipped into the crowd, which quickly ushered her out of sight. Storm immediately flew back up to a safe altitude, while two women pulled Miriam into a safe house.

"Ah, you camel dung!" Pilate screamed at the soldiers who let their prisoner escape right before his eyes. Angrily, he grabbed a spear from the hands of a guard and threw it toward the soldier with the whip, piercing his abdomen. Frustrated at his lost opportunity to force Tabor to reveal the location of the Ark, and at his bungling guards who'd lost a battle with a bird, Pilate turned abruptly to go back inside before the crowds began to heckle him. Pointing at Tabor, he shouted as he walked off, "If I can't have the Ark, *no one* will! *Crucify him!*"

# CHAPTER 28



*Friday, April 7, A.D. 30*

Before Koda and Daniel were within sight of Tabor's home, the putrid smell consumed them. "Ugh, what is that, Father?" Daniel asked, pulling his sleeve across his nose and mouth to block the stench.

"Death weighs heavy in the air," Koda said, hoping to prepare Daniel for the horror that awaited them.

One by one, they followed the trail of rotting sheep carcasses, most riddled with arrows. As they drew ever closer, first Koda, then Daniel, saw ahead a gut wrenching sight that pierced their souls. Strung from the pole he had used many times in the past to clean slaughtered sheep, Koda recognized the woman he swore to protect with the last words he'd spoken to his brother.

As the two stood close enough to recognize the body, Daniel asked what he already knew, "Is that Ruth, Father?"

"Yes."

Suddenly realizing his cousin was nowhere to be seen, Daniel asked, "Evia? I don't see her. Do you think she got away before the Romans came?"

Shaking his head gravely, he replied, "I doubt it, Daniel. If she *had* escaped, she would have sought refuge in our home by now. She may be here somewhere, or they may have taken her with them. Either way, she is surely dead." Koda looked at his son, realizing how cold he must have sounded, but the shock of the devastation around them and the discovery of Ruth's body left him empty.

"I'm going to look for her," Daniel said, running off to look for Evia.

Koda did not respond or even acknowledge Daniel's decision. He could not. His morose walk up the hill toward Ruth's body was marked by no thought or sensation, other than a grief transcending words. When he arrived at the pole, he cut the single rope that had held her upright for days, easing her body to the ground. Going inside the home, Koda brought out a large blanket and wrapped Ruth in it. Carefully, yet with ease, he lifted the body of the petite woman and carried her to the back of the cave behind the home.

"Father!" Daniel called from outside. Koda stepped through the doorway to see Daniel running toward him. Again his son hollered, "Father, I can't find her!" Tears washed over the young man's face.

At the bottom of the hill near the stream, two corpses of Romans lay rotting on the ground, one of which was decapitated. "Do you think Evia killed those two soldiers before they took her?" Daniel asked, lifting his robe over his mouth to try to mask the putrid smell.

"No, not Evia," his father replied. "I only pray, whoever killed these men rescued Evia as well."

"Start a fire where most of the sheep are lying, Daniel. We need to burn them before disease plagues the valley."

"And the Romans?"

"We'll burn them too."

For the rest of the afternoon, the two men drug carcasses to the fire, where they watched their very connection to life turn to ashes.

"Father," Daniel asked, "shouldn't we seal the cave where Ruth is buried?"

"We will, Daniel, but not yet. I fear we will soon have more to bury. You run home and stay with your mother. I'm going to Jerusalem to find what has become of my mother, and to see if there is word of Tabor."

Blood streamed down Tabor's chest and back from open wounds brought on by repeated whip lashes, as he labored to remain conscious under the weight of the torturous wooden cross. Each step forward seemed to invite the crack of another whip against his back. Climbing the slope of

Calvary Hill, outside the walls of the great city, was arduous. Deep within his being, he prayed each step would be his last.

"That's far enough." the Roman soldier who had been whipping him declared.

Relieved that his suffering would soon end, Tabor collapsed on the ground. Another soldier took the heavy wooden beam that had been strapped to Tabor's back and positioned it on the ground beneath the post that had held many Jews before him.

Two other soldiers pulled Tabor by his arms and dropped his back on the center of the beam, stretching out his arms to either side. After lashing both forearms to the crossbar, a soldier began pounding a long iron spike through each wrist.

With Tabor's weakened condition, he couldn't reward his executioners with loud cries of pain, but his body heaved upward with every pounding of the mallet. After stripping off his clothes, a soldier pointed to the arrow wound in Tabor's chest and said, "I thought this was the one who nearly died from an arrow. That wound looks completely healed." Those standing around ignored the comment and focused on preparing the man's execution.

Two ropes were then tied to metal eyelets at either end of the cross, both of which were strung through similar eyelets at the top of the post. Two men pulled the ropes from behind the post, lifting Tabor by his arms until the cross was in place. Suspended by his arms, he immediately began to suffocate, unable to pull in enough air to sustain consciousness.

Quickly, a soldier hammered a flat wooden pedestal where his feet dangled, allowing him to support his own weight, thus relieving the strain from his arms. "There," the soldier viciously told Tabor. "We wouldn't want you to die too quickly."

From high up on the cross, Tabor looked down to see his mother, Miriam, holding Koda's arm, as they slowly walked to the foot of the hill. However, Roman guards prevented them from getting any closer. Corpuscles burst in Tabor's eyes as his body strained and clung to life. During one conscious moment, Tabor saw far off in the distance a wooden bench outside the city gate, where a small boy pointed in his direction.

Suddenly, the cross shook, as a ladder was being propped up against the cross member. A guard climbed the ladder and nailed a plaque above Tabor's head, announcing the crime of theft. Soon after the ladder was removed, Tabor felt a man's hands move one of his feet to be in front of the other, followed by the excruciating pain of a metal spike passing through the bones of his ankles.

After nailing his feet to the cross, the wooden pedestal was removed, leaving the iron spikes in his feet and wrists to support his weight.

When the hammering stopped, the throbbing in his wrists and ankles pulsed with every beat of his heart. "They freed Barabbas for Passover, and killed me instead." Hearing these words, Tabor realized Ishmael was already being crucified directly to the right of him. Somehow, he had not seen the second cross.

"Death will free me from a life, once worth living," Tabor answered with short, painful breaths. His lips were cracked and blood replaced saliva to moisten his swollen tongue.

Caiaphas had walked the path from Jerusalem's outer wall up to Calvary, shadowed by two temple priests. When he was stopped by a Roman guard at the base of the hill, Caiaphas forcefully said, "I *need* to speak to that man," pointing to Tabor.

Without offering a response, the guard lowered his spear to block the priests from approaching the condemned men.

"Stand aside, I said!" Caiaphas shouted, challenging the guard's authority.

The guard stood his ground, and a second soldier moved closer to the disturbance. Neither man spoke to the Chief Priest, but both knew failing to follow their orders would mean certain death.

Suddenly, a waft of wind passed over Tabor's neck and hair. Turning his head to the left, a moment of happiness blessed him. "Storm, it's so good to see you."

Storm walked sideways down the wooden beam to get as close to Tabor's head as the cross would allow. Her body leaned forward and she reached for his mouth. Opening her beak, she let a few droplets of water drip onto his lips, which had continued to crack deeper as the morning sun strengthened.

Walking back along the beam to his left, she took flight, returning minutes later with another beak full of water. Tabor gratefully opened his mouth to feel the water sooth his swollen tongue. Time and time again, as the morning turned to afternoon, Storm cared for him as a mother bird would do for her own hatchling.

Miriam watched Storm through her tear-filled eyes, thankful the bird she once tolerated only for her young son's sake was now working hard to keep him alive, as he had once done for her.

"What's that bird doing there?" one soldier finally called out, pointing his spear to the eagle perched on the cross of the condemned man.

"Get it!" a second soldier yelled. The two men moved cautiously toward Tabor's cross, preparing to impale the intruder with their spears. As Tabor pushed against the iron spike securing both his feet to the cross, so as to lift his weight, he did his best to wet his lips, filled his lungs and whistled the command to take flight. "Storm! Fly! Be Free!"

Storm sidestepped her way quickly down the crossbar, distancing herself from the soldiers who were rushing toward her. With a lunge, she spread her wings and soared down the hill, barely clearing the heads of the crowd that had gathered to watch the giant bird on the cross of the dying man.

Following the road from Calvary, she glided above another condemned man who had collapsed on his back, under the weight of a cross, and wore a crown of thorns on his head. He watched the mighty eagle soar directly above him, in awe of God's creature.

This third man slated for crucifixion could barely hold onto the cross another man carried, as he walked his final steps. When the soldiers ripped the man's tunic from his body, Tabor could see the open wounds and blood flowing down his back. Even Tabor, suffering his final hours of life nailed to a cross, could barely stand the sight of the man's tortured body.

When the third man was laid on the cross for nailing, Tabor looked down, past his feet, and realized the face was that of Jesus of Nazareth, the man thrown into his prison cell in the early morning hours. His face was battered and bruised, his eyes were swollen shut, and blood encircled every tooth. Streams of blood ran from the punctures of countless thorns protruding through the man's skin, but still, Tabor recognized him—*knew* him.

Jesus broke his silence, crying out in agony, as Tabor watched the spikes being driven through his wrists. Then, as just Tabor had endured, the wood beam of the cross with Jesus suspended was hoisted up and attached to the vertical post in the center of three crosses.

Again, the same Roman guard did to Jesus what he had done earlier to Tabor, nailing his feet to the pole with a crude metal spike.

Tabor suffered for long hours of agonizing torment, enduring the repetitive cycle of lifting his weight with his feet, pushing against the spike that nailed his ankles to the cross—so as to pull in a breath of air—

followed by an exhaustive release, when he'd let his weight fall to hang suspended by the spikes through his wrists. Nonetheless, his body tenaciously held onto the life Tabor so desperately wished to release.

As the afternoon sun reached its peak, Tabor heard Jesus call out to the heavens, "Father, forgive them—they do not know what they are doing!"

With those words, Tabor knew Jesus had already done what he had asked earlier of him. Even within his own anguish, in that moment, Tabor felt an upsurge of emotion, to relinquish his hatred and rage. "God, give me the strength," Tabor prayed aloud. Looking down directly to the soldier who stood in front of Jesus, he called out, "Centurion!"

The guard turned and walked to the base of Tabor's cross. He asked, "What do you want, Jew?"

Tabor took two short breaths, before mustering, "I forgive you— you and all others of your kind."

The centurion guard cocked his head and sneered at Tabor, unsure how to respond to such a statement. Perplexed and confused, he returned to his post in front of the center cross.

For Tabor, the reward was immediate; his heart was relieved and his soul was cleansed. He lifted his head and saw Jerusalem and all its inhabitants as a place and people to be loved, not feared. Not since John the Baptist had baptized him in the River Jordan had he felt such peace.

Suddenly, Tabor heard the other condemned man, Ishmael, ridiculing Jesus. "Are you not the Christ? Why don't you save yourself and us?"

Jesus said nothing in his own defense, but Tabor rebuked the man, "Do you not even *respect* God, since you are under the same sentence of condemnation? We are suffering justly for our crimes, but this man has done *nothing* wrong. He is dying because they are afraid of what he might do if he *lives.*"

Turning his attention to Jesus, Tabor said, "Jesus, please remember me when you come into your kingdom."

Having heard the words of forgiveness from Tabor to the centurion, Jesus responded, "Truly I say to you, today you shall be with me in paradise."

Miriam could barely bring herself to look upon the three bloodied, bruised and savagely beaten men, hanging before her on Roman instruments of torture and death. She only saw her first-born son, wincing in agony. Holding her eyes upon Tabor, she recalled how, as a toddler, he'd escaped certain death by mere hours when Jonas had rushed her and their child from Bethlehem before Herod's slaughter of the innocents. Now, thirty-five years later, she felt helpless in her role as a pained, grieving witness to death claiming its victory.

"Miriam?" A familiar voice sounded in her ears.

Miriam turned to see a woman lowering the headdress of her mantle. "Mary?"

The two women embraced with open arms, clinging to one another in their sorrow and compassion for the broken men before them, both sobbing quietly into each other's shoulders for a few long moments. They then turned to the three "criminals" hanging from the crosses. Looking up at the man on the cross next to Tabor, whose entire body was a tapestry for his own blood, Miriam could barely say his name. "Jesus?"

Unable to speak, Mary acknowledged her with a tearful nod. Turning her gaze up to the battered, disfigured man next to Jesus, she whispered, "Tabor?"

Miriam looked at her son and simply whispered back, "Yes."

"Why has Tabor been condemned to such a death?" Mary asked.

"He hid the Ark of the Covenant from the Romans," Miriam replied. Staring at the man she had not seen since he was a small boy, Miriam asked, "Why are they killing Jesus?"

Mary gazed at her son—crowned with thorns and violently trembling from his brutal torture and loss of blood—and answered, "He dared to change the world."

The crowd thinned, as many who had followed Tabor and Jesus to watch their execution returned to Jerusalem to enjoy the Passover festivities. Lifting his head and opening his eyes, Tabor saw in the distance a shepherd leading a herd of sheep into the valley. He sighed deeply, his heart full of longing, then began to lower his eyes once again.

But beneath him at the foot of his cross, he saw his mother, and the mother of Jesus, who clasped hands as they suffered the terrible anguish of watching their sons' purposely torturous execution. Turning to his right, his attention was drawn to the lone woman kneeling beneath the feet of Jesus with her face pressed against her hands, wailing with the cries of insufferable loss.

The woman's crimson headdress, ornately framed with golden tassels, barely clung to the back of her head. Yet as he looked down upon her, he sensed she knew something of the purity of love. And through witnessing the heartache and pain she so openly expressed, he found, at long last, the strength to forgive himself for the sins of his life.

Behind the dwindling crowd, Tabor saw a young girl carrying a newborn lamb in her arms. Her long black hair hung uncovered, in contrast to her shimmering white tunic. She smiled, oblivious to the dying men looming above her on wooden crosses. Slowly, she turned to stand next to Miriam. When the young girl lifted her eyes from the lamb to face Tabor, he realized Ruth was there, waiting for him.

To his right, the body of Jesus hung lifeless. To the front, the beauty of his wife blinded him to the soldiers who approached with a club to break his knees, bringing a rapid end to his suffering.

High above Calvary Hill, beneath the dark swirling clouds that gathered to block the sun, a golden eagle cried out, as Tabor closed his eyes and released his last breath.

# ABOUT THE AUTHOR

Dixie was born in Germany and later moved to the United States with her family. She earned her certification as a Radiological Technologist in Lexington, Kentucky, and currently resides in Huntsville, Alabama with her husband and children. A mother of three and grandmother of three, she has proudly served her local church as a teacher for over thirty years. It was through her love for children and storytelling that she found her passion for writing fiction and reading the classics.